Praise for Kieran Larwood

'**A joy to read** and absolutely **world-class**.'
Alex, age 10, *LoveReading4Kids*

'Will entertain everyone ...
already feels like **a classic**.'
BookTrust

'The **best book** I have ever read.'
Mariyya, age 9, *LoveReading4Kids*

'**Jolly good fun.**'
SFX

'I just couldn't put it down.'
Sam, age 11, *LoveReading4Kids*

'**Five stars.**'
Dylan, age 12, *LoveReading4Kids*

'Great stuff and definitely **one to watch**.'
Carabas

'An original fantasy with ... **riveting adventure**,
and genuine storytelling.'
Kirkus

'A **great** bit of storytelling.'
Andrea Reece, *LoveReading*

'Rich with custom, myth, and a little touch of **magic**.'
Carousel

'A story for children who enjoy fantasy, quests.'
The School Librarian

THE TREEKEEPERS

KIERAN LARWOOD

Illustrated by Chris Wormell

faber

First published in 2022
by Faber & Faber Limited
Bloomsbury House,
74–77 Great Russell Street,
London WC1B 3DA
faberchildrens.co.uk

Typeset in Times by M Rules
Printed by CPI Group (UK) Ltd, Croydon CR0 4YY

A CIP record for this book is available from the British Library

ISBN 978–0–571–36456–5

2 4 6 8 10 9 7 5 3 1

For my parents

FR

BITTERBLIGHT

THE

THE ROTLANDS

THE
UPTURNED SEA

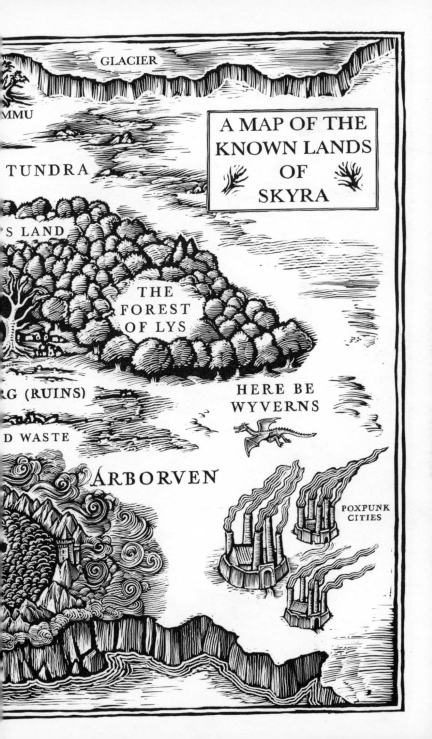

I

'All magic begins with the Tree.'

The Book of Undren

There was a mountain.

Not a pointed, snow-capped peak like the one you've just imagined.

No. More a solid slab of rock. A giant volcanic loaf, pushing up out of the ground, its top cloaked in mist. Millions of years old, hundreds of feet high. Hard as iron, smooth as glass, unforgiving as death.

And halfway up it, on a ledge no wider than the palm of your hand, stood two figures. Woman and girl: mother and daughter, even, judging by their matching green eyes, copper-brown skin and shoulder-length tangles of hair, matted and braided into warriors' locks.

Above them, the rockface yawned away to the summit, somewhere in the candyfloss mess of clouds. Below them was a fall on to knife-edge shards of broken stone. A long fall: one in which you would have plenty of time to think of how you were about to burst open like a rotten tomato, and exactly how much it was going to hurt.

There were no ropes or ladders to show how they had come to be there, standing side by side on that tiny wrinkle of rock. The mountain face was silky smooth all around: impossible to even think about climbing.

Yet there they stood, toes curled over the edge, backs pressed against the stone, the girl with her head bowed, nodding as if being given a lesson, the mother gesturing with her hands, making them swoop and turn through the air.

'Are you ready?' the mother said, reaching back to grasp the hood of the fur cloak she wore.

'Of course,' said the girl with a shrug that meant she probably wasn't but was trying hard to fake it.

'Then let's go.'

The mother pulled her hood over her head, revealing the ears and nose of a russet-furred fox. The rest of the cloak fell over her shoulders: a strange mix of scales and feathers, as if the skins of several animals had been stitched together.

Then, as the cloak covered her body, there was a changing. A *folding*, as the outline of her human body shifted and shrank, wrapping itself in the animal hide and becoming something other.

One minute, an adult woman stood on the ledge, the next there was a griffyx. An ancient creature – long lost to the world except in myths – it looked like a mix of fox, dragon and eagle. Head and snout of fur, body of scales, feathered wings and a thick brush of a tail.

The creature paused for a heartbeat, staring at her daughter with those same green, flashing eyes her human form had owned. A brief nod of the head, and then the mother griffyx spread its wings and dived from the ledge, plummeting downwards, becoming a speck in the time it took to blink.

'For Tree's sake,' muttered the girl, watching the winged beast disappear. 'I'll never catch her now.'

Ignoring the wind that threatened to whip her off the narrow ledge, the girl pulled her own cloak up and over her head, feeling her body tingle and ripple with magic energy as it spoke to the animal skin and remade itself.

Even as her bones were melding into paws, even as she felt the wings come alive on her back, she pushed herself off the rockface, out into nothingness where she hung for an instant, waiting for gravity to grab hold of her and snatch her back to earth.

Her wings snapped out, caught the air and sliced it, and she sailed after her mother, off into the open sky.

*

'Come on, Liska! Keep up!'

Her mother's voice came back to her, whipped by the wind, making it hard to hear.

Liska was a hundred metres or so behind, just close enough to watch the ruffling feathers in her mother's wings, noting how they tilted just so, keeping her soaring as she searched out the currents of warm air that would give her lift. Close enough to see the glowing bands of the stripes that blazed on her forelegs.

Shapewalkers like Liska and her mother were gifted the marks of gleaming colour for great deeds of courage and heroism. Liska hadn't earned a single one yet, but oh, how she longed to. Seven at least, like her mother. Possibly ten or more, if only she could find enough epic adventures to grant them . . .

'Stay focused! You're daydreaming again!'

Liska flipped back to reality with a yelp, realising she had flown into a patch of cold air. She lost height rapidly, had to flap her wings with fast, swooshing beats to stay aloft. The effort pulled at her muscles, making her strain and growl.

'You've lost the thermal! Bank to your left!'

'I'm . . . trying . . .' Liska muttered through gritted teeth as she battled back up to proper height. The warmer air began to rush under her wings, helping her rise until she was level with her mother again. She shook her head. Flying was *hard* . . .

'That's better,' her mother called. 'Now bring it around. We're going to head for the Undrentree.'

The distant form of her mother turned, soaring in a gentle curve and beginning to sink gradually lower. Liska raised her left wing, dipped to the right and tried to follow.

Below them lay a circular basin three miles wide, ringed by the towering granite Shield Mountains. A scoop of earth filled from one edge to the other with a flowing sea of green leaves. Tree upon tree clustered together, and in amongst the branches peeped the glow from thousands of lights. Strings of lanterns, candles in windows, street lamps and flickering torches. The place was home to a throng of people; a city among the forest. Arborven.

In the centre stood the Undrentree.

Even though she had seen it thousands of times, it still filled Liska with wonder.

Almost as tall as the mountains that enclosed the valley, it dwarfed everything around it. Its thundering great branches spread out like open arms covered in sprays of jade leaves that rose high enough to touch the clouds.

From this distance it tricked your eye, looking like any ordinary tree just a few metres away. That was until you noticed there were walls and roofs of buildings all over it. And not just huts or shacks, either. Temples with turrets and steeples. Whole villages of three-storey houses running along branches. Bridges of rope and plank wider than any highway strung between them. Castles and mansions built amongst the roots. And scurrying everywhere, the flea-sized specks of figures that were hundreds upon hundreds of people.

The thing was monumental. God-sized.

Surrounding it, in a ring, was the first of the city circles. A round string of oak trees that belonged to the group of magic users known as arbomancers. Giant, gnarled trunks holding houses of dark wood with roofs narrowed into the steepest of points. Most honoured, most respected, this tribe lived closest to the tree which gave them their powers.

Around that was the second circle: the bushy, round-leaved hazel trees of the stormsingers. They lived high in the branches, in spherical houses like teardrops covered in silver pennants that fluttered in the breeze.

Then came the barkmages, the sapsmiths and the mossherders, with circles of rowan, birch and elm that stretched the city right up to the steep sides of the mountain walls. Each with their own styles of building, from craggy huts that seemed formed from the trunks themselves, to six-storey towers that swayed like the trees around them, decorated with streamers of shaggy lichen and sprays of coloured moss.

Liska stared down at it all as she passed above.

She saw flocks of forest birds fluttering everywhere, searching out spots for roosting. Bats had begun to whirl above the branches, snapping up the juicy moths that were attracted to all the glowing lanterns. Squirrels sat at the doorways of tiny houses that had been built especially for them, cleaning their tails and staring down at the bustling world around them with bright, beady eyes.

Liska marvelled at its order, at the way it all worked in harmony. The Undrentree gave its magic to the wizards of Arborven, and they used it to tend the trees, the wildlife and keep the city thriving. Each thing helped the other to survive. Balance and partnership.

Although it wasn't perfect, she knew.

The farther away from the tree you lived, the less magic you had. The poor mossherders were considered weak and worthless by the mages who lived near the Undrentree, and the sapsmiths weren't much better. They in turn were jealous of the arbomancers and stormsingers. Like a family with several children, petty arguments and squabbles were common.

*

Relaxing, feeling the air tickle through her pin feathers, Liska looked up from the spread of flowing leaves below, staring out towards the ring of granite mountains that surrounded Arborven.

They were crowned by a halo of thick white mist, but she knew there was a world out there. Beyond.

A scary one though.

The Blasted Waste to the north, packed with fire-breathing wyverns who liked to snack on flame-grilled humans for breakfast. The Poxpunk tribes to the east, with their smoke-choked cities of metal and junk. And to the west . . .

. . . she didn't want to think about that.

Instead, her eye caught the silhouettes of more shapewalkers out flying patrols along the mountain ranges. Warriors wearing the form of long-dead beasts. *Her* people.

She could just about make out the shape of the Noon Fort, nestled on the northern wall. That was where she and her family lived, along with the other griffyxes and the manticores. There was a squad of these doing manoeuvres in the distance: lion manes flowing and eagle wings soaring, with those brutal scorpion tails trailing behind.

Root-chewing manticores, Liska cursed. *Always thinking they're better than us griffyxes. Just because they're five times our size.*

She turned her head away, looking off to the right where some other shapewalkers – these ones from the Stormfort to the east – circled way up above.

She could see the curved beaks of griffins, with their clawed paws and cats' tails. And was that a peryton amongst them – a winged deer with a grand spread of antlers?

All these creatures must once have been as common here as the foxes and squirrels. Liska tried to imagine the valley as it was then, packed with roaring beasts. Wild ones that weren't just humans wearing their forgotten shapes.

At least the Undrentree remembers them, she thought. The sacred tree had changed the furs and skins that the first shapewalkers brought to it, so the legend went, turning them into copies of the mythical beasts that once filled the skies. And then the skins were handed down through the families, given to the youngest when they were ready for their bonding ceremony.

Seems such a long time ago now. Liska cast her mind back to when she had received her skin, after her ceremonial bath in oil from the tree. How the magic had sung through every pore in her body. How the cloak she wore became a part of her. A second skin, another piece of—

'Watch it, Liska!' her mother shouted back to her. Daydreaming once more, she had drifted off course, heading out over the west of the city instead of around towards the towering bulk of the Undrentree.

Liska growled under her breath and swung about, swooping down to brush the tops of the highest trees with her paws. They were over the second circle now, the home of the stormsingers. She could see the outlines of their houses through the leaves, the glimmer of lanterns and candles shining up at her.

As she passed one especially tall tree, she noticed a pod had been built in its topmost branches. A round bulb of wood, it was just big enough for a child's bedroom and there, sure enough, was a little face peering out across the treetops.

The mages in the city below looked down on the shapewalkers, Liska knew. Even though they protected them from all the outside threats. Even though they risked their lives fighting off wyverns and everything else. They weren't treated as part of Arborven. They were lower than mossherders. Creatures less than human. Beasts from scary tales told to children at bedtime.

Well, let's see if I can change that, shall we? Liska hardly ever came down to the city, so she was determined to make this visit count.

She swung closer to the bedroom window, making

sure she was spotted, and was rewarded by a gasp of surprise. Keen to show off her flying skills, and to prove that shapewalkers weren't all scary monsters, she flipped her wings around in what she hoped would be an impressive barrel roll.

Except her rear paw caught on a stray branch and she wobbled badly, crashing into the foliage for a moment before struggling free in an explosion of leaves and twigs. Instead of gasps from the child's bed-pod, she heard howls of laughter, making her blush hard under her fur.

'For Tree's sake, Liska, can't you concentrate for even a moment?' Her mother. Again.

Maybe it was the animal side of Liska, maybe it was just because she didn't like being told what to do, but something snapped inside her then. She felt a bubble of rebellion surge up and take her over. With a fierce snarl on her lips, she decided to show her mother that she knew *perfectly well* how to fly properly no matter how much trouble it would land her in.

Beating hard to build up speed, she climbed almost vertically until her mother was a gliding shadow sixty metres below.

Then she pointed her nose downwards, folded her

wings into her body and went into a dive, picking up speed as she plummeted like an arrow, like a furry javelin thrown by an angry giant.

The air screamed past her face, whipping her fox ears back and washing her with the thick scent of bark, moss and leaves from the forest.

The trees zoomed up towards her, threatening to swallow her up. She zipped past her mother, made her yelp in surprise, and then jabbed out her wings just in time to stop herself colliding with the forest.

She was still speeding like a bolt of lightning, and she shot away over the treetops. Somewhere behind, her mother was shouting, but she was too fast and far away to hear. The Undrentree was right in front of her now and nothing could stop her.

It had been a moment's decision, made in a blink. A single instant that would change the entire course of her life. But right then, hammering across the forest city, she had no idea about any of that.

Liska threw back her fox head and barked with laughter.

*

As she neared the Undrentree, Liska pricked her ears and focused her eyes upon the enormous branches.

13

Alongside the mages, there were other inhabitants of Arborven, ones that she always sought a glimpse of whenever she had a chance to visit the city: the treekeepers.

There were only a dozen of them and their job was to speak the will of the tree, to guide the quarrelling tribes that grew and tended the city. In a way, Liska supposed, they were the rulers of Arborven itself.

They lived in the Undrentree – on it and under it – in wooden buildings that towered above all the other structures, with rooms the size of barns and roofs like small mountains.

Just like the shapewalkers, they had been changed by magic. They had once been human mages – although Liska found that hard to believe – before being chosen by the Undrentree. Now their bodies had been turned to living wood, blending with the trees themselves to become a mixture of plant and human. Their faces peering out from the bark and grain like moving carvings.

Three times taller than an adult person, they had hair of moss and creepers and limbs of gnarled branches. They were almost as old as the tree and moved with slow creaking steps; spoke with measured, booming voices. Everything about them oozed power. The magic in their scent made Liska's animal senses tingle, filling her nose with electric zaps, as if she had just inhaled a nest of tiny fire ants.

She had spotted Edda, the leader, before. And Twiga, Taproot and Aspen. She had always wanted to see Craggit though. She had heard he was half the size of the others, twisted and covered in moss thicker than hair.

As she curved her flightpath around the Undrentree, she kept an eye on the house-covered branches, on the walkways and rope ladders that sprawled everywhere like spiders' webs.

She saw arbomancers casting hexes on limbs and leaves to make them grow into new platforms and paths. They drew patterns of green light that hung in the air. They sang songs in the language of root and twig.

Hanging in baskets from the highest branches, mossherders coaxed lichen into swirling patterns. Their long hair and flowing beards, as green and shaggy as the moss they summoned, waved in the evening breeze.

Further down the tree, sapsmiths were draining amber-coloured liquid from taps set into the bark. They poured it into vats and buckets, down pipes and chutes that led to the factories and breweries below, where it would be used to make potions and syrups, mead and ale. They left a cloud of sweet, sticky scent in the air that gummed up Liska's whiskers as she sailed through.

Everywhere there were crowds of tiny figures going about their business, but no sign at all of the hulking treekeepers.

Round the outside of the tree she flew, passing over the colossal roots as they grew over one another in endless twining layers. Where temples, libraries and workshops balanced among them in clusters. She saw the arbomancer Academy, the printing workshops of the stormsinger scribes, the hanging gardens of the mossherders … sights and wonders everywhere she looked.

Further still, she came to Undren Square – a wide open space between the smallest roots and the beginning of the first tree circle that was used for gatherings and ceremonies.

Night was beginning to draw on and it was mostly empty now. Just a few figures clustered at the edge. Two mages and … was that a treekeeper with them?

Liska flew closer, gliding down until she was ten metres or so from the ground. She flew under the lowest of the tree's branches, where it was dark and cool. Clusters of hanging lanterns – each one larger than her own bedroom at home – cast pools of warm, yellow light on the forest floor and the air was thick with the spicy scent of magic.

It *was* a treekeeper! With long, thick legs, gnarled and carved with spirals. With an ivy beard that almost reached the ground. Strings of green glowing runes ran up and down its arms, matching the gleam of its deep-set eyes. Magic poured out around it in an aura that Liska could almost see, almost *taste*.

It looked like Edda – the oldest, most important of the Keepers. Liska recognised him from brief glimpses she had caught before.

Gliding silently, she drifted closer, circling around to try and see what was so important that Edda himself had come down from his palace on the tree.

As she passed around the edge of the square, she could see Edda stooping downwards, talking to a man in long, sweeping robes of black and silver. An arbomancer. An important one, judging by the amount of symbols embroidered on his cloak. He was waving his hands wildly and snatches of a raised voice drifted towards Liska's sharp, fox ears.

Someone was daring to shout at a treekeeper? She had to get closer. She had to find out more.

Tilting her primary feathers a fraction higher, she tightened the circle she was flying in, bringing her closer to the figures at the square's edge. With luck, they would be too involved with their argument to notice her sliding by, lost in the shadows of the Undrentree's lower branches.

As Liska came around, she could see Edda in more detail. His face looked human, trapped inside the wooden statue of his body. Although there were bark-like whorls and bumps all over his skin. His eyes glowed from deep pools of shadow under his mossy brows, and she spotted the brush of a squirrel, scurrying around in his beard.

The arbomancer was still yelling, and now she could pick up some of the words.

'... foolish not to try! What else are we to do? Wait for the rot to reach the Undrentree? Let the minions of Bitterblight walk right into our city and destroy everything we have created?'

The rot. Liska couldn't stop a snarl slipping from her mouth.

That was what lurked to the west of the mountains.

18

The greatest threat of all that the city faced. There, amongst the blackened, drained soil, was another tree: sister of the one that nurtured all of Arborven. *Bitterblight.* Nobody had ever seen it, or at least lived to tell the tale. But legends described it as a dark, shapeless thing. A void of emptiness more like a hole in the universe than a tree. Jagged scratches instead of branches. Black, flapping streaks of *nothing* instead of leaves. A stinking, toxic thing – opposite to the Undrentree in every way.

It killed instead of cared; destroyed instead of created. Its roots drained energy from the world, spewing it out again in the form of grey fungus and seeping, living oil. Poisons that spread ever outwards, hungry to reach the Undrentree itself and suck it dry.

Edda moved his head from side to side in a slow, ponderous shake. When he spoke, his voice creaked like branches rubbing together in the wind. It echoed as if it had travelled up from roots lost deep under the ground.

'The power of the shadow tree cannot be harnessed. It is not for us to touch. Our law forbids it. Any creature who tries to use or control it will be destroyed by it in the end. This is known. This has always been known.'

The robed arbomancer shook his head. Liska had arced round behind Edda now and could see the mage's face. Pale skin, bald head. Dark eyes that flashed with anger.

'But nobody has even tried! My research shows that it might be possible. That the rot from Bitterblight can be channelled ... used ... made to work for us, even! Wouldn't it be worth an attempt at least? Imagine if we no longer had to worry about the Undrentree being killed off? What if we controlled its armies and were able to use them against the wyverns and the Poxpunks?'

Liska could see the back of Edda's head beginning another of its slow shakes as she sailed past. She had time for one last look down at the group before her orbit took her back out over the square. She was surprised to notice someone else was present. A silent, dark shape who stood some way off, half hidden in a pool of shade.

Peering into the gathering shadows, she tried to catch a glimpse of the third figure. If it hadn't been for her sharpened griffyx senses she might not have been able to see anything in the gloom, but as it was she picked out the slender wiry shape of a woman. Dressed in leather armour, with short spiky hair,

20

she was leaning on a barbed spear, appearing to be very casual – bored, even – but Liska could see her needle eyes watching every move that Edda and the arbomancer made.

Looking closer, Liska noticed some kind of scar on her face. It twisted down from her mouth to her throat, puckering the skin in what looked like the trails of claw marks.

Leather armour. Spear. Scars. She didn't seem like any kind of mage Liska had ever seen. And she definitely wasn't a shapewalker.

But she held herself with the same kind of quiet confidence. That of a skilled warrior. Muscles ready to spring at the slightest danger. Twitching, looking for threats and weaknesses. What was someone like that doing here at the Undrentree? A place that was supposed to be sacred and peaceful?

Intrigued, Liska leant harder into her turn, trying to come around for a better look.

As she did so, the woman looked up. Had she sensed Liska there? Had her passage through the air made some kind of noise?

It didn't matter. The woman had seen her now. Those sharp, predator's eyes locked on Liska and the pose of their owner changed instantly. A fighting stance, the spear gripped and ready to launch, to strike Liska from the sky.

By pure instinct, Liska drove her wings down, sending herself up high out of range. But, with her eyes locked on the dangerous figure below, she forgot completely that she was flying beneath the boughs of a gigantic tree. She had a sudden sense of a very large and solid object in front of her, and then there was a crunching *smack* as her head met hard, unmoving wood.

Sparks danced in front of Liska's eyes and her whole body jarred. Dazed, she expected to begin the long tumble to the ground, but instead she felt her back paws being gripped tight.

Head spinning, she found herself swinging *up* through the air rather than down. Dangling by her feet she thrashed her head around, frantic to see what had snared her. Up, up, up she went, until part of the tree came into view. A branch, draped in creepers, patterned with moss and ... was it carved into a man-like shape? Were those arms? A head? *Eyes?*

'Hello, tiny shapewalker.' A thrumming, timeless voice echoed through her dazed head. 'Did I hurt you?'

Liska, upside down still, stared into the glowing eyes of a treekeeper. Her nose filled with the scent of bark, living wood and musty age.

Of all the places to crash in the whole of Arborven she had chosen the one that would get her into the most trouble possible.

Another sound met Liska's ears, a distant one that was growing steadily closer. One which she recognised instantly, this time.

It was the sound of her mother yelling with rage as she flew towards her.

2

'We walk the path of the warrior,
the mages walk the path of magic.
We both protect the Undrentree,
but in our own ways.'

Shapewalker Military Manual

The day after the treekeeper 'incident' was pure torture.

After shouting at Liska for the entire flight home, her mother's fury had fossilised, becoming cold and silent. Her father had been deeply disappointed. Her older sister, Ylva, had almost burst with smugness.

'Of all the things you could have flown into, you

picked the most stupid,' she had said, smirking her face off.

Of course, *she'd* never done anything wrong in her life. Perfectly behaved, top in all her flight and combat classes. She'd even earnt a stripe already, after helping chase off a wyvern on her very first patrol. It was Liska who was the clumsy one. Liska the useless baby. Liska who had to stand there while everyone scowled and pouted and smarmed at her . . .

Now she sat on the stone balcony of her room looking down at the forest city below, feeling very sorry for herself.

Liska's family lived in the Noon Fort, an age-old castle built on top of the northern range of the Shield Mountains. The bottom floors were centuries old and they had been added to over the generations: shapewalkers building up and up and up, until the structure was like a mountain itself. The top turrets were lost in the fog, frosted in ice and snow most of the time. The place bristled with turrets and launching platforms with catapults and trebuchets. Liska thought it was the strongest and safest place in the world.

And the coldest. Her family had chambers halfway up; tapestry-covered rooms with high ceilings and thick stone walls, full of chill that made your breath steam even in summer.

From the balcony Liska could see the whole of Arborven stretched out beneath her dangling feet. In the winter, when the leaves were bare, it looked like a firepit stuffed full of kindling. In the spring, when mists covered the trees, it reminded her of a witch's bubbling cauldron. Today, in its clothes of summer green, the city could have been a giant dish of salad, artfully arranged in circles of slightly different colours.

She watched as a trio of shapewalkers strode out on to one of the launching platforms below. They whipped their hoods on and folded into their manticore shapes, becoming three snarling lions with sweeping wings. One by one they launched themselves into the valley below, then soared up and over the mountains, roaring as they went. The final one spotted Liska watching and tossed its mane in the evening sunlight. Somehow manticores managed to add a bit of arrogance into everything they did.

It made Liska feel even worse about her clumsiness. *I didn't* mean *to fly into the treekeeper,* she thought. *It's not something I would do on purpose. I was only trying to listen to that arbomancer and what he was saying. And then that hunter lady spotted me . . .*

Even after all the yelling, Liska had the sense that the mage's argument with Edda the Ancient had been important. Could he really have been suggesting an experiment with the energy of Bitterblight, the shadow tree? Wouldn't that be a serious threat to them all? And weren't shapewalkers supposed to guard the city from threats?

But nobody had wanted to listen to her side of the story. Forget about protecting Arborven . . . No, all the shouting had been about the embarrassment she had caused. The shame upon the griffyx families. How the manticores downstairs would never let them forget about it.

Liska sighed, adding a small cloud of steam to the wisps of mist that always seemed to drift past the Noon Fort.

From behind her, she heard the chamber door open. Her mother's footsteps as she walked into the room. And her father's. And her sister's.

Uh oh.

'Liska. We need to talk to you.'

She turned to see her family standing with their

27

arms folded, faces stern. All except Ylva, her sister, who looked as though she were about to laugh herself to death. This was not going to be good.

'There's been a meeting of the Noon Fort elders,' said her mother. 'They have decided there need to be consequences for what you did. Your flight and combat training are going ... as well as can be expected. But your behaviour at the Undrentree ... Well, you obviously need to understand more about ... certain things.'

'What things?' Liska understood how to change her shape, how to fight and – apart from little accidents – how to fly. What else was there to know?

'Things about how Arborven works,' said her father. 'About why you should act with respect when you go down to the city.'

'But I *was* being respectful!' Liska jumped up from the balcony and faced everyone, fists on her hips. 'I didn't *mean* to crash into the treekeeper! I didn't do it on purpose!'

'It doesn't matter.' Her mother raised a hand to silence her. Her stern expression melted, just a fraction. 'I know you didn't *mean* to do it, child. But you know full well what the mages think of us. How they judge us

28

every time we venture into Arborven. There's already been gossip about us because of what happened. And the manticores ... they aren't happy. They take these things very seriously. Too seriously, perhaps. But it's been decided. You shall go down to the city tomorrow to learn about its history and customs along with the mages' children.'

Liska couldn't believe what she was hearing.

'They're sending you to tree-wizard school!' Her sister spoke through gusts of laughter and had to stagger from the room bent double. Liska glared as she left.

Young shapewalkers began training in combat and flight as soon as they were old enough to wear their second skins. Survival, first aid, tactics ... every day they had drills out on the mountainside, or even in the Blasted Waste. They never learnt from books and scrolls like the mage children. They had no use for spells and sagas – only battle moves, flight formations and which bits of an enemy were easiest to bite off.

'This kind of learning is usually only for mages,' her father began. 'If you think about it, it's actually an honour to attend such a place ...'

'No, it isn't!'

29

'You will learn many things about how the city was made . . .'

'No, I won't!'

'You'll meet lots of other children your age . . . you might make a friend . . .'

'The mages hate us shapewalkers! And I hate *them*!'

'Enough!' Her mother's shout was filled with the snarl of a fierce vixen. Both Liska and her father closed their mouths instantly and looked sheepish.

'I know you don't like it, Liska. But you're not supposed to. It's a punishment, remember?' Liska looked away, hot tears burning the corners of her eyes. The shameful sense of being a disappointment to her family, her clan.

Her mother sighed, then strode across and pulled her into a tight hug. The fur of her cloak tickled Liska's nose as she tried not to sob into it.

'Darling, I understand. You've probably already learned your lesson and it was an accident after all. But the elders have decided. They wouldn't change their minds, no matter how much I argued.'

'And she *did* argue,' added her father.

'You will attend your first class tomorrow morning at the Undrentree temple. You will hold your head high.

30

You will learn what you can, and you will show them all – mages, manticores, elders – that the griffyx clan take responsibility for their actions. They follow orders. They show respect. And then you can walk away from this whole thing with pride. Can you do that? For me?'

Liska gave a silent nod. There didn't seem much to be proud of, especially with Ylva still giggling her stupid head off in the other room, but she would try.

'That's my girl,' said her mother and, to Liska's great surprise, she squeezed her tight and kissed her.

*

The next morning Liska woke early, hoping to leave before having to endure another round of smirking and sniggering from her sister. Her father was waiting for her at the launching platform, to give her a final hug and whisper in her ear.

'We're proud of you, cub. Your mother is too. Even if she doesn't show it sometimes.'

Too choked to do anything but nod, Liska shifted into her griffyx form and let herself fall from the platform, dropping forty, fifty metres before spreading her wings and gliding down towards Arborven once again.

She landed in Undren Square, empty at this hour, the mages all still sleeping in their wooden tree houses.

Padding on silent paws, she sniffed her way towards the tree, to where rows of buildings towered amongst the roots.

From the ground everything seemed so much larger. The Undrentree's trunk made the Noon Fort look like a doll's house. Its roots loomed like hillsides all around her. Each leaf on the enormous branches above was bigger than Liska herself. She suddenly felt very small and very alone.

The school was part of a complex of buildings next to the arbomancer Academy, her mother had said. It was easy enough to find. The Academy towered over all the surrounding houses and was covered in enough silver-plated carvings to make the thing topple over. It made everything else look very plain and humble. The school was just a simple longhouse beside it.

Liska had no intention of being the first student there. She also didn't think it would go down very well if she turned up in her griffyx form. That meant waiting for a while before shifting back. Changing too quickly could be dangerous for shapewalkers.

Following her nose, she wandered in amongst the roots looking for a spot to rest.

*

32

An hour or so later, having found a perch on a moss-covered tendril, she looked down on to the square as the mages began to wake up and go about their business. Crowds of them, in their different coloured robes, wandered out of the tree circles, milling around like a kicked ant hill before streaming off into the various buildings and workshops that poked out all over the roots.

Several queues formed under the branches, making Liska wonder what they could be up to. Her curiosity was answered when platforms began to descend from the branches above. As soon as they touched the ground, mages swarmed into them, filling them to bursting, before they were winched back up into the clouds of leaves. Up, down, up, down, the lifts began to work non-stop, the sound of creaking ropes even louder than the chattering of the mages.

How ridiculous, Liska thought. *I could fly up there in a few heartbeats. And they think us shapewalkers are backward.*

She watched several younger mages arrive with their parents, waving them goodbye before heading into the school building. Her new classmates. Most likely her new enemies.

A wave of dread washed over her at the sight but she fought it back, hopping down from the root and shifting shape as she landed. *Time for school,* she thought to herself and headed in.

*

Once inside the building, she found the class was being held in a wooden hall full of thick beams and pillars, carved all over with leaves and vines. Peering through the doorway, she could see that desks filled the floorspace, arranged in rows, and there were windows along each side that let in streaks of dust-filled sunlight.

To Liska, used to mountain tops and rooms built from age-old slabs of stone, it seemed stuffy and small. The smell of wood was overpowering, mixed with chalk, varnish and parchment.

At the front was a blackboard with a diagram of the Undrentree drawn in green. Labels and bits of writing were scrawled all around it, but Liska had never been very good at reading. She knew her letters and could struggle through a simple book, but the words had a habit of jumping around on her that made her head hurt and her patience fray. She was much better at fighting and being disobedient.

An old sapsmith was standing at the front of the

class, introducing himself. Apparently his name was Master Ambrose and he was to be their teacher. He had a bald head, straggly white beard and robes of gold and yellow. At least three necklaces of amber fragments hung around his neck, clinking and rattling as he walked. His eyes were watery and weak, and his voice trembly. The kind of voice Liska could very quickly fall asleep listening to.

She had another peep around the classroom.

There were twenty or so students wearing mage robes of all the different circles. Like the city itself, there seemed to be an order of where they sat.

The arbomancers had taken the front seats, closest to the teacher. Silver-robed stormsingers were behind them, then the barkmages and so on . . . all the way to the mossherders in their robes of green.

Taking a deep breath, Liska stepped in and found all the seats were full apart from a row at the back. As she walked further into the room, there was an instant hush, as if a boulder had suddenly dropped through the roof. The mages' eyes locked on to her, following every step.

You will hold your head high. Her mother's words echoed in her head, and she did just that, making her way

35

to the back of the class without catching the eye of any staring mages. She pulled a chair out and sank into one of the empty desks, finding herself all on her own except for a scrawny-looking boy dressed in shades of brown. He had pale pink skin, overly big eyes and close-cropped, wispy blond hair. He looked like he'd been hidden in an underground cave for most of his life and had escaped just to sit in this sweltering, stinky classroom. But at least he wasn't glaring daggers at her like the others.

'I think we are all here now, so I shall begin.' Master Ambrose's voice trickled out over the class like a stream of wheezy syrup. The mages had all turned their attention back to their teacher, leaving Liska peacefully ignored. 'Welcome to the first of seventy-three sessions on the historical, geographical and social history of Arborven. Let us start with the creation of the planet Skyra's magical core, at least fifteen billion years in the past ...'

Here we go, Liska thought as she made a pillow out of her arms on top of the desk. *At least nobody will notice if I have a quick nap.*

*

'... and so, we come to the creation of the trees *Quercus Divinus* and *Quercus Maleficius*. Our Undrentree, for example, whose roots reach down to the well of magic

36

energy at the centre of the planet, and its opposite in nature: Bitterblight, the shadow tree in the Rotlands which drains energy and creates harmful creatures in the form of seepers, shulks, gorgaunts, and so on ...'

'Excuse me, sir?' For the first time in what seemed like three hundred years, Ambrose's voice was interrupted by one of the children. Liska raised her head from her desk, trailing a string of dribble from her bottom lip. She had been having a dream about lying in the boughs of a dusty old tree full of fat orange-and-yellow bumblebees that buzzed in her ears.

'Yes?' Ambrose squinted out at the rows of desks in front of him, seeming surprised to have had his droning interrupted.

The child with her hand up was a green-robed mossherder. One or two of the arbomancers tutted and shook their heads. 'Excuse me, but my father said that Bitterblight and the Undrentree will destroy each other one day, and our city will end. Is that really true?'

This might actually be interesting, Liska thought, sitting up in her chair. Across from her, the pasty, brown-robed boy flipped open a notebook and waited with his pencil poised.

'Hmmm. Well ...' Master Ambrose ran his fingers

through his beard several times as he thought. Liska noticed he wore rings on all his fingers, each with a softly gleaming lump of amber set inside. 'The answer,' he finally said, 'would have to be . . . "perhaps". There have been many pairs of such trees before, you see. It seems to take three to four hundred years for them to fully grow. Then the process begins in which the shadow tree sends out its minions to attack the tree of light, attempting to destroy it.'

'But can't the shadow tree be stopped?' the mossherder asked again. 'Can't we use our magic?'

'We are indeed trying to use our magic,' said Ambrose. 'There are whole sections of the temple whose only purpose is to find a way to destroy Bitterblight before it becomes too powerful. And if it does reach its peak – should that day come – there is always the last resort.'

'What's that, then?' The mossherder's hand was still up and she was now getting lots of angry stares from the children in front. She didn't seem to notice.

'Well, the last resort, as I thought you would have known, is for someone to take the heart of the Undrentree – the glowing seed at the very centre of its trunk – and plunge it into Bitterblight's core. The shadow tree will then be destroyed completely, as will all its hideous creations.'

'Then what will happen to our tree?' asked the mossherder, her voice quivering.

'Ah,' said Ambrose. 'Then, unfortunately, our tree will die. And the city will die with it. Of course, this is very unlikely to happen. We are bound to come up with a way to stop Bitterblight before then.'

Liska's mind flashed with the scene from the other day – the argument on Undren Square that had landed her in so much trouble – and before she knew it, her own hand had gone up.

'Is it true that some of you mage-folk are planning to use the powers of Bitterblight as a weapon?' There was a sudden, complete silence in the classroom. Her voice seemed to echo about the rafters and every single pair of eyes turned to stare at her again, to burn right into her flesh. The arbomancers, in particular, looked livid with fury. A bulky, scowling boy at the front was going a ripe shade of purple.

'A weapon?' Ambrose squinted in her direction, his head turning to and fro like a blind mole, popping out from its tunnel into the sunlight. 'Wherever did you hear that?'

The angry faces stared daggers at Liska. This was the point when she should mumble something about making a mistake and put her head down. But Liska was never very good at doing what she *should*. The thought of it usually made her do just the opposite.

'I saw one of you talking about it with a treekeeper. Well, shouting, actually. It was a bald man in black robes. An arbo-whatsit, I think. He was saying how he wanted to try and control the forces of Bitterblight himself. I don't think the treekeeper was too happy.'

'Ah,' said Ambrose. 'Ah, yes. *That* unfortunate incident.' His watery gaze turned to the big arbomancer child in the front row. The one who looked like he was about to climb out of his chair and thump Liska very hard. 'There was some talk about that recently. Fortunately – or unfortunately, perhaps – the mage in question seems to have . . . left the city. Shall we move on?'

No, thought Liska. *We definitely shan't.* 'But what if he's left the city to do just what he said? What if he's messing around with Bitterblight right now? Shouldn't the treekeepers be hunting him down? Shouldn't he be thrown in a dungeon somewhere?'

At this, the arbomancer boy actually slammed his fist on his desk. The rest of the class gasped.

'Now, now,' said Master Ambrose, flapping his wrinkled hands. 'That's quite enough. Calm yourself, Odis. The matter has been dealt with and we are getting distracted from my lesson plan. Where were we?'

Ambrose resumed his mumbling about the forces of magic, tree roots and circles of power and gradually all the children turned away from Liska, back to the notebooks and scrolls on their desks. All except Odis, who continued to stare at her from under his mop of black hair for another long minute.

Liska stared back, her fingers idly playing with the fur collar of her cloak. *Let him try to do anything to me,* she thought. *He'll soon learn not to mess with shapewalkers.*

Another, less fierce, part of her mind wondered what his connection to the bald mage might be. Friend? Nephew? Son?

Whatever it was, Liska had a feeling she would soon find out.

*

In the end, it took much less time than she expected.

After they had listened to another hour or two of wittering, they were allowed outside to have a bit of fresh air.

There was a patch of muddy earth next to the classroom, walled in on all sides by other wooden temple buildings. Overhead hung the branches of the Undrentree, like some kind of dappled green sky. Wavering puddles of light seeped through the overlapping leaves. Everything was tinted green, speckled with floating seeds and flitting insects.

As soon as they were released, the mage children wandered into familiar groups, each in their own part of the playground. Mostly, Liska noticed, they stuck together with others from their circle. The arbomancers seemed to strut around the centre, full of self-importance, while the lesser mages huddled at the edges.

So young, and already obeying the order of the city, Liska thought. Although there were some who didn't seem to bother who they played with. She watched as an arbomancer conjured several tree shoots from the ground and then weaved his hands through the air, making them twine into a ball. A barkmage came over and spoke a few words. The shoot-ball hardened itself, snapping off and rolling across the earth. A stormsinger hit it with a blast of wind, making it fly into the air and then the three children were running after it, kicking it backwards and forwards and laughing to each other.

Liska was about to go over and join in when a shadow fell across her. She looked up to see the big arbomancer boy blocking her path, along with a cluster of others. They looked like his followers, copying his every move. The way their faces were set into mean, hard scowls. Why did bullies always seem to have a flock of smaller bullies around them?

'Who do you think you are, you flea-bitten shapeshifter? Coming down into our city and spreading filthy lies about people better than you?' The boy's voice was full of hate. His eyes were dark and sour, almost hidden by a sweep of black hair. Liska noticed his hands were at his sides, clenching into fists.

'It's not a lie,' she said. 'I saw it. And you should be careful how you speak to shapewalkers. Just because we don't live in your city, doesn't mean we have no magic.'

Her fingers moved to the collar of her cloak as if she was about to flip on her hood, and she was rewarded by all of the mages taking a quick step backwards.

'You don't scare us,' said the arbomancer boy. 'You're nothing more than a monster from a fairy tale. We'll teach you to stay in your mountains, just you see.'

Before Liska could do anything, the boy brought

43

his hands up, twisting them in a strange pattern. Liska thought she saw a hint of green light sparkling in the air, and then there was a crunching sound as two thick vines burst up from the ground.

Stepping backwards, Liska tried to pull on her hood, tried to take her griffyx shape, but the vines were too quick. They snapped themselves around her shoulders, pinning her arms to her body. Round and round they whipped until she couldn't move her upper half. She was even having trouble breathing, as the vines squeezed her so tightly.

'Greetings from the stormsingers,' said a girl in silver robes. She reached up towards the sky, then dragged her hand down in a fist causing a tiny storm of raindrops to lash Liska's head, soaking her to the skin.

'And the barkmages,' said another. He touched the vines and they hardened like iron. All Liska's strength couldn't make them budge.

'Don't forget the mossherders,' added a girl in green robes and streaks of lichen in her hair. She hummed under her breath and Liska felt a wet, furry moustache form over her top lip. Compared to what the others had done, it seemed a bit pathetic.

'H-hey! You fellows! Y-you really should leave her

alone, you know. Master Ambrose might give you all extra homework. Or tell your parents, maybe.'

As Liska spat the fresh-grown moss away, she saw the brown-robed boy who had sat across from her edge up to her attackers. He was trembling like a new-formed leaf on the Undrentree. The mages immediately burst out laughing.

'What are you going to do, worm-face? Throw maggots at us?' The big arbomancer clapped his hands and guffawed. All his cronies laughed even harder. The boy seemed to shrink into his robes, as if he was about to shrivel up and disappear.

'What's going on here?' From the classroom doorway came Master Ambrose's voice, no longer weak and brittle. His old eyes flashed with anger as he glared towards them. He began to stomp over and the bullies instantly scattered, leaving Liska – still wrapped in hardened vines – and her would-be rescuer.

'Who did this to you?' Ambrose asked, stepping up to Liska and putting a hand on the wooden cocoon that bound her. She felt the strips of vine begin to vibrate as if something inside them was twitching, then one by one they snapped and fell to the floor.

'Oh, nobody really,' she said. Even though she had

45

begun to hate that arbomancer and his friends, she knew better than to tell tales. She would much rather settle the matter on her own. 'Some kids were just showing me their *amazing* powers.'

Ambrose looked at her long and hard before nodding his head. 'If that's the way you wish it,' he said. 'But I would like to apologise on behalf of all of us that live in the city. I know the way shapewalkers are treated – why they don't often come down here. The young ones – and some of their parents – don't really understand what your people do for us. The danger you face so that we may be safe. The bravery and sacrifices you make on our behalf, and the way you do it without any thought of reward or praise.'

Liska gaped. She had no idea anybody in Arborven felt that way. She had grown used to the idea of being despised and ignored. 'It's nothing—' she started to say.

'It most certainly isn't "nothing",' said Ambrose. 'You warriors risk your lives for us all the time. Don't think that it's not appreciated . . . no matter how some of us may act.'

He nodded at Liska, and then walked back to the classroom, leaving her to rub her sore shoulders, bruised where the vines had squeezed them.

'Flukes and nematodes,' said a quiet voice next to her. 'That was close.' Liska had forgotten about the brown-robed boy. He was still standing there, blinking at her with his puppy-dog eyes. His hands were still trembling and a tiny vein had started to twitch on his forehead.

'Thanks for trying to help me,' she said. 'But I had the whole thing under control.'

'Oh, did you?' said the boy. 'Because it looked a bit like Odis and his friends had you trapped and were about to kill you. Anyone who even mentions his father is risking their life.'

'So, the shouty mage was his father? That figures. I'm Liska, by the way.' She held out a hand, expecting him to grasp her wrist in a warrior handshake. Instead he took hold of her fingertips and gave them a tiny wiggle. It was a bit like shaking hands with a breeze.

'I'm Lug,' he said. 'Pleased to meet you. You're the first shapewalker I've seen. Up close, that is.'

'What type of tree wizard are you, then?' Liska asked. 'I didn't know there were any who wore brown robes.'

Lug sighed a little as he answered. 'I'm a vermispex,' he said. 'There aren't very many of us. And we're not very ... well known.'

47

Liska raised an eyebrow. This was something she'd never heard of before. 'What's your power?'

Lug blushed. For a moment Liska thought he wasn't going to tell her, but then he knelt and tapped on the ground as if he were knocking at a door. When he stood again, there was a plump, glistening earthworm coiled on the palm of his hand.

He began to waggle his fingers and the worm reared up, waving its head from side to side like a snake-charmed cobra. Then it wound itself into a ball and began to roll around. Finally, Lug knelt back down and released it. The poor thing hastily buried itself in the soil, disappearing from sight.

'Worms,' said Lug. 'We summon and control the worms in the soil of Arborven. They keep the earth fresh and full of food for the trees, you know. Without us, the city would probably shrivel up and die. You'd think everyone would appreciate that a bit more. But they don't.'

'So, do you have a circle to live in? How close to the tree is it?'

'Well,' Lug began to squirm. 'It's not a circle exactly. And it's probably not as close as it could be. In fact, it's quite far away. Behind . . . behind the mossherders.'

'*Less* important than the mossherders, eh?' Liska laughed and gave Lug a friendly punch on the shoulder that almost knocked him over. 'Don't worry. *My* people are as far away from the tree as you can get. It doesn't bother me where you live or what your powers are.'

'That's just as well. Or you'd have to ignore me like the others all do.' Lug gave her a half smile. 'Did you really see Odis's father argue with the treekeepers?'

Liska nodded and proceeded to tell Lug all about her fateful flight around the tree, and the row she had overheard. He listened with eyes gleaming, then gave a low whistle as she finished.

'It's been the talk of the city,' he explained. 'Everyone knows Noxis – that's Odis's father, by the way – has been dabbling with dark magic. We heard that he had fallen out with the treekeepers and then, just a day ago, he disappeared. That's why Odis is so touchy – he thinks people are talking about his family behind his back. Saying they are traitors, poisoned by the rot.'

'What about the hunter lady?' Liska asked. 'Who was she?'

'That must have been Thresher,' said Lug with a shiver. 'She's a scout who actually ventures out of the city into the Blasted Waste and beyond. She reports to the treekeepers sometimes about how far the rot has spread. Most people are afraid of her. They say she got her scars from a wyvern that she killed. Her throat was almost torn out and now she can hardly speak.'

'And she's working with this Noxis? Trying to find a way to control the rot?'

'Could be,' said Lug. 'She comes and goes, so nobody would notice if she was missing too.'

Liska thought for a moment, playing the scene under the tree through her mind for the hundredth time. 'I don't understand why the treekeepers would be so cross with them. At least they're trying to defeat Bitterblight somehow. I can't see anyone else doing much to help.'

Lug gaped at her, as if she'd said something terrible. 'Are you joking? Even *thinking* about using the rot is forbidden,' he whispered. 'It's against every law in Arborven! Noxis wanted to control it, to bring it *inside* the city. He could have destroyed us all! Just thinking about it makes me want to faint . . .'

'Keep your robes on,' said Liska. 'I was just thinking aloud. I'm as worried about the rot as you are. But what else is there to do? Are you mages just going to sit around waiting until you have to take the

50

Undrentree's heart and destroy Bitterblight with it? Is that the great plan?'

Lug stared at her for a moment, and then glanced around the playground as if making sure nobody was listening. He beckoned her closer until his mouth was just inches from her ear. 'The treekeepers are probably working on a plan,' he whispered, 'but they're taking their time about it. I've heard of another way, though. Top secret. A way to kill Bitterblight *without* having to sacrifice the Undrentree.'

'What?' Liska lowered her voice too, even though she half-thought this strange boy might be crazy. 'Tell me what it is!'

'Not here,' whispered Lug, looking all around again, his eyes full of fear. 'Come to my house after school. I'll tell you all about it then. And don't mention it to *anyone.*'

Before Liska could reply, Master Ambrose appeared at the doorway again, this time with a hand bell which he rang loudly. On cue, the children began to shuffle back into the classroom to hear more tedious tree histories. Whatever Lug's deadly secret was, it would have to wait.

3

'And one day the Mighty Worm
shall return. And all shall cower
before its Glorious Segments.'

The Legend of Nematus

The rest of the day passed so slowly, Liska felt she was one of the dead prehistoric insects frozen forever in the amber beads of Master Ambrose's necklace.

From her place in the farthest corner of the classroom she cast glances across at Lug, but he was absorbed with the notebook in front of him. Scribbling and doodling away. Liska hoped he might be writing a message for her detailing his secret plan, but none came.

She did catch Odis, the arbomancer's son, looking at her though. His lip was curled in a sneer that grew deeper each time she saw him. Liska matched it with a snarl of her own. *Fancy trying to stare down a shapewalker,* she thought. *Us mountain warriors invented glaring.*

Finally, *finally*, Ambrose's voice trailed off and he dismissed them from the classroom with a wave of his hand. Liska and Lug waited until Odis and his friends were gone before making their way out between the desks.

'Do you think he's going to ambush me?' Liska asked. 'Jump out from behind a tree? Because I'll be ready if he does.' She was thinking about shifting into her griffyx form, just in case. Let him try and wrap her in vines when she was swooping through the air, snapping at him with her jaws . . .

'Bless my wrigglers, I hope not!' Lug began peering at the shadows all around him. That little vein in his forehead had started pulsing again.

'Relax,' said Liska. 'He won't really. He's a bully, and bullies are nearly all cowards. He won't try anything if he thinks there's a chance I'll hurt him.'

'I suppose so,' said Lug. He took some deep breaths to calm himself. 'Besides, he's probably run home to avoid all the gossips. Everyone is still wondering where his father is.'

'Hmpf,' said Liska. She had been quite looking forward to getting her revenge. 'So, are you going to tell me your secret now? Your plan for getting rid of Bitterblight and saving the Undrentree?'

'Not *here*!' Lug hissed, eyes darting around the empty corridor. 'The trees in Arborven have ears! I'll tell you when we're back where I live, where it's safe.'

He led them out of the school, in between the jumble of roots and on to the Undren Square. Liska looked up to where the titanic branches of the tree blocked out the sky, hundreds of feet above, and imagined herself swooping and gliding between them. Part of her wanted to spread her griffyx wings and take off, but she had to admit she was intrigued by Lug's secret. If he wanted to keep it so badly, surely it must be worth hearing?

She glanced across at the scrawny boy. The way his round head seemed to wobble on his skinny neck. His habit of twitching his hands up inside his robe sleeves. He didn't *seem* like a person who would know deep,

54

dark, hidden things. But then – as shapewalkers like her knew better than most – people weren't always what they appeared to be.

The pair made their way across the open ground and into the first circle of trees that curved before them like a leafy wall. They were all oaks, as thick and gnarly as any Liska had ever seen. Some must have been hundreds of years old.

Most were built around with the houses of the arbomancers. Each of these had several floors and extra rooms jutting up all over the place in miniature turrets. They lined the branches and swallowed the broad trunks of the trees, and all were of the same style: dark oak planks, trimmed with silver-painted carvings.

Wide, arched windows with coloured glass panels let Liska peer into libraries, kitchens, greenhouses, studies, bedrooms, conservatories ... every room you could possibly imagine. The furnishings were of the highest quality, the paths and gardens swept and trimmed. Not a blade of grass was out of place. It made Liska want to scratch the place up a bit, just to make it look real.

One or two buildings were shops selling food, flowers, gardening tools or tomes and scrolls filled with scribbled spells. They paused at a baker's to buy a paper twist of almond and nutmeg cookies, which they munched as they walked. In between nibbles, Liska peered at the city folk, fascinated by how different they were to the military shapewalkers of her home fort.

Mages wandered in between the trunks, dressed in black robes, lined or embroidered with glittering silver. Men and women, old and young, they all held themselves with supreme confidence. Whenever one of them spotted Liska and Lug, they raised their eyebrows as if wondering what such lowly creatures were doing in the circle of the arbomancers.

'Doesn't it annoy you?' she asked Lug, 'that the arbomancers think they're the best just because of where they live?'

Lug winced. 'Don't say that so loudly!' He cast a nervous glance at a passing mage strutting by with her silver staff and an angry-looking rook perched on her shoulder. Then he leant in to whisper in Liska's ear. 'Of course it's annoying. And unfair. I mean, being able to grow and shape the trees ... well, that's an important power. But they shouldn't look down on everybody else the way they do. We all play a part in Arborven.'

'Do the circles ever change? Do groups of mages ever become more powerful?'

Lug shook his head. 'It's always been this way. Power comes from the tree, and those closest have more of it. They'd never want to move, not unless they were forced out of their houses. Besides, arbomancers *need* the most power. Their kind of magic uses up lots of it.'

It did indeed seem unfair to Liska. But then, she supposed, it was a bit similar to the shapewalker families. The cockatrices and manticores thought they were stronger and better than the rest, and that would never change. Nor would they ever give their precious skins to anyone outside their family. Power, or the thought of it, was hoarded by shapeshifters like a wyvern hoarded gold.

Soon they passed out of the first circle and into the second. The trees changed from oak to hazel: smoother bark, ramrod-straight branches and catkins dangling from sprays of bushy green leaves. The sun made rippling streaks of light as it shone through the canopy and Liska's feet seemed to sink in the spongy soil. Red squirrels dashed up and down the tree trunks or scurried about the ground burying stashes of hazelnuts for the winter, and chirping birds of all colours flitted through the branches.

How different it was from walking on granite mountaintops and through stone-paved hallways as she was used to.

The tree houses here were of a different style, too. Still built of wood, they were all pods or spheres, hanging from the branches or clustered about the trunks. This was the circle of the stormsingers: mages who were a bit more familiar to Liska. She often saw them visiting the mountains where they kept the mists swirling around the outside of the city, hiding its presence from hungry wyverns.

Here, in their circle, were traces of their magic. Weather charms hung from twigs everywhere and there were random patches of fog, drifting on stray gusts of wind. Liska even saw a tiny thunderstorm, crackling with baby lightning, as it hung over one of the rooftops.

'Don't you wish you could learn another kind of magic?' she asked Lug. 'Then you could move into one of these circles. You could swan around in silver robes and sneer at everyone else.'

'It's not that simple,' said Lug, stepping aside as a stormsinger lady and her child barged past, noses in the air. 'The kind of magic you do is in your blood.

Sometimes people from different circles get married and move, but mostly we just stick to our own.'

'Us shapewalkers are a bit like that too.' Liska swished her cloak, showing off the scales and folded wings. 'I'm of the griffyx clan, and we keep to the Noon Fort. If I was a simurgh, I'd live in Cliffside to the south. I'd probably think having a peacock body and a wolf's head was the best, and I wouldn't dream of swapping my skin. And I'd definitely never want to be a flightless mage.'

'Not even if you could be a powerful arbomancer?' Lug's voice held just the tiniest trace of envy.

'Not even,' said Liska with certainty. 'Why, would you like to be one? Are you fed up of being looked down on the whole time?'

Lug was quiet for a few steps before he replied. 'A bit,' he said. 'I suppose. I wouldn't really want to change ... I do love worms ... but I'd like to show all the others just how powerful vermispexes can be. I'd like to ...'

'Go on,' Liska urged. 'You'd like to what?'

'To summon the god worm,' Lug mumbled under his breath.

'The what?'

'Nematus,' said Lug, blushing crimson. 'The god worm. He's an earthworm the size of a mountain. Us vermispexes believe he exists somewhere beneath the ground. If one of us could just summon him ... then the other mages would have to think again about us being the weakest. I know it's just a stupid daydream, really, but ...'

Liska slapped him on the back, knocking him into a tree. 'It's not stupid, Lug. Everyone should have a dream. Nobody should just bumble along because that's the way "things have always been done". How would the world ever change?'

'What's yours, then?' Lug asked, rubbing his head where it had just bounced off a branch. 'What's your dream?'

'That's easy,' said Liska, grinning. 'To have an incredible adventure and earn a stripe. And then another and another, until I have the most ever.'

Lug's face was blank so Liska explained to him all about shapewalkers and how they could win stripes of coloured fur by doing great deeds. She told him how her mother had gained hers, and about all the other shapewalker families and their quirks. She was just describing the ceremony in which shapewalkers first receive their skin when they walked out from the final circle of elm trees.

Before them, a few hundred metres away, rose the sheer granite face of the western Shield Mountains. Up there, Liska knew, hidden in the clouds, was the ruined fortress known as The Breach. Guarded by winged pantherine and cockatrice shapewalkers – some of the fiercest fighters of her kind – it was the most important of all Arborven's defences. Because, on the other side of the mountains, lay the Rotlands. Home of Bitterblight itself and teeming with the poisonous monstrosities the shadow tree had created.

The land between the mountains' feet and the last circle of the forest-city was peppered with the odd leafless, stunted tree and hummocks of straggly grass. Wisps of mist crawled over the ground, and beneath it could be seen stagnant pools of dirty water and churned-up patches of wet mud.

'Well,' said Lug with a sweep of his arms. 'We're here. This is the Scrubbings. Home sweet home.'

'You live in a *swamp*?' Liska had been expecting a humble tree house. Maybe a little copse. This place looked like a scene from a horror story about demonic frogs.

'It's nice and moist,' said Lug, flinching at her reaction. 'Good for the worms.'

'It's ... um ... lovely,' Liska lied, trying not to wrinkle her nose at the damp, putrid stink.

That seemed to perk Lug up a bit. 'We live in a burrow by that stump over there,' he said. 'Would you like to come in for a cup of tea?'

The thought of being trapped underground anywhere, let alone in a foetid marsh hole, walls seeping with mildewy water, filled Liska with horror. She was used to open skies, fresh air and freedom. Even walking between the Arborven trees had made her feel a bit claustrophobic.

'That's very kind,' she said, 'but I should be flying back home. The sun is almost setting. Perhaps you could just tell me your secret now and then I can be off.'

'Oh,' said Lug, blushing again. 'Yes, of course. The secret.'

Liska sat on a nearby hummock of dry grass and folded her arms, waiting.

'Well, it's actually more of a legend, you see ...' Lug began. 'A story, or a myth ... about another set of twin trees, far in the north ...'

A frown began to wrinkle Liska's face. Had she really walked across the whole of Arborven to hear an old fable?

'You *said* it was a secret. You *said* you had a way to kill Bitterblight. I thought you meant something real, not just a bedtime story.'

Lug twisted the sleeves of his robe in his hands, beads of sweat on his head, trying to find words to explain himself. 'The legend isn't the secret. It's how I found out about it. And that I don't think it *is* a legend. It might actually be true. But I can't tell anyone *how* I know without getting into serious trouble . . .'

Nothing Lug said was making any sense and he was getting more and more upset. Liska realised she was going to have to calm him down somehow. With a sigh, she unfolded her arms and tried to look less threatening, a skill she wasn't naturally very good at. 'Look, start from the beginning. Take a deep breath and tell me what the legend is.'

'Yes.' Lug stopped flapping with his robe and nodded. 'The beginning. So. There's a story about another pair of trees, just like our Undrentree and Bitterblight, except far, far to the north where the snow and glaciers are. Have you heard it?'

Liska shook her head. She had never been very interested in legends or any other part of the world that wasn't the Shield Mountains.

'Well, the ice there moves in giant sheets – slow but unstoppable – and eats up everything it comes across. Cities, villages, farms, all vanish beneath it as it shifts. And of course it destroys sacred trees too.'

'So the trees up there are gone?'

'Just the shadow tree,' said Lug, his wide eyes beginning to gleam. 'It got swallowed by the ice before it could attack. Which means the light tree is still there. Nammu it was called. Just think . . . a spare tree, with a heart inside it that could be used to destroy Bitterblight! We could kill it with Nammu's heart and leave the Undrentree untouched!'

Liska took one of her locks between her fingers and rolled it back and forth, thinking. *If it sounds too good to be true, that's because it is.* Her mother said that all the time. And she could see at least three major faults with Lug's story already.

'How do you know the glacier hasn't swallowed this Nammu as well?'

Lug flinched. 'Well . . . I suppose I don't. Somebody would have to go up there and see. But I know it was still there some time ago. And glaciers move *very* slowly.'

'And what about the city that owns Nammu? Don't you think they'd be upset if we turned up, cut the heart out of their tree and ran off?'

Lug's eyes gleamed again. He did a little jump from foot to foot. 'There *is* no city! That's the amazing thing! The people who lived there had to flee the glacier and move south. Nammu is just sitting there, waiting to be frozen . . . its heart doesn't belong to anyone!'

Liska shook her head. 'I'd like to believe you, Lug, I honestly would. But this does sound like some kind of fairy tale. If it was true, don't you think the treekeepers would have been to this Nammu tree themselves?'

'That's just it!' Lug looked as though he might pop at any moment. 'Everybody thinks it's only a story. Nobody takes it seriously! Except I *know* someone who's seen it. I know it's really true!'

'How?' Liska asked. 'Who is this person you know? And why don't they just go and tell the treekeepers themselves?'

Lug fell silent again. His cheeks flushed and he shot Liska a guilty look. Then he gave a guilty glance over her shoulder.

Liska followed his gaze and saw he was looking at a patch of scruffy woodland in the distance. Separated from the circles of the forest, it was sandwiched in between the mountains and the swampy Scrubbings.

'The Cryptwood?' Liska had flown over the deserted patch of trees before. She had seen the dead branches with their iron-grey bark. She had heard the owls hooting between its misty, cold trunks and had listened to the spooky stories about what lived within. All the time she had thought it was just creepy nonsense to scare tiny children with.

'I did something I'm not supposed to,' said Lug, his eyes fixed on the ground. 'I heard something I probably shouldn't.'

Liska was about to press him for more when she heard a familiar noise. One which usually spelled danger, even death.

Crrrrrrrrackkkkk!

'Rockslide!' she shouted, leaping up to grab Lug and shield him. Only after she had wrapped her arms around him did she realise they weren't three hundred feet up, balancing on the sheer mountain face, so they were probably quite safe.

In the distance, a cascade of small boulders tumbled

and smacked their way down the mountainside, breaking into fragments before splashing into the swamp with muddy, sticky explosions. *Splap! Splap! Splurp!*

By instinct, Liska followed their trail with her eyes to see if any more were coming. That was when she spotted the figure standing on a ledge fifty metres up, at the bottom of a jagged split in the granite.

'There's somebody up there,' she said, releasing Lug who jumped away as far as he could, still squirming.

'Where?' he said, peering up at the rock.

'On that ledge,' said Liska, pointing. 'Someone in black robes. And he's doing something . . . magical.'

The figure was gesturing, moving in the way Liska had seen mages do when they summoned up their power. It looked as though he was trying to open up the granite mountain behind him, as though he was forming some kind of a gateway.

Lug, squinting upwards, had seen him now. Suddenly his face went even paler than usual. 'Is that . . . could it be . . .'

'The arbomancer! The father of that bully from the playground!'

'Yes, Noxis. But what is he doing?'

The pair watched as the mage finished his spell. Then he stood aside and waited. Waited for something to come through the tunnel he had made.

Liska and Lug moved closer and clutched each other again. They stood with their necks craned upwards, breath held, staring at the spot where the thing would emerge.

Both of them had an idea what it might be, but the actual sight of it made them step backwards in terror.

A tendril appeared first. Like the first shoot of a plant or tree, sightlessly feeling its way around its new world. Except this one was made of shadowy darkness. A dark grey, flowing liquid, wisps of smoke seeping from its edges.

'It's true!' Liska fought back the urge to scream. 'Everything I heard him say at the Undren Square! I *knew* the city was in danger! I knew it!'

'The rot ...' Lug could only manage a strangled whisper. 'He's bringing the rot inside the city. That thing is a seeper ...'

More of the sludge emerged. The tar-like goo had formed itself into a humanoid shape. A featureless head, writhing grasping arms that slapped and stuck to the stone as it hauled itself through. It lurched and wobbled as it moved, stretching itself then shrinking, so that one moment it was taller than the mage that summoned it, the next half his size.

Others filled the tunnel behind it and Noxis beckoned them onwards, out on to a path that led down the mountainside towards the Scrubbings and into Arborven. The second walked on all fours like a beast, the third had seven or eight limbs that waved in the air as it shuffled and slithered along. They were formed differently but all were made of the same slimy, oozing goo.

'It's a sneak attack,' said Liska. 'He's smuggling those things in to kill the treekeepers!'

'Bitterblight must have cast a spell on him,' said Lug. 'Possessed him. Made him turn against us. That's why it's forbidden to experiment with rot. That's why the treekeepers were furious with Noxis!'

'The shapewalkers won't have seen him,' said Liska. 'They only expect attacks to come *over* the mountains. We have to warn everybody. Raise the alarm . . .'

She looked back into the forest. The Undrentree was so far away . . . by the time she reached it, there would be a whole flood of rot creatures pouring down from the tunnel.

Then she looked upwards, up where the clouds hid the broken fortress. There were hundreds of shapewalkers up there, primed and ready for battle . . .

'Lug!' She pulled her new friend towards her, making him look away from the horrors that were frothing out of the tunnel mouth. 'I have to fly up to the fortress and sound the alarm. You need to warn the treekeepers. Run back to the Undrentree, shouting all the way. Get the mages to come here. We have to stop Noxis before he lets too many of those things through!'

'Yes,' Lug stammered. 'R-right.' He looked as though he might be about to turn his robe an even deeper shade of brown. But Liska didn't have time to worry about him. She pulled her hood over her head and dropped forwards, letting her cloak fall around her shoulders. The pull of the animal skin called her, washing over her until she felt herself begin to melt away . . .

Lug watched the transformation with his hands clapped over his mouth. He had seen magic before but nothing quite as dramatic as Liska's change. Her cloak seemed to coil itself around her body as if it were alive, and then she folded inwards, shrinking, bending. The hollow, floppy limbs of the griffyx fur started to pop and jut with bones and muscle. The dead, feathered wings on its back began to flap and flutter. The empty sockets on the fox-fur head were suddenly filled with Liska's eyes. Bright green, fierce and now wide with fright.

Finally, the ears pricked, the jaws snapped and a puppy-pink tongue flashed. Where the fierce girl had stood a moment before, a winged, scaled fox now crouched, tail swishing, nose twitching.

'What are you standing around for?' the griffyx said with Liska's voice. 'Get running!'

Then it hunkered down, beat its wings and shot off upwards, heading for the mountaintop.

4

'To the west stands the Breach. Brave
fortress. Our first defence against
the Rotlands, and the home of our
fiercest shapewalker guardians.'

A Guide to Arborven by Obediah Dawnsoul

The fortress known as the Breach was as old as the
city itself. Built from man-sized chunks of carved
granite, at some point in its history it had been damaged
in a wyvern attack. Split in half down the middle, one side
of the stocky tower had slid sideways, crashing through
walls and smaller buildings, threatening to topple down
into the valley below but not quite managing it.

That had been hundreds of years ago, and it still hadn't fallen. Shored up, reinforced and built all over with layer after layer of new stone, the lopsided fort now bristled with landing platforms, flags, banners, catapults, ballistae and lookout points. Not to mention extra turrets and observatories where stormsingers brewed their protective mists and master mages peered out at the Rotlands, trying to estimate how fast the black plague of Bitterblight was spreading.

Its battlements and walkways were patrolled by the prowling forms of shapewalkers dressed in leather armour criss-crossed with straps and buckles. They carried no weapons but wore cloaks of fur and hide that trailed behind them. Claws and fangs glinted in the scraps of sunlight that broke through the fog and cloud. *Those* were their weapons, hungrier and deadlier than any spear or blade.

Liska made for them now, pounding her wings against the air, fighting to climb as fast as she could. There was no time to glide in circles, rising on thermal currents, as she had been taught. Every second she spent flying, another one of those *things* could be oozing its way through Noxis's tunnel.

Panting for breath, she reached the lowest walkway

of the fort and crash-landed, spilling into a tumble of legs and wings and cracking her snout on the flagstones. Scrambling up, she tucked her wings away and began scampering on paws up stairway after stairway, following trails of scents, desperate to find somebody, anybody who could raise the alarm.

Bursting on to the wide rampart that ran along the top of the mountain wall, claws skittering, she nearly collided with two shapewalkers who had been standing there looking out across the cloudscape of white mist that stretched away over the Rotlands, cloaking the advance of Noxis and his seepers below.

'Hey, steady there, young fox-thing,' one of them said. 'You shouldn't be up here!'

Liska looked up to see a battle-scarred walker with her locks pulled up into a topknot. Her hair was shaved to the skin on either side in the warrior style, revealing a nasty scar where she had lost the top of one ear.

'Alarm ...' Liska's chest heaved as she fought to get words out. 'Below ... Stubbings ... seepers ...'

'What are you talking about?' The second shapewalker bent down to scowl at her, his eyes flashing with fury. 'Griffyxes aren't allowed on the Breach! Get back to your foxhole!'

Being talked down to reminded Liska of the way her parents kept on treating her like a helpless cub. It made her temper flare. With a growl of her own, she wrenched herself out of her animal form, rising up on two legs and flinging back her cloak. Even as her body rippled back into its human shape, she was shouting in the second shapewalker's face.

'Don't tell me where to go! I'm trying to save you all! There's seepers and rot creatures coming through the mountain down below, in the swamp! A tunnel has been opened and they're inside the city, right under your stupid noses!'

The effort of changing shape so quickly, coupled with her frantic flight, overcame her and she felt her knees give way just as she spat out the last word. She toppled to the stone of the walkway and the first shapewalker leapt to grab her.

'Is this true?' she asked. 'It's not some silly fox-cub trick?'

'Please ...' was all Liska could say. She could almost *feel* the oily creatures below her pouring into Arborven.

The first shapewalker pulled Liska into her arms. She smelt of oiled leather, mountain mist and ... cat.

'Abra!' She snapped at her partner. 'Don't just stand there! Light the signal fire! Sound the alarm ... we are attacked!'

Abra stared down at them for a second before realising she was serious. Fear and anger flickered over his face, and then he was away, pulling his cloak over his head as he ran. From her place on the floor, Liska had a glimpse of two clawed legs, a whiplash tail and a pair of enormous bat-like wings appearing. The thing jogged along the parapet before taking off, looking back as it launched: it had a beaked, feathered head and the leathery comb of a rooster.

Cockatrice, Liska thought as her woozy head swam. *I've only seen them in the distance before. They're so much bigger than I'd imagined.*

'Child, I must go and help rouse the warriors.' The woman's face was just a few centimetres from her own and Liska noticed her pupils were slitted, like a cat's. 'Will you be alright if I leave you?'

Liska managed a nod and a groan. Her head was still spinning, and each muscle in her body burned like lava, but she didn't care about herself. She wanted every shapewalker in the Breach to swarm down to the valley below. Now.

'You did well, little sister,' said the woman, leaning Liska against the cold stone parapet and briefly clasping her forearm in the greeting of warrior comrades. 'Selka of the pantherines is proud of you.'

Liska didn't know what to say. A warrior like Selka . . . praising *her*? Her mouth opened and closed a few times, like a fish gasping for air. Selka just smiled, then stood up and drew her own cloak around her, melting into her beast shape more swiftly and elegantly than any walker Liska had seen.

In a blink, a black-furred panther stood there, almost buzzing with power and strength. Dozens of glowing blue stripes covered her two front legs. From her back, a pair of eagle wings quivered. She stretched them out, revealing a span at least three times that of Liska's.

The pantherine threw back her head and thundered out a roar that thrummed through the stones around them. With a lash of her tail she pounced up and over Liska, swooping off the battlements and up towards the bulk of the ruined fort, sending a wash of air that blew Liska flat on to her face.

She turned her head to watch the pantherine go and saw, behind Selka, a plume of flame burst up from the tower's summit.

The signal fire is lit, she thought. *I did it. Mother might finally be proud.*

*

As Liska waited for her head to stop spinning, noise erupted from the fort around her. She heard the clanging of alarm bells, roars and crows from shifted shapewalkers, the flapping of leathery wings ...

Pulling herself up to peer over the battlements, she saw scores of flying creatures pouring from every landing platform, spilling from windows, leaping off turrets. Cockatrices, pantherines, griffins ... even a lamassu. Each and every one tucked their wings as soon as they were airborne and dived straight down, vanishing into the layer of mist that spread out from the mountain top.

Liska strained her ears, trying to pick up the clash of battle from below. But human hearing was so weak and useless. All she could make out were war cries and the crowing of the cockatrices.

Got to get down there, she told herself. *See if I can help.*

It wasn't good for shapewalkers to flit in and out of their two forms so quickly. Melting yourself from one thing to another took a lot of energy and doing it too often could cause shape sickness. There were even cases of walkers who broke themselves in the process, ending up stuck forever as a beast, or worse, as a human.

It was only sensible for her to stay where she was. Rest and gather strength before trying to shift again. She had done her part; nobody could say otherwise. Her mother might actually be proud of her, and she would definitely be glad Liska was safe, out of harm's way.

Roots to that, Liska thought. There was no way she was going to sit up here, where she couldn't even see the fighting. And if she flew below and managed to destroy a seeper or two . . . there might even be a stripe in it for her.

Legs trembling, she stood and reached for her cloak hood.

As she pulled it over her head, she felt the familiar tug of her animal form. Except, for the first time, her human body seemed reluctant to answer it. She pressed, *pushing* herself towards the change and was rewarded with the familiar sense of vertigo, that feeling somewhere between sleeping and waking, when your mind drifts, tethered to your body by the thinnest of threads and you feel as though you could become anything: human, animal, monster even . . .

The shift began, although instead of melting, her muscles felt as though they were being torn: pulled and twisted, as if she was being dragged over a barnacle-covered rock by her ankles.

Liska yowled and snapped, feeling her snout and sharp teeth forming, crackling into place. She writhed and turned until, with a gasp of relief, she collapsed to the parapet floor again, this time as a griffyx.

Tenderly she stretched out one paw, then another. She flexed her wings, twitched her ears, shook her tail. Everything was in place but, Tree above, it all *ached* so.

With her fox hearing she could pick out the sounds of fighting much more clearly, even though it was muffled by the layer of cotton cloud. Her new senses *saw* the scent-trails of the shapewalkers like streaks of rainbow colours twisting off the battlements and bending sharply downwards.

Gingerly, Liska climbed to the parapet edge, took a breath and jumped off.

Compared to Selka's roaring launch, it seemed more than a little pathetic. But, after a few tender flaps, she was airborne. It felt as though the wind might rip her wings right out of their sockets. They ground and popped as if her joints were full of sand. Still, she tucked them in and fell towards the clouds, their cool dampness soothing her muscles a fraction.

For a while she saw nothing, and then – as if a blindfold had been ripped from her eyes – she dropped out of the cloudy blankness and into the battle below. The sight made her catch her breath and brake, back-pedalling with her wings.

The shapewalkers from the Breach were in full attack. They swooped in lines down to the spot on the mountainside where Noxis had opened the tunnel. Roars and yowls of fury followed them, bouncing off the granite walls in overlapping echoes.

Below them were a crowd of gloopy seepers spreading from the tunnel and down a narrow path to the swamp below.

Standing on half-formed legs, they reached up with arm-like tendrils that lashed the air. Pantherines and cockatrices were dodging the filthy whip-arms and slashing with their own claws, jaws and beaks, tearing streams of gluey rot from the seepers and spattering it against the mountainside.

Judging by the thick coating of smoking goo, many seepers had already been destroyed, but more kept coming through the tunnel mouth.

From where she hovered, Liska had a glimpse of Noxis himself, waving his arms, trying to conjure up tree vines or roots to help his army. But he was on rock, not soil, and there was nothing for him to work with.

We got here in time, thought Liska. *He won't be able to keep this up. We're going to win!*

Even as the thought entered her head, she saw something else appear in the tunnel entrance. A different creature, much worse than the seepers.

Stooping, crawling, it was trying to force its way through the tiny gap. Out poked a hand, an arm . . . the thing was massive. If it got through, it would dwarf the seepers. It might turn the tide of the battle.

A gorgaunt, thought Liska. *It must be.*

Hulking giants, the size of ten men or more, the gorgaunts were made from poisoned fungus grown from the roots of Bitterblight itself. They had stubby, half-formed limbs, heads that bulged from neckless shoulders. Their faces were melted lumps of fungus, their shambling bodies covered in layers of overlapping toadstools like scales on a fish. They stomped and crushed everything in their path: mindless, relentless. Liska had seen them in pictures during her combat training. You could stab them, slice chunks off them, burn them ... they would just keep on storming forwards. The only way to fight them, she remembered, was to drop rocks and boulders on them from the air. Smash their soft, mushroomy flesh into pulp.

But the shapewalkers were too busy swooping and clawing at the seepers. They hadn't noticed what was scrambling its way through the tunnel.

'Gorgaunt!' Liska yelled. 'Gorgaunt in the tunnel!'

Nobody seemed to hear her. She had to get closer.

Tucking her wings for another dive, Liska dropped lower, in amongst the airborne crowds of troops. She waited until she was almost in the thick of those waiting for their turn to dive, then began screaming at the top of her voice.

'Beware! Gorgaunt coming! A flipping great gorgaunt! Can't you see it?'

'Move, cub!' A hulking male pantherine, limbs bulging with muscle, swooshed past her, sending her spinning in his wake. Another followed, pausing to growl at her, then a third.

This one, she recognised by its torn left ear. It was Selka, the warrior who had helped her.

'What are you doing here?' Selka growled. 'You're supposed to be resting!'

'Selka, the tunnel!' Liska flapped madly, trying to keep level with the hovering pantherine. 'A gorgaunt is coming through! You need to drop rocks on it!'

Selka turned her cat-eye gaze to the tunnel entrance and saw the arm of bulging, stinking fungus trying to gouge its way through. She yowled in anger and changed her path, flying straight through the ranks of shapewalkers.

'Bombardiers!' Liska heard her shouting. 'Bombardiers to the tunnel!'

As Liska watched, twenty or so cockatrices broke away from the swooping and diving flock, heading down to the spot where the Shield Mountains met the swampy Stubbings. They pounced on the soft ground, raking it with their curling, clawed feet, then taking to the air again with hunks of muddy rock clutched beneath them.

Flapping hard to gain height, they flew in line above the tunnel and let their loads drop. Boulders and shards of razor-sharp granite tumbled from the air, smacking against the mountain and bursting into splinters. Some hit the gorgaunt's gargantuan arm, thudding into it and breaking off clumps of stringy, fungoid flesh. Liska had a glimpse of gaping, meaty gashes that quickly filled up with the same gloop that the seepers were made of. She thought she heard roars of pain from deeper in the tunnel.

'It's working!' she shouted, although nobody could hear her.

For a moment she considered flying down, finding a rock and adding to the barrage. But then she realised she would only be able to lift something small. To the gorgaunt it would be like getting hit by an acorn.

Perhaps she could swoop and bite at a seeper instead? The air was thick with bigger, faster creatures, but maybe she could find a space . . .

She was just about to slot into the attack line, when she heard a chorus of roaring coming from behind her. Turning in the air, she saw the shapewalkers from the Noon Fort, her home, flying in to join the battle. A pride of manticores with their lion bodies and dragon wings and, behind those, the griffyxes. Her family would be somewhere among them.

As Liska watched, the manticores dived down, grabbing more rocks in their huge paws to add to the bombardment. The griffyxes, flying in tight arrow formations, soared straight towards the seepers, ready to dive and fight in waves along with the pantherines.

'Liska!' her mother's voice broke through the cacophony of roars and shrieks. 'What are you doing here?'

Liska flew towards the griffyx ranks, hovering above as her mother broke away to approach her.

'I saw them come in, mother. I raised the alarm. Please don't be angry!'

But instead of anger on her mother's face, there was fear. Terror, even. Not of the beasts that were attacking. Not of the thought of battle, but for *her*. She was terrified Liska might have been hurt.

'Darling, you shouldn't be here! It's far too dangerous. Fly back to the tower now. Do as you're told – that's an order!'

'But I want to help! I want to fight!'

'You're too young for this! Do as you are told!' Her mother snapped at her paws, driving her backwards before she veered away to join the attack.

There was nothing Liska could do except watch now. If she tried anything else, she'd end up in tree-wizard school for the rest of her life. She might even get her wings clipped.

Although it didn't really matter. The battle was almost over. Just a few of the seepers remained, clinging to the cliffside and flailing with their lashing arms. The rest had been shredded to ribbons, hanging from the rock in layers of spattered goo.

A rain of boulders was crashing down on the gorgaunt, smashing it to a pulp. One giant manticore sent a rock almost as large as himself spiralling end over end. It hit with a meaty *thump* and the arm broke off completely in a cloud of flesh and spores. The gorgaunt withdrew, howling all the way.

Liska saw Noxis, his face creased up in fury, wave a fist at the sky before following his wounded creature back down the tunnel. The rest of the boulders fell, blasting the entrance shut and burying it in a mound of broken rock.

It was done. Finished. Arborven was safe.

*

The flocks of shapewalkers circled for a bit, checking the area, before gliding, one by one to the ground.

From the forest city the sound of many footsteps and voices could be heard. Liska swooped lower and lower until her own paws touched the spongy earth just as the circle of trees parted and a crowd of mages, led by the towering form of a treekeeper, emerged.

The group stood for a moment, staring in horror

87

at the scarred mountainside, with its fresh tumble of broken rock and the smears of dead seepers. Then the treekeeper, Edda himself, spotted the ranks of shapewalkers who were now gathered around the swamp's edge, all panting for breath. He bent over in a deep, creaking bow, honouring them.

A victory cry went up – a raucous noise made of roars, yowls and barks. It echoed back off the Shield Mountains and through the swamp. It stirred a cloud of bats from the Cryptwood, sending them flapping madly through the dead tree branches.

Even the mages joined in, clapping, cheering and waving. Amongst them, standing next to Edda himself, Liska caught a glimpse of Lug trying not to get trampled by the dancing arbomancers. She waved her tail at him and caught a glance of him waving back, and then they were both swallowed up by the cheering crowds around them.

5

'Treekeepers know best.'

Arborven proverb

'Stand up properly! Straighten your cloak out!'

Liska's mother fussed around her, hissing in her ear. Liska squirmed and tried her best not to say anything rude. She had just helped save the city and now here she was, having her armour arranged for her like a four-year-old.

They were standing in a grand hall with towering wooden columns carved in spirals. Banners of the different schools of mages covered the wooden walls. One whole side of the structure was taken up by the trunk of the Undrentree itself. Liska could see the ridges of its bark, each one thicker than her entire body. Moss and lichen had been grown in patterns of interlocking circles all over it. There were hundreds of different colours in every shade imaginable. A living, growing work of art.

'Stop staring at the tree! You look like a halfwit.'

Liska sighed. All this was because she had saved the city from attack. Everyone had been happy at first. There had been parties and feasting at the epic victory. Liska thought she might be awarded a stripe for her bravery. Maybe even two. But it hadn't even been mentioned, and the celebrations didn't last all that long either.

In the whole of Arborven's history, this was the first time the rot had crept past the Shield Mountains. It was the first time one of the city's own mages had betrayed it.

Something had to be done. Measures had to be taken.

So a council had been called for the leaders of all the mages, of the shapewalker families and the treekeepers. And, of course, Liska and Lug had been invited as well, to tell their version of events in public.

She glanced across the chamber and saw Lug also standing with his parents. The three of them were dressed in robes of earthy brown and Lug's father had some kind of hat on his head. It looked like a giant worm, coiled round and round into a cone shape. Lug's mother was licking a handkerchief and using it to wipe a tiny speck of dirt from his face. He caught Liska's eye and grimaced.

The great hall was slowly filling up with important-looking people. They all had very long, very ornate robes on. Liska spotted the different colours of the mages: black, grey, silver, amber and green. There were many beards of extreme length and lots of staffs covered with runes and crystals. The air sparkled with the scent of magic.

At the front of the hall were three enormous chairs. Each one was big enough for a small family to live under. As Liska submitted to more of her mother's fussing, three treekeepers strode in through the arched doorway. The mages parted as they creaked their way to their seats. Edda was first. The second looked like the one she had crashed into and the third was a woman with hair of purple-leaved ivy that spilled down her wooden back. Twiga perhaps. Or maybe Liche.

They took their seats and a hush spread throughout the room.

'Greetings,' said Edda, his voice slow and booming. 'Thank you all for coming to this council.'

'As you know,' said the long-haired treekeeper, 'there has been an attack on Arborven. One of our own has turned against us.' Her voice was softer than Edda's. It reminded Liska of the wind sighing through the forest leaves.

'We are here to discuss what needs to be done,' Edda continued. 'The time of peace we have enjoyed is now over. Bitterblight and its rot have come to our door and we must fight for our survival.

'Before the planning begins, however, we should like to hear from the two youngsters who raised the alarm and saved us all. Would you please step forward?'

Edda gestured with an oaken arm, his twiggy fingers beckoning, his eyes glowing soft and kind. Liska felt her mother give her a gentle shove and she began the long walk up to the treekeepers, feeling her heart begin to rattle against her ribcage as she went.

This could be it, she thought. *I didn't get a stripe before because Edda wanted to do it in person. In front of all the mages, too!*

She puffed out her chest and tried to look as brave as possible. At some point Lug appeared beside her. Was he going to get a stripe as well? Or perhaps the vermispex version of one. A new pet worm maybe?

He blinked at her in terror, his large eyes bulging even more than usual. Liska could see his jaw trembling.

'Don't worry,' she whispered to him. 'We're heroes, remember?' Saying it made her feel a bit better, and she saw Lug swallow deeply before letting out a high-pitched squeak of agreement.

'Welcome, little shapewalker and vermispex,' said Edda, his normally booming voice soft. He leant forward smiling, bringing his head close enough for Liska to see the human face trapped inside the living tree. Whorls and circles of wood grain covered his cheeks, but she could almost picture his features as they had once been. *Just replace the moss and leaves with eyebrows and a beard and he might even be a kindly grandad.*

Edda's eyes glowed with powerful magic, flickering and gleaming as he studied the two youngsters. The runes carved into his arms and chest pulsed and seemed to shift, as if they were constantly rewriting themselves. 'My young friends. Would you please tell us,' he said, 'of what you saw the day of the attack?'

Liska glanced over to Lug, whose face was frozen in a mask of pure terror. A faint, whining sound was whistling out of his throat. It looked as though he might never move again, let alone speak, so Liska cleared her throat and began to talk.

She told Edda of their walk through the city, and how they had paused at the swamp's edge. She described the rockslide in great detail, seeing as she knew so much about them, and how they had seen Noxis emerge and beckon the seepers through. She was just getting to the good bit – flying at top speed up to the Breach – when Edda held up his gnarly hand.

'So, it was, without a doubt, Noxis the arbomancer you saw?'

Liska nodded. 'Yes, sir. I mean, lord . . . I mean, your majesty . . .'

'Edda is fine,' said the treekeeper with a twitch of his wooden cheeks that might have been a smile. 'And have you come across Master Noxis before? To be able to recognise him so certainly?'

Liska nodded again and explained her embarrassing incident at the Undren Square. She left out the part about crashing into one of Edda's friends, although the treekeeper on the right of him was smiling behind his hand.

'Ah, I remember that evening.' Edda gave a chuckle that made the floor under Liska's feet vibrate. 'That was you, was it? You have certainly been making a name for yourself.'

Liska cringed, imagining the expression that would be scrunching up her mother's face right now. But Edda didn't seem to be too bothered about it. He sat back up and nodded his thanks to them, gesturing at them to return to their families.

With a sinking heart, Liska realised there would be no stripe-giving. This event was a crisis meeting, not an award ceremony. She and Lug were just there as witnesses: children who happened to have been in that particular place and had been asked to tell their story before the grown-ups discussed what to do about it.

Well, I'm not having that. Liska knew she might never have an audience with a treekeeper again, let alone one so important. She decided to make the most of it.

'If you please, sir. I mean ... Edda.' The towering treekeeper looked down at her once more. 'My friend

Lug here has a plan to destroy Bitterblight. Perhaps you could consider it in your council? It's a good plan, one that won't force us to use the heart of the Undrentree at all. I can tell it to you if you want?'

She felt Lug go rigid beside her. He gripped her cloak with his hand, so tight that the bones began to crack, and hissed at her through gritted teeth. 'Liska! What in the Tree are you doing?'

'A plan?' Edda leant forward again. 'Yes, young vermispex, I would like to hear. As long as it is brief.'

'I . . .' Lug began. Beads of sweat formed on his brow, and Liska thought his eyes might actually pop out of his sockets and tumble down his cheeks. 'It . . . I . . . argh . . .'

'What he's trying to say,' Liska jumped in to help, 'is that there's this *other* sacred tree, way up in the north. The shadow tree that should be fighting it has been frozen, so its heart is there for the taking. We can use *that* to kill Bitterblight instead of taking our own.'

'Ah,' said Edda. 'The legend of Nammu.' He gave his floor-rumbling chuckle again, and many of the mages in the room behind them joined in. 'I am glad you have been paying attention to Master Ambrose's history lessons. But I am afraid that story is just a fable. The glacier was almost upon it centuries ago. Everything there will be far under the ice by now. Too good to be true, alas ...'

He waved his hand again to dismiss them, and this time Liska felt her mother step behind her and practically drag her away. She managed a quick glance at Lug and saw him glaring daggers at her. She wanted to go over to him and explain, but her mother was already whisper-shouting in her ear.

'... dare you bother Master Edda with nonsense? On your special day as well!'

'But, Mother!' Liska hissed back. 'I had to try! Lug says ...'

'I don't care what that skinny worm-botherer says! You had a chance – a *second* chance – to impress the treekeepers and the other walkers and you ruined it with nonsense about fairy-tale trees!'

'It's not nonsense!' Liska was pleading now. 'Lug knows something! He's got a secret ...'

'What secret?' Her mother glared at her, daring her to prove herself.

Liska silently cursed. 'Well. He hasn't actually told me yet ...'

'I knew it!' Her mother shouted that part, then went

back to angry whispering once heads began to turn towards them. 'There is no tree in the north. Everyone knows that's just a story. You're too young and stupid to know better! I don't want to hear another word about this Lug or other trees again. Leave the business of saving Arborven to the grown-ups! Now, go outside and wait for us on the Undren Square. And try not to get into mischief this time!'

Liska pulled away from her mother's grip with as much force as she could muster. All the hope and excitement of the day had curdled into anger and disappointment. No stripe, barely any thanks for saving everyone and now – yet again – she was being treated like a naughty child.

She slunk between all the mages, who had already begun to call out their plans and suggestions to the chamber. Nobody even noticed as she walked out of the hall, even though they would have been eaten by rot and gloop if it hadn't been for her. And they would probably still all die just because they were too stubborn to listen to her.

She stood in the doorway for a bit thinking up the rudest curse she could imagine, until Lug walked past her, heading for the staircase that spiralled around the

Undrentree's trunk to the ground below. He deliberately avoided looking at her, which made her even angrier.

'I think it's time you explained your guilty secret properly, worm-boy,' Liska muttered to herself. She tugged the straps of her armour tight and hurried down the stairs after him.

*

'Lug, wait!'

She caught up with him as he was walking out of the temple entrance into a wide space between the Undrentree's roots that had been turned into a beautiful ivy garden. Leaves of all different shades grew around them, water trickled gently through streams, spilling into ornamental pools, and carved wooden statues of treekeepers stood watch over it all.

'Stop storming off! I need to speak to you!'

When Lug finally turned around, his face was set in the fiercest glare he could manage. He clearly wasn't very good at it.

'Is that your best angry look?' Liska couldn't help giggling. 'You look like you've just wet your robes. Try scrunching your eyebrows up a bit more. Curl your top lip. Show your teeth a bit ...'

Lug gave up and shook his hands at the sky.

'Nematus below, I'm *trying* to be cross with you! Why did you have to go and say that to the treekeepers? I *told* you it was a secret!'

'No, you said it was a legend. The way you *found out* about it was the secret.'

Lug buried his face in his hands. 'Yes, but now my parents are going to ask me loads of questions. They're going to discover what I did and then they'll be furious.'

Liska stood and watched him for a few minutes. When it looked like he wasn't ever going to take his hands off his face, she sighed and tapped him on the shoulder.

'You did promise to tell me, you know, back at the swamp, before the battle. You said it was to do with the Cryptwood and then Noxis appeared ...'

'You wouldn't understand,' Lug said from behind his fingers. 'It's vermispex business.'

'Try me,' said Liska. 'It convinced you the legend was real, so it might convince me, too.'

The sound of a sigh came from behind Lug's hands, and then he finally dropped them to his sides. 'Alright,' he said. 'But this is just between you and me.'

'Of course,' said Liska, crossing her fingers behind her back.

'Well,' Lug began. 'I told you vermispexes could summon worms. But that's not all we can do. We can also use our magic to connect with them. We can't see through their eyes because they're blind, but we can feel what they feel and hear through their ears.'

'Like tiny underground spies?'

'Yes, I suppose. Except that using such power is forbidden. One of our ancestors got into trouble with the treekeepers about it, and since then it's considered very wrong.'

A grin began to spread over Liska's face. 'But *you* used it, didn't you? Who did you spy on?'

Lug blushed a deep shade of crimson. 'I wasn't spying! Not really ... At least I didn't mean to.'

'Explain,' said Liska, folding her arms.

Lug blushed even more. 'It was a week or so ago now. I was playing in the swamp, training some worms, when I saw this girl in the Cryptwood. You remember how close it is to the swamp?' Liska nodded.

'Well, I saw her walking through the trees, and then she just disappeared. I thought she was a ghost but I saw her again the next day, and the next. Finally I asked my mother about it and she told me there were people living in the wood.'

101

'*Living* there?' Liska couldn't believe it. 'I thought the place was full of ghosts and tree spirits.'

'So did I. But it turns out there was this family, years and years ago, who had a whole estate there. Then there was a terrible accident – some kind of surge of magical energy from the Undrentree – and they were all killed. Stone dead.

'Except a few months later, they all came back to life. Part of the magical effects, I suppose. Nobody understood it and they didn't really want them around, so they were just shut off from the city and ignored. All the stories about ghosts sprang up later. You can understand why: the Cryptwood looks so creepy . . .'

Liska was shaking her head. 'Wait – they were all dead . . . and then they came back to life?'

'Yes,' said Lug. 'Although not properly alive like you and me. My mother said they were "undead". They never grew old or even died. That girl had probably been that way for hundreds of years.'

'So, these half-dead, half-alive people . . . they were the ones you spied on?'

Lug nodded. 'The story just fascinated me. I wanted to see where they lived . . . I really didn't mean to snoop. I sent some worms into the soil under the

Cryptwood, trying to find their house. It took me weeks and weeks – it's so old that it's completely buried – and then when I found it, I just listened in a *smidge*. Just to hear them talk about their old lives.'

Liska stepped closer. She could smell something interesting … the start of an adventure maybe. One that might – this time – be finally enough to earn a stripe.

'What did they say? What did you find out?'

'Well,' said Lug. 'There seem to be a few of them, but most of them sleep nearly all the time. I heard lots of names mentioned but only two or three voices. One of them was the girl. I think her name was Elowen.

'Anyway, they were talking about things they'd seen, places they'd been to when they were alive. Cities outside the walls, palaces, rivers, other light trees. And then they mentioned going to see Nammu. The tree in the north, waiting for the glacier to swallow it. The girl, Elowen, even said it was a shame they hadn't brought its heart back with them when they had the chance. That means it's really there …'

'… and it could be used to kill Bitterblight!' Liska finished. She rubbed her chin, thinking. 'If the glacier hasn't eaten it already. It depends how long

103

ago this Elowen went up there. We need to speak to her properly. And then we need to go and find it for ourselves. Because there's no way anyone else is going to believe us now. Not after what just happened in the hall. No, we're going to have to do this on our own. Maybe she would come with us ... show us the way ...'

'Hey!' Lug waved his hands in Liska's face. 'Hey, wait! Nobody said anything about *us* going up there! The treekeepers need to do it! Have you any idea how dangerous it is? There's wyverns and Poxpunks and Tree knows what else. Not to mention the rot creatures ...'

Liska snorted. 'Didn't you hear them laughing at us back there? My own mother forbade me to ever *mention* other trees again. I'm not even supposed to talk to *you*. Besides, they're going to be too busy fighting off Noxis. He's bound to attack again. No. *We're* the ones who need to get Nammu's heart. *We're* the ones who are going to save the city. Again.'

'Absolutely not.' Lug began to stagger backwards, shaking his head. 'No way. Never. We're just children. I'm just a vermispex. We can't leave Arborven! We won't last five minutes out there! Do you have any idea how many allergies I have?'

'Lug.' Liska took him by the shoulders. 'Don't you remember telling me how you wanted vermispexes to be recognised? To have the other mages realise you were just as powerful?'

'Yes, but ...' Lug squirmed, looking like he was about to cry. 'Not like *this*. I just wanted to show them ... to make them see ...'

'This is your chance!' Liska gave him a shake. A very gentle one but, even so, his teeth rattled and his head wobbled like a stricken tadpole. 'What better way is there to make them notice you than saving them from Bitterblight? Just imagine the glory! Imagine how proud your parents will be! The vermispexes will probably be given their own tree circle! We'll be heroes forever!'

'Well,' said Lug. He swallowed several times and blinked his big eyes. 'Well ... well ...'

'That's good enough,' said Liska, grabbing his hand. 'Come on, let's go.'

'Where ... where to?' Lug asked, his voice shaking.

'The Cryptwood, of course! We need to speak to this Elowen, right away!'

Liska was just about to drag the reluctant Lug after her when they both heard a loud rustle from a nearby ivy bush. They stopped and stared at each other.

'Was that ...?' said Lug.

'... a spy?' Liska finished. They ran over to the bush. Whoever had been eavesdropping was long gone. Liska knelt to examine the ground and saw, pressed into the loamy soil, the trace of a footprint.

'Quite a large foot,' she said. 'Not an adult, but big for a child. If I shapewalk, I'll be able to smell them out.'

'Don't bother,' said Lug. 'I think I know who it was. I saw him skulking around outside the hall before we went in.'

'Who?' Liska asked.

'Odis,' said Lug. 'The son of Noxis. The one who bullied you. If he heard us, maybe he'll go and tell his father.'

'How can he?' Liska said. 'Noxis is on the other side of the Shield Mountains with all the rot. Whatever Odis heard, there's nothing he can do about it.'

'I don't know ...' Lug began, but Liska had already leapt up and grabbed his hand again. She dragged him after her in the direction of the Cryptwood before he could change his mind about helping her.

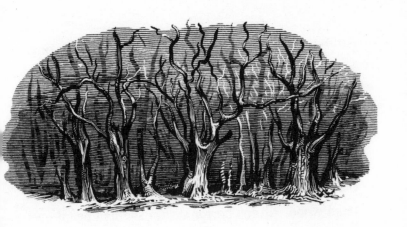

6

'Cold wood, dead wood, roots of bone.
If you play in the Crytpwood,
You'll never come home.'

Children's rhyme

'Are you sure about this?'

They stood at the edge of the Cryptwood. It loomed before them, all dead trees with bark like bleached stone. Crackly skeletons of ancient bushes covered the ground, woven through with hanks of long, brittle grass, stems rattling quietly in the breeze.

Behind them, from the lush, green leaves of the forest city, they could hear the background noise of nature: fluttering wings, birdsong, insects buzzing, foxes barking. Even the nearby Scrubbings had its own soundtrack. Frogs croaked, reeds whistled, mud bubbles *plorped.*

But the Cryptwood was silent.

'Of course, I'm sure!' Liska tried to sound brave but even she was wary about setting foot in the cold, dead wood. All the horror stories she had heard over the years came rushing back to her in a horrible jumble of phantom beasts and evil spirits. She swallowed hard and tried to put on a brave face. Lug was already on the verge of running back to his underground swamp house and never coming out. If he smelt any weakness from her, that would be it. 'Now. How do we get in?'

'There's a p-path,' said Lug, pointing with a shaking finger. 'That's where I first saw the girl. Elowen.'

Liska could see a gap between the trees where the faintest of tracks wound its way through the bushes, deeper into the woodland. It looked as though nothing but foxes had walked on it for many, many years.

'Come on, then!' She put on her best chirpy voice, as if they were off for an afternoon picnic by the river rather than plunging into a haunted wilderness. She kept tight hold of a corner of Lug's robe the whole time.

Mostly so that he couldn't escape, but also (a tiny bit) because it made her feel better.

It was difficult to walk along the path without getting snagged on twigs or thorns, although there were signs that someone had tried to keep the way clear. Branches had been pruned, brambles had been bent inwards. A few steps in, they came across a delicate yellow primrose that had been carefully planted by hand. Even though the petals were already wilted and falling, it was a splash of colour amongst all the lifeless grey.

'Did Elowen do this, do you think?' Liska asked, bending to examine the flower.

Lug nudged the petals with his foot. 'Do you think it might be a trap? Might a hungry ghost have planted it to lure us in? So it can eat us?'

'Ghosts don't do gardening, stupid,' said Liska. 'Look. There's more, further down.'

Liska pointed at a row of pansies dotted along the track. Something about the specks of vibrant colour in such a wasteland – the loneliness of it – made her feel sad. Even though she had never met Elowen, she felt she understood a little of what it must be like living out here in isolation amongst the dead, haunted trees.

'Come on,' she whispered. 'Let's follow them.'

Walking from flower to wilted flower, they made their way through the Cryptwood.

*

'I think this is it,' said Lug as they stepped into a clearing. There were more primroses and pansies planted around the edge, although most of them had shrivelled away, leaving showers of blackened petals on the ground.

'I can't see a house,' said Liska, looking around. 'Where does she live?'

The clearing was ringed with thick clods of dead bushes. Limbs of skeletal trees reached their bare fingers up to the sky. The silence of the place was like a cold, suffocating blanket.

'There.' Lug pointed to what Liska had thought was a hummock of earth. She now saw it was the rough shape of a triangular prism: the top metre or so of a roof, jutting from the ground. The rest of the house must have been slowly swallowed by the earth, and what remained was coated in so many overlapping layers of moss and lichen, its edges were blurred and unrecognisable.

Next to it were the topmost branches of an oak

tree – bare, dead, so old they had almost fossilised to stone. At one time, Liska imagined, tree and house could have stood, built around each other like the mages' houses in Arborven. There might have been a whole cluster of buildings just the same. A lonely woodland village outside the city rings, now forgotten and crumbled.

'There's a way down,' said Lug. He had begun edging closer to the house's remains but now shuffled behind Liska, letting her go first. She peered at one end of the mossy lump and saw a deep hole had been cut into the earth, complete with steps. It led down, down, until it reached a heavy door, banded with strips of ornate, curling iron.

'What do we do?' Liska found herself talking in a whisper. 'Just go down and knock?'

'Oh, I wouldn't do that,' came a voice from behind the dead oak. 'They're all *fast* asleep at the moment.'

Lug let out an ear-wrenching shriek and wrapped his arms around Liska. They both stared in the direction of the voice, trembling as a ghostly shape began to emerge from behind the lifeless branches.

It was a girl, or at least a creature in the shape of one. No older than Liska herself, with skin of the purest, smoothest white – like porcelain – and wisps of ashen blonde hair floating around her face. Her eyes were ringed with shadows of deep grey and purple, her irises so pale they almost faded into the whites. She drifted, silent, through the undergrowth. Quiet as a breeze, soft as a secret.

She was dressed in layers of faded snowy fabric. Tattered lace and fraying embroidery, bows of dusty ribbon everywhere. Some kind of corset tied with plaits of tattered cord. She looked as though she had just floated from a long-buried tomb or stepped through a tear in the centuries. A being from another time.

Liska peeled Lug away from her. He fumbled with his robes and blushed crimson.

'Actually,' Liska said, trying to keep the tremble out of her voice, 'we've come to see *you*. You are Elowen, aren't you?'

The girl blinked those milk-white eyes at them in surprise. 'However did you know that?'

Liska held out a hand. 'I'm Liska and this is Lug. He's a vermispex. One of your neighbours. He's the one who found out all about you.'

Elowen stared at them some more before reaching out to shake Liska's hand. Not a warrior's wrist clasp as Liska was used to; just a light brush of her porcelain fingertips. The ghost girl's skin was icy cold. And smooth like a statue.

'I'm so sorry,' Lug stammered. 'I didn't mean to ... I wasn't being rude ...'

'I don't understand,' said Elowen. 'People sometimes come to speak to my parents or my aunts and uncles. But nobody has been for ... well, such a long time. And they're nearly always asleep now, you see. I don't think anyone has ever come here asking for *me*. However did you discover my name?'

'Allow me to explain,' said Liska and, as Lug grimaced and tried to hide his face in his sleeves, she told Elowen all about the worms and how she had been eavesdropped on.

Both Liska and Lug half-expected her to lose her temper when she heard about the spying, or at least complain, but instead she seemed thrilled, even tapping her fingertips together in excitement.

'I *knew* I sensed some magic in the walls. I *knew* it!' she said, beaming at them both. 'What was it you heard? Is it why you came here today?'

'I wasn't trying to listen, I promise,' said Lug. 'I'd spotted you in the woods and wondered where you lived. I was just trying to find your house ... And then – when I did find it – some words accidentally fell into my ears. I honestly wasn't trying to spy or anything like that!'

'I'm sure you weren't,' said Elowen, smiling. 'Tell me, what did you happen to hear?'

'Well ...' Lug wriggled about in his robes a bit. 'You were telling someone about a trip you made to the sacred tree in the north – to Nammu – back when you were ... um ...'

'Alive?' said Elowen. She didn't seem to be bothered about what had happened to her although, Liska thought, it must have been quite upsetting to say the least. 'Yes, we travelled there once. Not long after Arborven was founded. We had heard that there was a tree of light there whose opposite had been frozen in a glacier. The city elders thought we might be able to use its heart to stop our own shadow tree before it had grown enough to start spreading its corruption.'

'But you didn't,' said Liska. 'Take the heart, I mean. Why not?'

Elowen shrugged. 'When we arrived, we found some of the local people still living near the tree. Just a handful. There had once been hundreds of tribes

114

there, they said, but nearly all had fled as the glacier got closer. Still, we didn't think it would be fair to take their tree's heart from them. It would have killed the poor thing. And besides, the Undrentree and its opposite were only small then. Saplings, really. Using the heart of an ancient tree might not even have worked.'

The Undrentree ... a sapling? Liska couldn't even imagine how long ago that must have been. Just how old was this undead girl she was talking to? 'But later on, when the trees had grown ... Didn't someone think to go back for it?'

'Perhaps,' said Elowen. 'Except by then my family had suffered the ... accident. Nobody in Arborven really listened to us much after that. And over the years the story of Nammu became a bit of a legend. I don't think anyone really believed it was true.'

'They still don't,' said Liska. 'When we found out that Nammu was real, we tried to tell the treekeepers but they all laughed. Now everybody thinks we're useless children who believe in fairy tales. Except the city is really under attack from the rot, and nobody even wants to *try* to get Nammu's heart. Apart from us, that is.'

'Oh, yes,' said Elowen. 'The attack. I felt the

commotion through the ground. When I came up to investigate, I saw the brave shapewalkers battling the invaders. It was quite terrifying. The rest of my family slept through the whole thing, of course.' She paused and looked long and hard at them for a moment, her head cocked to one side. 'Are you *really* thinking of going to find Nammu yourselves?'

'Of course not,' Lug began. 'That would be ridiculous. Although Liska did mention it, but I'm sure she didn't mean . . .'

'Yes, I did.' Liska cut him off. 'And we *are* going. This might be Arborven's only chance. Somebody has to try it and it clearly isn't going to be the adults. But we were wondering . . . would you be able to come with us? As our guide?'

Elowen did the clappy thing with her hands again, and this time added in a happy dance. 'I was hoping you would say that! How exciting . . . of course I'll come!'

'Hang on,' said Lug. 'Doesn't she have to ask her parents first? Don't *we* have to ask our parents?'

'If we ask them, they'll say no,' said Liska. 'In fact, my mother will probably lock me in the Noon Fort until I'm eighteen. And then I'll never get a stripe.'

'And I, Master Lug,' said Elowen, 'am five hundred

and seventy-eight years old. I don't have to ask anyone's permission to do anything.'

'Yes, but I ... I mean, *my* parents ...'

'Lug,' said Liska, taking him by the shoulders again. 'I've explained how amazing this could be for the vermispexes. We've both seen that nobody except us is willing to try it. And we all know that, if somebody doesn't act soon, Arborven and the Undrentree are doomed. Now. Are you going to give up and come along with us, or do we have to tie you up and kidnap you? Because those are your only two options.'

'You'll be very safe,' said Elowen. 'I'm sure things outside the city haven't changed too much in the last five hundred years.'

Lug opened and closed his mouth a few times as he tried to think of another excuse. He looked like a beached fish gasping for air. Both girls just stared at him, hands on hips, as immovable as the granite of the Shield Mountains.

In the end, all he could do was slump his shoulders and sigh.

'We'll take that as a definite "yes",' said Liska, grinning, and led them all back out of the Cryptwood.

*

They paused at the entrance to the old wood to say their goodbyes.

'It was *so* nice to meet you,' said Elowen. 'I can't even remember the last time I had a visitor. When shall we leave upon our adventure?'

Lug looked as though he was about to say 'never', so Liska quickly spoke over him. 'As soon as possible,' she said. 'Tomorrow maybe?'

'But how will I know what medicine to bring?' Lug wailed. 'There could be things out there I don't know I'm allergic to! And how do we actually get out of the city?'

'Oh, that's simple,' said Elowen. 'I know a pathway through the mountains to the east, just below the Stormfort. We need only bring blankets and spare clothing. And some food and water for you both. I myself do not need to eat or drink.'

'I can easily catch small animals to cook and eat when I'm in my griffyx shape,' said Liska, grinning. 'We won't need to bring any meat. As long as you don't mind the taste of rabbit. Or rat.'

'Hang on,' said Lug. 'Just how long are we going to be gone? I've never even spent a single night away from home! My parents will be worried sick!'

'Leave them a note,' said Liska, rolling her eyes. 'I'm sure we'll only be a few days. Right, Elowen?'

Elowen waggled her fingers. 'Maybe a bit longer than that. It is quite a journey. Although it will be much quicker if we can ride along with one of the travelling-merchant caravans. I'm sure they've kept the northern road in good repair.'

'Excellent,' said Liska before Lug could object any more. 'We'll meet here tomorrow with all our supplies. Just remember not to tell anyone!'

This last sentence was aimed at Lug and she backed it up with a fierce glare.

'Until tomorrow, then!' Elowen leant over to give them both a peck on the cheek – her button nose was like a tiny icicle – and then skipped back into the grey depths of the Cryptwood. Liska and Lug stood looking at each other for a moment.

'You'd better be here, Lugworth,' said Liska, giving him a stern frown.

He studied a patch of nearby grass, trying not to meet her eyes.

'Or I'll have to climb down into your swamp burrow and drag you out.'

Lug gave a final grimace before turning and heading

off into the Scrubbings. Liska watched him go and then pulled her fur hood on, shifting into her animal shape before flapping off over the treetops, startling a flock of roosting starlings.

When they had all disappeared, the vines of a nearby bush began to twist and writhe, folding back on themselves to reveal a black-cloaked figure hiding within. A boy, eyes hidden beneath a drooping fringe, stepped out brushing stray leaves from his shoulders. He looked around and, when he was sure nobody was watching, set off across the Scrubbings towards the mountain wall.

*

It wasn't until later that evening, back in her chamber at the Noon Fort, that Liska realised what she'd actually done.

Caught up in all the excitement of Elowen's story – in the idea of an epic, stripe-winning adventure – she had basically decided to run away.

No wonder Lug was so worried, she thought to herself as she gazed out of the open window at the green disc of Arborven below. *I told him to leave his home, his family. I told him to put himself in danger just so* I *could get what I wanted.*

But it wasn't *only* about that, was it? They were trying to save the Undrentree and the whole of Arborven too, weren't they?

Yes, but Lug was right. We're just children. We shouldn't be the ones doing it. If only the adults would listen to us.

Maybe if she went back to her parents with evidence. Maybe if she told them about Elowen – made them fly to the Cryptwood and hear her story . . .

'They still wouldn't believe it.' She spoke the words into the evening breeze, imagining the wind carrying them away to the patch of brown mud in the distance that was the Scrubbings. Where Lug was probably crying himself to sleep right now.

Liska looked over to the corner, at her backpack that she had hastily stuffed with blankets, spare socks and underwear, along with a water bottle and her father's pocketknife. She tried to imagine herself out in the wilderness of the Blasted Waste, surviving on rabbits and wild garlic. She tried to imagine *Lug* doing it.

They wouldn't last five minutes.

With a growl of frustration, she slammed the window shutters closed and flopped on her bed.

It had been *such* a good idea. Such a chance at

adventure . . . But she'd let herself get carried away by it, like a stupid child. Lug had been right to worry all along.

'Root and branch!' she yelled into her pillow, then wrapped herself in her cloak – being careful not to change shape – and buried her face in its musky fur.

Her parents weren't back from the council yet, but when they finally arrived she would try one last time to convince them about Nammu's heart. Perhaps they would believe her and send a party of warriors up there. Perhaps they would ignore her and carry on with their own plans to defeat Bitterblight and Noxis. Who knew? But whatever happened, it would be up to them. She was done with it.

Lying there, exhausted by all the excitement of the day, by all the plots and plans that had been zipping through her head, Liska gently drifted off to sleep.

*

Screams.

Liska sat bolt upright.

It was deep in the night. She had been fast asleep and somebody's screams had woken her.

Was it a dream? *No, I can still hear them. It's coming from outside.*

Liska ran to the shutter and threw it open. The sky outside was painted bright orange and for a moment she wondered why. Then she remembered what was built on the mountain's ridge, alongside their tower.

The signal fire!

Liska turned from the window and ran out of her room. Her sister, Ylva, was in the hallway strapping on her leather armour and cloak. The doorway to their apartments stood open, letting in the chaotic sounds from outside, along with a whiff of smoke, cold mountain air ... and the unmistakeable, acrid stench of rot.

'Ylva!' Liska ran up to her sister. 'What's happening?'

'I'm not sure ...' Her sister, normally so arrogant and sure of herself, looked shaken. 'We're under attack. Mother and father hadn't been home long when the alarm was raised. They ran out to fight ...'

With her cloak clasped firmly at her neck, Ylva began to stride out of the front door. She turned to Liska before stepping outside. 'You should stay. It might be dangerous out there.'

'I've seen a battle before!' Liska shouted.

'Not like this,' said Ylva. 'I haven't got time to argue. Close the door after me and stay put.'

With a flap of her cloak, Ylva was off, her footsteps echoing as she ran up the stairs outside the apartment. Liska waited a few seconds, until her sister was definitely gone, and then headed out of the door herself.

*

Feet pounding on the worn stone, Liska raced up the spiral steps of the Noon Fort; round and round until she emerged on the roof with its flagpoles and launching platforms jutting out all around like stocky, stone diving boards.

There were shapewalkers everywhere, in human and beast form and everything in between. Shifting from one to the other, leaping off the platforms with wings outstretched, or loading and firing the giant crossbow-like ballistae at targets down below.

Captains stood at the battlements yelling orders through megaphones. Signallers waved coloured flags, sending messages to the shapewalker troops who were already airborne.

Liska ran to the edge and peered out from the battlements.

Despite the glare from the signal fire, it was still night. A star-speckled sky, complete with gibbous moon, served as a backdrop for the battle.

Looking down, Liska could see the boiling waves

of magically created mist that helped to protect Arborven. Looming out of it were moving shapes: heads, shoulders and arms of giant *things*.

Gorgaunts, Liska thought. Like the one that had tried to come through the tunnel the other day. These ones must have climbed the mountains, hauling themselves up with their fungous, rotting limbs. Now they clung to the rocks, flinging handfuls of . . . of what?

One of the missiles exploded against the granite at the foot of the tower, directly below Liska's vantage point. She looked down to see a giant-sized handful of that grey, smoking sludge that the rot was made of. As she watched, it congealed, shaping itself into something roughly human-sized.

'They're throwing seepers at us!' Liska shouted. The thing that had been launched by the gorgaunt turned to the tower and began trying to climb its way up, slapping its sticky hands and feet against the stone. Luckily a flying manticore spotted it and swooped down, ripping it to pieces with its fierce front paws.

'The north and west of the city is under attack,' said a shapewalker next to her. He was loading a crossbow, ready to shoot from the battlements with it. 'The commander thinks they're testing our defences.'

'Will they hold?' Liska asked. Her eyes scanned the flocks of flying shapewalkers, looking for her parents, her sister.

'Let's hope so,' said the walker. 'You should probably get down below, just in case. This is no place for young cubs.'

Stay put, get down below... Liska was sick of being told what to do. She was about to complain to the walker when an injured griffyx came spiralling down to crash on the tower roof. Its shape began to melt even as it landed, and Liska was horrified to recognise her mother.

'Mother! Are you hurt?' She ran to her and saw one of her legs was covered with the grey seething liquid that the seepers were made of. She was grimacing in pain. Liska grabbed her hand as two healers rushed over and began trying to scrape the smoking, stinking substance off her body, dousing it with buckets of water as they worked.

'Roots below, it *burns*,' her mother said through gritted teeth. 'Liska! Darling! What are you doing here? Are you hurt? Are you keeping out of danger?'

'The battle woke me,' Liska said, blinking back tears and squeezing her mother's hand. 'Will you be alright?'

'This will need oil from the tree,' said one of the healers. 'She'll have to go to the infirmary.'

'I need to *fight*!' Liska's mother tried to stand but the other healer held her down.

'You're no use like this,' the healer said. 'Get treated and fight another day.'

'There might not be another day,' Liska heard her mother mutter, and it made Liska's breath catch in her throat.

'Is this it? Are we going to lose?'

Two more healers with a stretcher had come over and began shifting Liska's mother on. With all four of them holding her down she finally gave up struggling and let herself be lifted.

'Liska,' she said, pulling her daughter into a desperate hug. 'Listen to me. We're fighting our hardest, but if the city falls, if we can't stand ... promise me you'll run. Don't try and fight these things. You're too small, too young ... Find a mountain cave or somewhere safe. Away from the rot ...'

If the city falls ... Could this really be it? 'Mother ...' Liska broke her grip to stare into her mother's eyes. 'What about Nammu's heart? Why don't you come with me to find it? We'd both be safe and we might save Arbor—'

'Not that again!' her mother snapped, snarling at the pain in her leg. 'You're not listening! I need to be here to fight! And you're too young for battles and quests! Get somewhere safe and if the city falls ... run. Do you understand?'

Liska couldn't speak. She could only stare at her mother as one of the healers gently separated them both and the stretcher was carried away. Her mother raised a fist to her heart in the shapewalker's salute, but all Liska could think about was her backpack stowed behind her room door, filled and ready to go.

If Arborven was going to fall, if she was going to have to run anyway ... well, it might as well be north. And there was a chance, just a slim one – but still a chance – that she and her friends could stop all this before it even came to that.

She *had* to do it she realised. She had to at least try. If she didn't, everything she knew and loved would be lost. And if she did, she would prove once and for all that she wasn't 'too young' for *anything*.

Forgetting about waiting for morning, she ran for the stairs to fetch her pack, find her friends and save the Undrentree.

*

Gliding low over the treetops, backpack clutched in her fox jaws, Liska came in to land on the scrap of rough ground between the Cryptwood and the mossherders' tree circle.

Even though it was pitch dark out here, past the edge of the city, she could see perfectly with her night vision. The barkless trees of the Cryptwood glowed white in the moonlight. Its scents came alive in her new nose. It smelled of age, dry wood, old bones and a faded gleam of tree magic.

It was easy for Liska to pick up the trail they had left on their walk to Elowen's house. She scampered along the path, into the clearing and down the earthen steps to the hidden front door. Staying in her griffyx form – there was no time to change – she scratched at the wood with her paws, dropping her pack to bark and whine as loudly as she could.

After what seemed like an age, the door creaked open and there stood Elowen, a white smudge in the darkness, holding a candle up to light her way.

'Hello, baby fox,' she said, kneeling and holding out a hand. 'What are you doing here deep in the dead wood? And look, you have wings!'

'It's me,' Liska said, rolling her eyes. 'Liska. You know – from yesterday?'

'Oh, yes!' Elowen stood up, beaming. 'I was forgetting you were a shapewalker. So this is your beast form? It's so beautiful!'

'Never mind that,' said Liska, unable to keep an edge of panicked growl from her voice. 'We have to leave *right now*. The rot creatures are attacking Arborven again, and this time we might not be able to hold them back!'

'Ah,' said Elowen. 'I wondered what was going on. I was walking in the wood earlier and saw all the mages from the swamp go running into the city. I think your friend was among them.'

'Lug?' Liska sniffed the air, trying to pick up his scent. 'We have to find him! We need to leave tonight!'

'Really?' Instead of objecting, Elowen reached behind the door for a pack of her own. She slung it on to a shoulder and then picked up Liska's too. 'What are you waiting for, then? Let's go!'

*

They ran through the trees of Arborven, heading for the Undrentree in the centre. Before they even got close, they could hear the rumbling of hundreds of voices. The whole of the city had been called out and were gathered in the square.

Standing at the edge of the treeline, Liska could see the towering treekeepers rearing up from the mass of bodies. They seemed to be guiding cockatrice and manticore shapewalkers as they swooped down from the sky, landing briefly so that mages could leap on to their backs before beating their way skywards again, back to the forts.

'They're sending them to use their magic in the battle,' said Elowen, her face lit up with excitement. 'How clever!'

'It's not a circus,' snapped Liska. 'The whole city could be destroyed.'

'Sorry,' said Elowen. 'It's just ... I've hardly seen a soul for over a hundred years. All these people ... the Undrentree ... it's just as I remembered. So exciting!'

'Come on,' said Liska, her nose to the ground. 'We need to find Lug.'

She dashed around the edge of the gathering, sniffing every blade of grass. Finally she picked up a swampy, nervous smell she recognised. A few seconds later she spotted Lug standing by a pile of baggage looking terrified.

'Lug!' she shouted, running up to him. 'What are you doing here?'

'Liska! And Elowen!' Lug jumped at the sight of them. The worm mage was a trembling wreck. 'The city is under attack!' he blurted. 'All the mages have been summoned. My parents are in there, ready to help fight. They made us evacuate the Scrubbings in case the rot creatures break through the mountain wall.'

'What are you doing here on your own?' Liska asked, looking at the mound of vermispex bags and boxes next to him.

'I'm ... um ... supposed to be watching everyone's stuff,' Lug said. 'It's a very important job, actually.'

'Well, forget about being a baggage boy,' said Liska. 'We've decided we need to leave *now*. I wasn't going to go at all, for a bit, but then the attack started and my mother's hurt, and she told me to run ...'

'Wait. What? We're going *now*?'

'Yes,' Liska pawed at his robes. 'The city could fall at any minute. We would have to run anyway so we might as well go now. If there's a chance to get Nammu's heart and stop all this ...'

Lug looked around at the shouting, clamouring mages. At the shapewalkers swooping down, the treekeepers beckoning and pointing. And beyond them, in the distance, to where the signal fire from the

Noon Fort could be seen blazing in the sky like a giant candle.

'But my parents ... the baggage ... I can't ... I shouldn't ...'

'Lug.' Liska stood on her hind legs and did her best to stare into his eyes. 'If you stay here you'll never be anything other than someone who gets to watch the luggage. Or worse, you'll be eaten by a gorgaunt for breakfast. This is your chance. Come with us. Save your family, be a hero. Or stay here and be nothing.'

'I ... I guess ... I guess you're right,' he said finally. In the darkness Liska glimpsed the gleam of tears in his eyes.

'Well done, Lug,' she said. 'Get your things. And be quick. Your parents will understand. This is the best thing we can do for them. This is how we save them.'

With a nod, Lug grabbed one of the packs, emptied it out, then began stuffing it with spare robes and what looked like a stuffed, cuddly worm. A few seconds later, the three of them were running through the shadows, heading for the eastern wall.

7

'Although no mage in living
memory has seen one, the valley
of Arborven was once home to an
ancient race of talking felines.'

A Guide to Arborven by Obediah Dawnsoul

They sprinted through the gaps between trees,
running through circle after circle. Everywhere
they saw house doors open, mages dashing towards
the Undren Square clutching staffs and scrolls. Others
herded crowds of children still in their nightwear
towards the safety of the temple.

Liska felt the muscles of her legs burning with

effort. Her fox tongue lolled as she sucked in lungfuls of air. Lug also panted for breath beside her, while Elowen seemed to flit effortlessly between the trunks like a patch of white mist.

'Are you sure you know where we're going?' Liska asked. 'Will the path still be there?'

Elowen turned to look at her, her eyes so pale in the darkness they almost looked blank. 'We're going to the Oddment Caves where the mages throw their broken pottery and bottles. There's a hidden passage there which leads up to the mountain top. That's if they haven't managed to fill the caves with rubbish in five hundred years.'

'They probably have,' muttered Liska. The mages were careful to reuse or fix most of their broken goods, but half a millenium of smashed dinner plates would still make a pretty enormous pile of junk.

Still, they had to trust that Elowen knew what she was doing. Dodging groups of mages coming the other way, they continued to dart between the trees.

They were just leaving the sapsmiths' circle when Lug gave a shriek. Liska skidded to a halt, spinning round almost on the spot. Expecting to find her friend tumbled over a tree root or tangled in a patch of ivy, she was horrified to see him clutched in the grip of a black-robed figure.

Is that ... Noxis? Her first thought made her hackles rise and she bared her fangs, a fierce snarl building in her throat. But then she peered closer and saw that this mage wasn't quite tall enough to be an adult and beneath his hood was a mop of black hair.

'Odis,' she said. 'Here to do some of your traitor-father's dirty work?'

For a second the boy's eyes boggled as he was faced with a talking mythical animal, and his grip on poor Lug tightened. Then he realised who – or what – Liska was. He let Lug fall to the floor and stood, shoulders slumped.

'No,' he said. 'No. I'm not going to hurt you. I just wanted to get your attention. I've come to warn you.'

'About another attack from Daddy's friend Bitterblight?'

Elowen had helped Lug up from the ground and then pushed him behind her, shielding him. Liska flared her wings wide, green eyes flashing with fury. 'Too late. It's already started. The whole of Arborven is in danger. Are you happy now?'

Odis clenched his fists and slammed them against

his thighs. 'Just *listen,* will you? It's *you* that's in the most danger. All three of you. And it's . . . it's my fault.'

Liska snorted. Her eyes flicked around the surrounding trees looking for enemies, worrying that she'd led them into a trap. 'Explain yourself,' she said.

'I heard you,' said Odis. 'You and the worm boy. Talking outside the Undrentree. I heard what you said about the Cryptwood, so I followed you. And then I heard you talking to that . . . that girl.' He glanced at Elowen and then looked away quickly, as if the sight of her unnerved him.

'Oh, yes?' said Liska. 'And what did you hear exactly?'

Odis shrugged. 'About your plan. About the other tree in the north and how you were going to get its heart. It sounded stupid, you know. Everybody's heard about that dumb legend, but no one believes it.'

'*You* must,' said Liska. 'That's why you're here to stop us. What's going to happen? Are some seepers going to jump out and get us?'

'I'm not trying to stop you! I'm trying to save you!' Odis clenched his fists again, but this time he seemed more upset than angry. It even looked like he was about to cry.

'Your plan sounded pathetic,' he said, 'but I needed a story to tell my father. I thought that it might get his attention and then maybe I could change his mind. I thought, if I could just talk to him for a bit he might ... come back to himself. Forget about the rot and Bitterblight. It's all he's been on about for months, and then he left the city. And you said he was there when the seepers attacked. That means it's true – all the gossip about him betraying Arborven. But I had to *try*! I couldn't just let him become ... become evil!'

'What did you do, Odis?' Liska took a step towards the older boy. 'What did you tell him?'

Odis made a sobbing, choking sound, and rubbed at his eyes with his knuckles. 'I went to a place in the mountains, one he'd told me about, and I sent a signal. He came to me but he was with a horde of those things, those seepers. They were under his control, like he was leading them.

'I tried to speak to him. I told him about how much mother and I missed him, that we forgave him, but ... but he didn't care. He was just full of anger, and his eyes were all grey and misty. Like he'd been filled with that seeper sludge.

'He made me tell him why I'd summoned him. He

made me tell him everything I knew. I had to do it or he would have killed me. He really would. His own son . . .'

'So, he knows about our plan?' Liska said. 'He knows we're going to get Nammu's heart?'

Odis nodded. 'I never imagined he'd take it seriously; you have to understand. I just wanted to talk to my father . . .'

'He believed you, then?' Lug was peeping out from Liska's shoulder. 'What is he going to do to us?'

'Yes, he believed me,' said Odis. 'And he must think it's a real threat to him. He said he was going to stop you. He said he was going to set Thresher on you. The hunter. The one who started all this with her tales of the Rotlands. He's sending her to kill you.'

There was a long moment of silence. Liska could feel Lug trembling behind her, small, squeaking noises coming from his throat. While Elowen was calmly observing everything as if it were another scene in a puppet show.

Finally Liska spoke. 'Why did you warn us, Odis? Why didn't you stay in the Rotlands with your father? You could be helping him with the attack right now. Getting yourself in his good books . . .'

'He's not my father any more!' Odis screamed, drawing looks from all the passing mages. Then he buried his face in his hands. 'He's gone. Been taken over. My father would never order three children to be hunted down and killed. That's when I knew. He has become someone else. Someone cold and dangerous. I ran back here and not long after the attack began.'

Liska watched the boy crying, wondering what it felt like to see his father become a different person, a stranger. It must have been horrific. 'I'm sorry, Odis,' she said. 'You did the right thing.'

'I've met her, you know,' he said. 'Thresher. She's terrifying. She was the one who made my father leave. Bitterblight must have gotten to her first. Now she serves the shadow tree and she'll never stop. Not until she's killed you all.'

'She won't catch us,' said Liska, trying to sound much braver than she felt.

Odis just looked at her with red-rimmed eyes. 'She's fought and killed *wyverns*,' he said. 'You three are just children. You're not even proper mages. You don't stand a chance.'

'We'll see about that,' said Liska with a snarl. *Another jibe about being children,* she thought. *Why does everyone in this place think our age is going to stop us?*

'What will you do now?' Elowen asked. 'You can come with us if you like.'

Lug and Liska stared at their new friend in horror but, thankfully, Odis shook his head. 'I have to go and see the treekeepers. It's time I told them everything about Father. All the things he's said. His plans. Some of it might help them save the city. Maybe.'

Liska nodded. Even though he had put them in danger, admitting his father was wrong and trying to stop him was a brave thing to do. Odis nodded back, then he turned and left, jogging off in the direction of the Undrentree.

When he was gone, Lug let out a long, shuddering breath. 'Well, that's it,' he said. 'It was a nice idea – very heroic and everything – but there's no way we can go *now*. Not with Thresher after us. We have to stay in Arborven, where it's safe. I'll just unpack my robes. And Mister Wriggles.'

Liska stopped him with a paw on his leg. 'Not so fast! The plan is still on. Do you think we're safe here? You might know this Thresher better than me but I got a good look at her. She won't let the fact that we're in here stop her. She'll hunt us down wherever we are. Our only hope is to move faster than her.'

Lug let out a long, frustrated whine.

'Do not worry,' said Elowen. 'I know the way very well. We shall easily outrun anyone trying to chase us. Besides, a little pursuit will add an extra bit of excitement to our adventure!'

'It's a life-or-death mission of extreme danger!' Lug wailed. 'Not a mage-school field trip! We're all going to die in horrible, painful, awful ways.'

'Oh, stop moaning!' Liska gripped a corner of Lug's robe and began to pull him along behind her. Elowen followed, blocking his path in case he tried to run off.

A part of Liska wished Lug wasn't so melodramatic, but then she remembered her glimpse of Thresher, of those cold, cruel predator's eyes. As they set off through the city again, she couldn't help casting a nervous glance or two behind them.

*

Just as Liska was beginning to think her legs might drop off, they stumbled out of the trees on the eastern side of the city.

The sheer, grey face of the Shield Mountains reared

up before them as bleak and tall as ever. Perched on the top somewhere was the Stormfort. A tower like her own, filled with warrior shapewalkers ready to defend Arborven from attack. There were no signal fires lit here, though. No sounds of battle or stench of rot. It looked as though Noxis was concentrating his attack on the other side of the city.

'The caves are over here if I remember rightly,' said Elowen. She skimmed over the rough patch of grassland between forest and mountain, towards a series of dark shadows amongst the slabs of tumbled, broken granite that had toppled down over the centuries. Liska followed and, as she got closer, saw that the shadows were actually deep holes in the rock. Most of them were clogged up with mounds of ... stuff. Broken jugs, glass bottles, washtubs, smashed plates, pots, vases, pieces of teacup. All the unusable rubbish of Arborven, probably dating from since the mages first moved in five hundred years or more ago.

'I never knew this was here,' said Liska.

'Nor me,' said Lug. 'In fact, I didn't really wonder where our rubbish went at all.'

'Most people don't,' said Elowen. 'Once it's broken they just buy new things and forget about the old.

Although there's a bit more here than I expected. I hope we can still find our way inside the caves.'

She led them to the third cave along, and then paused to open her pack and take out a lantern. Liska cursed under her breath – she hadn't even thought to bring candles or lamps, let alone anything to make fire. It made her wonder what other essential survival tools she might have forgotten.

When Elowen's lamp was lit, she set off into the cave with the others behind her. There was a tiny scrap of a path between the mounds of rubbish and the cave wall. Even so, they had to slip and slither over shards of china, glass and pottery. It broke even more under their feet. Tiny *tink, tink, tink* sounds and lots of crunching, as if they were walking on especially hard snow.

'Did anyone bring bandages?' Lug asked, his voice echoing inside the cave. 'If we fall over on this stuff, we could slice open an artery and bleed to death.'

'Are you going to worry about *everything* we do?' Liska asked, rolling her eyes.

'I'm just being realistic,' said Lug. Then added 'Someone has to be' under his breath.

The piles of broken rubbish reached up almost to the cave roof. As they went further and further back, the pieces of shattered pots and jugs became more and more buried in dust, rubble and what looked like rat droppings. From the flickering shadows cast by Elowen's lamp, they could hear scurryings and snifflings. Liska's nose twitched as it filled with the scent of rodents. That, and something else. Something . . . *feline*.

'The entrance to the secret path should be around here,' said Elowen. 'Unless it's been buried in old crockery. It's so hard to tell . . . the last time I was here, there were only a few cartloads of junk.'

'Why is there a secret path, anyway?' Lug asked. 'And why put it somewhere so . . . disgusting and dangerous?'

'Why, it's the best place for a secret,' said Elowen. 'Who would ever want to look here? And it was built to escape the city in an emergency. There used to be lots of wyvern attacks when I was younger.'

'That must have been before the stormsingers created the mists,' said Liska. 'We don't get any wyverns now.'

'Yes,' said Elowen. 'There were no mists when we first arrived here. Just hungry, flying, fire-breathing monsters.'

'I don't suppose you were one of the first

stormsingers?' Lug asked. 'Then you could magic a mist to surround us when we're . . . out *there*. To keep us safe from monsters.'

Elowen patted him on the shoulder. 'I'm afraid my magic is rather weak at the moment. It always is for a while once I have woken from one of my sleeps. It takes a few weeks for things to get back to normal when you're dead, you know.'

'But you *do* have magic, right?' Lug pressed. 'You can help us with some storm spells when we need it?'

Elowen ignored him, stopping to peer at a section of wall, holding up the lamp to see better. It plunged the rest of the cave into darkness, and the skitterings of small animals grew louder.

'Ah . . . this might be it,' she said, laying a hand on the wall. 'Help me push.'

It just looked like a featureless piece of rock but, with a shrug, Liska put her front paws against it and pushed. Lug came to join in and with all of them straining, the wall gave a sudden jolt and began to grind inwards.

'Slimy segments! There *is* a passage!' said Lug as the sliding doorway revealed a small room with some steep steps leading upwards at the far end.

'Of course,' said Elowen with a frown. 'Do you

think I'm making things up? Don't you trust my memory?' When neither Lug nor Liska answered, she huffed and stepped inside the doorway. 'Come on, then. We'd better shut this behind us. Make it harder for the hunter person to follow.'

One by one they squeezed inside, pushing the door shut behind them. A metal rod stood in a corner of the chamber and Elowen used it to bar the way behind them, 'just in case'. Then she held up her lamp again until it shone on the steep, stone steps, spiralling up inside the mountain.

'Where does this stairway go exactly?' Lug asked, peering up into the darkness.

'Why, to the top of the Shield Mountains of course,' said Elowen. 'It comes out by the Stormfort, but not close enough for them to spot us.'

'And then where do we go? We'll be stuck up *there*. We're supposed to be leaving the city!'

'We will,' said Elowen, smiling. 'There's a path down the mountain on the other side once we get through the Kittimew Kingdom.'

'The *what*?' asked Lug, looking more worried than ever. But Elowen had already stepped past him and was heading up the steep stairway.

'Up we go,' said Liska, giving Lug a firm nudge and wishing – for the hundredth time that night – that she could just spread her wings and fly, preferably leaving the moaning worm mage behind her.

*

Round and round, up and endlessly up.

Liska followed the glow of Elowen's lamp, trudging step after step. Her eyes watched the dancing patterns of light on the featureless rocky walls, letting them hypnotise her as she forced her tired paws to take one more step, then another, then another . . .

It started to seem like all she had ever known was the plodding walk up this rocky staircase, as if all her past life had just been a dream and she would trudge on and on forever, never reaching the top.

From somewhere behind she could hear Lug's whimpering. It had a rhythm of its own: a squeak every time he moved a foot upwards and a pained groan as he heaved his weight after it. Mixed with the scuffing and shuffling of her own paws and the whispering of Elowen's long layers of dresses against the stone, it made a kind of music: *squeak, shuffle, groan, shuffle, swish, shuffle, squeak.* And repeat, and repeat, and repeat.

I'm never going to take flying for granted again, she thought, remembering how it felt to soar down from the mountain top in just seconds, or to lazily circle on a thermal, rising up and up until she reached the top.

Just when she thought she was going to have to stop and scream, or at least have a little cry, Elowen turned to them and said, 'We're here!'

'Oh, praise the Tree,' gasped Lug. Liska heard him collapse on the steps behind her. She felt like having a lie-down herself. A very long one.

'Just another secret door to open,' said Elowen. She set her lamp down on the top step and gave the wall in front of her a push. This time it swung open easily and sunlight poured in through the opening, making them all squint and blink.

'It's morning!' said Lug. 'We were walking up those stairs all night!'

'Well, probably only for a couple of hours,' said Liska. 'It was almost dawn when we went in. But it was long enough to make my feet feel like they want to fall off. Come on, let's get out of this horrible stairway.'

They heaved themselves up the last few steps and walked out on to the top of the mountains. A familiar ring of jagged granite stretched off around them, jutting up from a writhing sea of mist. A hundred metres or so along the summit loomed the Stormfort, a towering structure of stone battlements and turrets that looked almost identical to the Noon Fort that Liska called home. Behind them was the tree-filled bowl of Arborven, a round dish of green that seemed to be still unscathed.

'It's . . . it's *incredible*,' said Lug, looking all around him. 'I can see so far! We're so high up! And I've just remembered that I'm terrified of heights!'

Liska was forgetting that her friend had never been anywhere except inside the city. To her, this view was just an everyday thing. She often forgot how impressive and beautiful it was: filled with the immensity and the power of nature.

'The city seems to be intact,' she said, peering down at the smudges of treetops. 'Maybe they fought off the rot army.'

'I doubt it,' said Lug. 'Bitterblight won't give up that easily. There will be more and more attacks until the whole of Arborven is covered in rot.'

'You're right,' said Liska. 'They'll be back as soon as night falls I expect.' She wondered how her mother was doing, lying in the infirmary. Were her father and sister safe? Or might they be injured as well? Or perhaps even worse …

'The fort has grown a lot since I was last here,' said Elowen, interrupting Liska's scary thoughts. 'And the mist! There's so much of it. I hope we won't get lost on the way down.'

'We're going *through* the mist?' said Lug. 'Won't it poison us?'

'Not us,' said Liska, turning away from the view of Arborven. 'But the wyverns don't like it. It's made to blind them and clog up their throats so they can't breathe fire.' She knew quite a lot about it, having grown up with the stormsingers who visited the towers and used them as bases to conjure up the constant fog. She often watched them, leaning out over their platforms, waving their arms in complicated patterns as clouds of smoky vapour billowed around them. 'We should be able to walk through it. Although it might make finding our way a bit tricky.'

'A bit tricky' was an understatement.

They walked across the humped back of the mountain's top, over to where the bleached trunk of an old tree stood. From there Elowen was able to find a faint path – barely more than a goats' track – that

151

spidered its way down the mountainside in zigs and zags. It looked treacherous enough, but after only a few metres it vanished into the swirling grey mist, making it even more deadly.

Liska decided it would be safer to tackle it with two feet. Enough time had passed since her last transformation, so she shifted back, taking her rucksack from Elowen and clutching it to her chest.

The three of them then edged their way down the ledge sideways, backs to the rock, one slithering step at a time, trying to squint through the mist as they went.

It was so thick – like trying to walk through cotton wool. Liska could feel it clinging to the back of her throat, clustering in cold drips to her hair and clothes. They hadn't been walking long before everything she wore was soaked through.

'I think we have to climb down this bit,' came Elowen's voice from up ahead. The path had reached a patch of fallen rock where a thick slab of granite had sheared off. There was nothing beyond but a steep drop, the bottom hidden in the mists.

'I can't do that!' Lug had crawled to the edge on hands and knees and was peering over. 'It could go down for miles and miles! There's only tiny cracks to grip on to!'

'I'll go first,' said Elowen as if they had just spotted a fun-looking mud slide to go down rather than a plunge to certain death. 'Let's tie ourselves together, just in case.'

She pulled a coil of gleaming, silver-stranded rope from her pack, and Liska cursed again. Another thing she had forgotten.

With the three of them tied to the line, they began to make their way down the rock. For Liska, it didn't seem too difficult. She had grown up on the sides of mountains after all, and climbing was almost as natural as flying. But Lug was struggling and nearly slipped more than once. It was a relief when the broken section of rock turned out to be only twenty metres high and they set foot on solid ground again.

'Is this the bottom of the mountain?' Lug asked, eyes shining with hope. 'That wasn't nearly as bad as I thought it would be. Perhaps this journey won't be so hard after all.'

Liska laughed. 'We've hardly started! Haven't you seen how high the mountains are? This isn't even halfway.'

The next section did have a much better path

however. It led them under some overhanging rocks and into a world of tumbledown boulders which was dotted with twisted, half-dead trees. Their way led in amongst the stony mess and looked like some kind of mind-bending maze.

'I'm not too sure of the route through,' said Elowen. 'Not with this mist covering everything.'

'Why doesn't Liska fly up and spot the way?' Lug suggested.

Liska waved her arms through the thick fog that surrounded them. 'What do you think this is, genius? If I fly up, all I'm going to see is white fluff. And I might never find my way back to you either.'

'Oh.' Lug pouted. And then his face lit up. 'But then we'd have to go back home, wouldn't we?'

'No,' said Elowen. 'Then we'd probably stay lost on the mountain and starve. Or this Thresher person would find us and slice us into sausages.'

Liska shook her head at Lug before returning to the problem of getting down the mountain.

'Perhaps we should leave a sign in case we double back on ourselves?' Elowen suggested.

Liska nodded and made a simple arrow on the pathway out of some rocks and a twig.

She worried for a moment that the hunter on their trail might use it to find them, but then figured it was more important that they didn't get lost. Besides, Lug was probably leaving a trail clear enough for anyone to follow with all his scuffing and slipping.

Keeping themselves tied together with the rope, they plunged into the misty maze.

*

The narrow path wound in between boulders the size of houses, around stacks of stones that looked as though they had been purposefully piled. It reminded Liska of something Elowen had said back in the stairwell.

'Is this the place you called the Kitten Kingdom?' she asked.

'Kittimew,' corrected Elowen. 'Yes, I believe they used to live somewhere around here.'

'What exactly are they?' Lug asked from the back of the line. 'Are they as cute as they sound? Do they have pink button noses and fluffy-wuffy ears?'

Elowen laughed. 'Definitely not. They can be very fierce. They were the original inhabitants of Arborven, you know. They lived around the Undrentree, but when us humans first arrived, they agreed to move to the mountains and the Oddment Caves.'

'Why would they do that?' Liska wondered. 'Why would they just give up their home?'

'They were quite happy to,' said Elowen. 'They knew that humans make lots of rubbish, and rubbish attracts rats.'

Liska remembered all the skittering noises she had heard in the caves. She hardly dared ask what the kittimews wanted with rats, but Elowen told them anyway.

'Yes, they love to eat rats. They consider them a delicacy. Fried, grilled, stewed, roasted, baked, raw. Rat soup, rat curry, rat pie ... I'm sure the kittimews will be most plump. That's if they're still around, of course. I thought we might have seen one by now.'

Liska peered into the whirling strands of mist as they walked. She had lived all her life in the mountains and had never even heard of kittimews, let alone spotted one. She was beginning to think Elowen might have made the whole thing up when they found themselves walking past some dead trees that looked very familiar. Sure enough, they came across the spot where Liska had left her arrow sign, except somebody or something had moved it. The rocks had become eyes; the broken twig, a mouth. It now looked like a smiley face.

'My arrow!' she shouted. She didn't know if she was more cross about having walked in a circle, or that someone had messed around with her sign.

'Who ... who did that?' Lug stammered, his wide, terrified eyes darting around, imagining Thresher the hunter hiding behind every tree.

'Oh, that will be the kittimews,' said Elowen, giggling. 'They do enjoy a bit of mischief!'

'That's lovely, but it means we're lost,' said Liska. 'And tired and hungry and achy. I would really like to get off this mountain and having someone messing with my signs isn't helping!'

She shouted her last words into the mist and thought she might have heard a quiet snickering noise in reply.

'I think I know where we made a wrong turn,' said Elowen. 'Let's have a rest, then try again.'

They sat at the foot of a dead tree and drank from Liska's water skin. It was blissful to stretch out their aching legs and rub their sore feet, but when Lug started to close his eyes and doze, Elowen made them get up again.

'Just a snooze ...' Lug moaned. 'A tiny nap. Forty winks. Please?'

'We can sleep when we're off the mountain,' said

Liska. She wanted to find somewhere safe before they made camp, just in case Thresher was on their trail already.

With a sigh of frustration from Lug, they set off on the path again. Liska recognised some of the boulders they passed, but then the mist thickened and it was hard to see anything at all. After another hour of walking they stopped and realised, to their horror, that they were back at the arrow sign again. This time the face had been changed to look more sinister: snapped twig crosses for eyes and a downturned mouth.

'Oh, very funny!' Liska shouted. 'A dead face? Why don't you come out here and show yourself? *Then* we'll see whose face is dead!'

'You really shouldn't shout at the kittimews,' said Elowen. 'They are an ancient and respectable people. You should treat them with kindness: leave them gifts and tributes, ask their permission when you cross their lands . . .'

'How can we ask their permission when they just hide in the mist and tease us?' Liska was on the verge of shifting into her griffyx shape. Then she'd be able to sniff these kitty-things out and give them a good biting.

Maybe even smell a path through the maze while she was at it.

'The pale one is right,' came a voice from somewhere in the mist. 'You is wrong to be shouting at us. You should be giving offerings and stuff, and being thankful we is not eating you for trespassing.'

Lug flinched while Liska whirled around, searching for the voice's source. It had come from somewhere behind them and, straining her eyes against the fog, she could make out a shadowy smudge coiled on top of a nearby rock.

'Who are you?' she asked it. 'Why do you keep messing around with my signs?'

A yawning sound, and the thing uncoiled. It slank down from its perch and padded towards them, stepping out of the mist and into plain sight.

It was a cat. Or at least something cat-like.

Wild felines lived in the trees of Arborven, climbing branches, catching mice and chasing flying squirrels. Some mages even kept them as pets, so Liska was familiar with the pointed ears, slitted eyes, striped fur and long, twitching tail. *This* creature, however, walked on two feet and wore an assortment of clothes. If the patched, darned and stitched fragments of tattered fabric it was dressed in could be called that.

It was about the size of a small child but had a sly, calculating look in its yellow eyes. Several rings glinted in its torn ears and the fur on top of its head had been smeared with some kind of ochre, stiffening it into a spiky crest.

'I is moving the signs because I is bored,' it said, then emphasised its comment with another yawn. Liska noticed its pink tongue and needle-sharp white teeth. 'Why is you humies walking through kittimew lands anyhow? You is never coming out of your trees normally.'

Elowen, to the others' surprise, knelt on one knee before the cat-thing and bowed her head. 'Please forgive us, noble kittimew,' she said. 'We are on a dangerous mission that has forced us to leave the city. We must travel through your lands on our quest north. With your permission, of course.'

'Dangerous mission?' said the kittimew, its tail twitching. 'Tell us what this mission is.'

'I don't really think that's any of your business,' said Liska. 'Just leave our signs alone and let us through.' She gave her cloak a swish to show she meant business, but the kittimew only wrinkled its nose.

'You *will* tell us,' it said. 'Or you'll never find your way through the boulder walk. We will make sure you is walking round and round it forever.'

Liska began to growl but Elowen held up a hand to stop her. Instead of arguing, she told the kittimew all about Noxis and Bitterblight, about how the Undrentree was under threat and that they were hoping to bring back the heart of Nammu to save it. She even mentioned the fact that Thresher was pursuing them with orders to kill.

All through her speech, the kittimew watched Elowen closely with its gleaming yellow eyes, not moving so much as a whisker. When she had finished, it stood silent for a few minutes more, deep in thought.

'If the humies want to pass, we will show them the way. But only if they let us come on the adventure with them.'

'What?' Liska couldn't believe it. 'Why do you want to come along? What has the Undrentree got to do with you? You live on a cliff next to a dump!'

'And what does he mean by "us"?' added Lug. 'Just how many talking cats does he want to bring?'

The kittimew opened its mouth and let out a hiss, then raised a paw towards Lug with claws flexed out. It was probably some kind of serious cat insult.

'Just me, you pasty fool,' it said. 'And the Undrentree

is where all kittimew came from. We would give our lives to protect it. Also I is very bored – as I mentioned earlier – and a good adventure will give me something to talk about at the next yowling.'

Elowen got to her feet, brushing down her dress. 'Well, I think that would be a lovely idea,' she said. 'A guide down from the mountain, another comrade and the chance to learn more about the kittimew way of life. What do you say, Liska?'

'Well,' said Liska. 'I suppose I don't mind.' If the kittimew became too annoying, they could always run off and leave it. Perhaps with Lug for company.

'Excellent,' said their new companion bowing deeply and swishing his tabby-striped tail. 'I shall show you the path through the boulder walk and down to the mistless lands.'

'We should probably introduce ourselves,' said Elowen, proceeding to tell the kittimew all their names. It listened carefully, nodding after each one.

'And my name is *Reeeeowwwreeeeeowwwwwoooo wwwoooowwwfsst Fssst Fsst*. In the kittimew tongue, that is.'

'I don't think I'm going to be able to remember that,' said Lug. 'What's that written on your chest?'

The kittimew looked down to where a splodge of greasy black paint had been smeared over the mishmash of wool, leather and cotton that passed for its jerkin. It looked a bit like the skeleton of a fish.

'That is the sign of my house,' said the kittimew, puffing out its chest. 'The family of the Half-Eaten Trout.'

'Fish bone,' said Liska. 'It looks like a fish bone. Can we call you that?'

The kittimew looked at her for a long moment, as if wondering whether to leap on her and scratch her to pieces. Then it blinked its eyes and bowed its head. 'Yes. That would be a good name.'

'Great,' said Liska. 'Fishbone it is. Can we get down off this mountain now, please?'

'Of course,' said Fishbone. 'We should probably hurry, I suppose. Or that hunter up there will catch you and kill you.'

Liska turned to look where Fishbone was pointing. As the mists shifted and swirled, she caught a glimpse, further up the path they had just walked down, of a slender figure hunched over the trail. She stared, heart pounding, as their tracker raised her head and looked down the path at her. Those blank, dead, ruthless eyes ... it was Thresher and she had found them.

The mist closed over her a second later but by then they were already running, chasing after the scampering tail of Fishbone as he darted in amongst the boulders. From behind them came the sound of pounding, hungry footsteps.

8

'A hunted kittimew is being more
slippery than a frog's botty.'

The Yowlings of King Reeeoowwrrrr the Third

Through carefully placed towers of stones they
sprinted, around boulders, beneath overhangs,
leaping across springs of water, scrambling between
toppled tree trunks. Liska's breath rasped in her throat.
Behind her, still attached by the rope, Lug sobbed and
sniffed, whimpering with terror. Every now and then
she had to stop and shout at him to hurry, or even haul
him along like a sack of soggy potatoes.

They followed Fishbone as best they could but they

were no match for his agility. He flowed up rocks and bounced off as if he were made of rubber. He *swished* between cracks that the others had to pause and squeeze through, every second waiting for a blade or spear to shoot out of the mist and hit them.

Finally he stopped running at the mouth of a narrow fissure in the granite. The split was in a giant slab twenty metres tall, and ran all the way through, like a sliced turnip. They would have to shuffle along it sideways to fit, dragging their packs behind them, and it would slow them down considerably. They would be sitting ducks if Thresher caught up with them.

'We have to go through *there*?' Lug wailed. 'We'll never make it! The hunter will catch us for sure!'

'Isn't there another way?' Liska asked Fishbone. After watching him bound through the rocks, her respect for the cat-creature had grown enormously.

'No,' Fishbone shook his head, but a crackle of mischief danced in his eyes. 'This is the only safe way down from the mountain. But us kittimews have a surprise in it. Quick now. In, in, in and start moving.'

He hurried them up with quick jabs of his claws. They were very sharp, the needly tips even piercing through Liska's leather armour. The three humans were soon edging their way through the crack, their noses almost brushing the solid rock in front, their backs squashed against the wall behind.

Shuffle, shuffle, shuffle – they made such slow progress it was painful.

Gradually the hole they had squeezed through began to fade into the distance. Liska kept her eyes fixed on it, waiting for Thresher's cruel face to appear.

Shuffle, shuffle, shuffle. The gap in the rock stretched above them: up, up, to where a strip of misty sky could be seen overhead. Liska willed Elowen to go faster. She longed to be out in the open again, with space around her to run, to change, to fly.

O, Undrentree, please don't let me die here, trapped like an animal, she prayed.

After the longest ten minutes of her life, she heard a gasp as Elowen finally stepped free. A few more wiggles and Liska felt her left toe emerge into the open. She was about to whoop with joy when her eye caught a movement at the far end of the narrow passage.

Something – some*one* – was there.

She stared, pausing in her shuffling, and a low moaning noise of horror escaped from her throat.

A silhouette of a tall, slender figure with spiked

hair, a barbed spear clutched in one fist. It blocked the entrance for a second, before stepping aside and making a beckoning motion with its hand.

That's Thresher, Liska thought. *But who is she calling? Who else is after us?*

The question should have been *what* else. As Liska watched, frozen, another form appeared. Liquid, shapeless, the thing edged into the gap, wisps of thin smoke trailing from its surface. It stretched itself as it moved, pushing out limbs, a head – all clumsily formed from the grey sludge of the rot.

A seeper? But it didn't look humanoid like the others. It was four-legged and scrawny, with a barrel chest and pointed snout. It looked like a hunting hound.

'She's here!' Fishbone shouted. 'Hurry, hurry!'

Even as the seeper hound set one gloopy paw, then another, into the passage, Fishbone was leaping, ricocheting from one wall to the other, high over Liska and Lug's heads. He landed in the open grabbed hold of Liska's cloak, trying to pull her free from the crevice.

That was enough to get Liska moving. Using every last scrap of strength she forced herself out, and then snatched up the rope that attached her to Lug. With

Fishbone and Elowen helping, they began to heave the vermispex out of the passageway.

'It's coming! It's coming!' Lug shrieked, frozen in place. Peering behind him, Liska could see the hound edging its way closer and closer.

'Don't just stand there!' Liska shouted at the petrified worm mage. 'Get wriggling!'

'Don't worry,' said Fishbone, through gritted teeth. 'We want it in there. But we have to get pasty whining boy free quickly or he'll be turned into humie jam.'

Wondering what he was talking about, Liska gave the rope a final heave. Lug popped clear like a sweaty, trembling cork from a wine bottle. As he tumbled to a heap on the floor, Fishbone laid a paw against the rock wall and made some cattish miaowing noises.

'Kittimew magic,' he said with a grin.

Back in the crevice the seeper hound was only a few metres away from them now, slipping and sliding between the narrow rock walls much more easily than they had done. Liska could see the thick, gelatinous liquid it was made of. There were tiny particles of fungus and mould suspended in it. They twitched and moved with a life of their own as their host stretched

169

and shaped itself, all the while steaming with wisps of poisonous smoke.

'Bye bye, rotten thing,' Fishbone said. He jumped back from the rockface and then, with a *crack* like a sudden burst of thunder, the crevice snapped shut. Now there was only a smooth wall of granite before them. No passageway. No seeper.

*

'Dear worms below, is it over? Has it gone?' Lug had both hands clamped over his eyes and had missed the whole thing.

'That was *amazing,*' said Liska. 'But are you sure there isn't another way for them to get through?'

Fishbone shook his head. 'They will have to climb over or go around. Both will take them much longer. We will be down the slide and in the mistless lands by then.'

'Slide?' Elowen tapped her fingers together in her *I'm so excited* gesture. 'I love slides! I haven't been on one for centuries!'

'You never been on one like this,' said Fishbone, grinning. Then he was off again, scampering on all fours, looking more like an actual cat than ever.

The others followed him, still joined to each other

by rope. They ran down a steep, narrow ridge with a sheer drop into the mists on one side. It zigged and zagged as it descended and looked as though it might carry on like that all the way down the remaining section of mountain, but after a few minutes Fishbone stopped.

'Here it is!' he said, pointing to a shallow groove that fell away from the path, down the steep rockface and into the wall of fog. 'Sit on your packs, lie back and slide!'

With that he lay on his stomach and pushed himself off the pathway, shooting down the smooth furrow like a bullet. In half a blink he was gone, just a cat-sized gap in the mist showing he had ever been there.

'This isn't going to be good for my vertigo,' said Lug. 'It looks very steep. And very dangerous.'

'You think *everything* is dangerous.' Even so, Liska had grown up on the mountaintops and slithering down a rock when you couldn't see what was below seemed like an incredibly stupid thing to do.

'Don't be silly,' said Elowen. 'Look how smooth it is! Generations of kittimews must have used it before, and they were all fine.'

If they're so fine, Liska thought, *where exactly are*

they? For all they knew, Fishbone could be the only kittimew left. The others could all be lying at the bottom of this slide in a heap of rotten bones.

'Well, I'm going to give it a go,' said Elowen. She swung her pack into the stony groove then sat on it, ready to descend into the unknown.

'Wait!' Liska shouted. 'We're still . . .' she was about to say 'tied together', but Elowen was already gone. The rope around Liska's waist began to stretch out after her, and she only had a few seconds to jump on to her own pack.

'Quick, Lug!' she yelled as the slide funnelled her, heart in her mouth, down into the mist. She felt the rope go tight behind her and then heard a strangled squawk and a *thump* as Lug was yanked off his feet.

Swishhhh . . . The sound of slithering stone filled Liska's ears as she sailed through the bank of white fog. She held her breath, staring in wide-eyed horror at the visible patch of mountain in front of her, expecting to see a bottomless drop appear at any moment.

Down, down, she went, although it was impossible to tell how fast or how far she had travelled. All she knew was that the slide lasted for longer than she could have thought possible.

It must go all the way to the bottom of the mou—.

Her thought was never finished as she cannoned into a soft lump of lace and flesh that turned out to be Elowen. Before she had time to roll out of the way, Lug crashed into *her* and the three of them tumbled – packs, rope and all – into a bundle on the ground.

They lay there catching their breath, a jumble of elbows, knees, wild hair and bruises. When her heart had stopped trying to crack its way out of her ribcage, Liska began to untangle and pick herself up. From the corner of her eye she saw Fishbone perched on a rock nearby, calmly licking his tail.

'You could have explained that a bit more,' she said to him. 'Or at least told us to untie ourselves.'

The kittimew shrugged as if their safety was nothing to do with him.

'That was such *fun*,' said Elowen, climbing to her feet and rearranging her complicated array of dresses and petticoats. Lug was still lying where he had fallen, face down. It looked as though he might be trying to kiss the ground.

'At least we've got down from the mountain,' Liska said. 'And made good time as well. Thresher will have a job catching up with us.'

'And now,' said Fishbone, hopping down from his rock, 'we is going forward. Into the mistless lands!'

Liska was about to ask whether the kittimew knew anything about crossing the Blasted Waste when a sound erupted that almost knocked her off her feet.

ROOOOOAAAAARRRRRGGGGGHHHHH!!!

The ground around them shook with the force of it. The mist itself bucked and swirled.

Lug had been gathering enough strength to stand up again, but had instantly fallen flat and was now trying to bury himself under the mound of packs. 'What ... what was *that*?'

'Wyvern,' said Fishbone, putting a finger to his lips. 'Quiet now. If it hears us, it is eating us.'

*

Following the slinking kittimew, they tiptoed through the mist, using rocks and boulders as cover.

The further they moved, Liska noticed, the thinner the fog became. Soon she could make out the landscape around them.

Compared to the lush forest of Arborven, it was a bare and lifeless place. Tumbled rocks from the mountains were dotted all over, and the ground was mostly dry earth speckled with clumps of bristly heather and straggly trees.

It carried on that way for as far as she could see, and the sight of it filled her with dread. *Open ground. No cover.* And with wyverns flying around looking for prey. But what had she been expecting? A lovely straight road all the way to Nammu? She might have known it wouldn't be that easy.

Fishbone had run ahead and was hiding behind a large boulder, peering around the side. They scrambled after him, keeping low to the ground.

'What can you see?' Liska asked. 'Is the wyvern there?'

She was answered by another earth-shaking roar. The thing sounded close. Far too close for comfort.

'Relax,' said Fishbone, spotting the terror on everyone's face. 'No danger. At least not from the wyvern.'

Wondering what he meant, Liska took a turn at peering around the boulder and what she saw made her duck back and hide.

There was a creature there. A lizard-like thing. Except it was at least fifty metres long. She had a brief glimpse of horns, snout, spines and tail. Thick scaly skin patterned with spots of blue and an overpowering reptilian stink. Hot and bitter; a smell that stuck in the back of your throat.

'It's ... it's ... *a monster*,' she managed to say. It made the cockatrices and manticores she had grown up around look like hamsters.

'Will it eat us?' Lug whispered. He looked like he was thinking of running back up the slide to take his chances with Thresher and her gloop hounds.

Fishbone shook his head. 'Look closer. The danger is not being from the fire lizard. That one is a dead thing.'

Liska peeked around the boulder again, this time taking a longer look.

Fishbone was right. The gigantic wyvern was lying flat on the ground, eyes closed. Its leathery wings were folded and she could now see they were bound with coils of thick rope. Shafts of spears and harpoons jutted out from its blue spotted hide, and there were *people* standing around it. Men and women dressed in scraps of metal and leather, with hair coloured in screaming shades of purple, red and pink. At first, she thought their skin was blue, but then she realised it was because they were almost totally covered in tattoos.

'Poxpunks,' she said. 'We learnt about them in

battle training. They live in the Blasted Waste, trapping wyverns.'

'We call them "lizard-hunting painted humies",' said Fishbone. 'Sometimes they climb up the mountain and shoot kittimews, too. They makes garments from our fur. Things they is wearing under their breeches.'

'Underpants?' Lug said. 'They make you into underpants?'

'Yes.' Fishbone made a hissing noise and spat on the ground. 'Big Mew curse the lot of them.'

'Big Mew? Who under the Tree is that?' Lug asked.

'Kittimew god,' Fishbone replied. 'He built the world from leftover mouse guts. Thunder happens every time he purrs. Lightning when he sharpens claws. Rain when he—'

'Alright, we get the picture! Now, what are they doing to the poor wyvern?' Elowen asked. 'And how can it scream so when it is dead?'

Liska took another look and saw that the Poxpunks were winding the wyvern's body on to an iron trailer with a mechanical winch. The contraption was being pulled by a ship-like wagon. It had six or more towering spiked wheels, a cabin with cannons and harpoon guns poking out from firing ports, and a deck with mast and sails. There were also tall pipes jutting from the top, puffing out clouds of oily smoke.

As the wyvern's body was winched up and secured on the trailer bed, Liska spotted a second beast behind it. This one was not even a quarter the size of the first. It had big, vulnerable eyes and stubby horns. Poxpunks stood on its back, binding its wings tightly and poking it with wooden rods. The poor thing looked terrified and helpless.

Liska told the others what she could see and soon they were all staring out from behind the boulder.

'That little one is just a baby!' Elowen whispered. 'Are they going to harm it?'

'Painted humies kill wyverns,' said Fishbone. 'They drag them back to their cities on their land boats and carve them up. Make clothes from skin, build things from bones, eat the meat and use oil to make their stinking machines run. Baby wyvern will get chopped in a minute.'

Liska was horrified. Even though she had heard terrifying tales about wyverns, the one in front of them now looked innocent and harmless. She couldn't bear to see it butchered in front of her, no matter how dangerous the Poxpunks might be.

'No.' She found herself standing up before she fully realised what she was doing. 'I'm not going to let them.'

Fishbone gawked at her for a second before grabbing her hand with his paws. 'Stupid humie! What is you doing? The painted ones will turn us all into bottom warmers!'

'They can try,' said Liska, sounding a lot braver than she felt. Clenching her jaw, she marched out from the rock, striding towards the baby wyvern.

'Wait for me!' Elowen trotted after her, and she could hear Lug's frantic protests as Fishbone prodded him to his feet with the help of a pawful of needle-claws.

The reptilian stink grew stronger as she marched. It was sour and acidic, mixed with a lizardy muskiness. The clanking sound of the Poxpunks' winch drowned out their approach so the trappers didn't notice them until they were just a few metres away.

Liska planted her feet and raised a fist. The other hand reached for the hood of her cloak, ready to flip it over if she needed to shapewalk quickly.

'Stop hurting that dragon!' she shouted in as commanding a voice as she could.

'Actually, it's a wyvern,' Elowen whispered in her ear. 'Dragons have four legs. These only have two.'

'Stop hurting that wyvern!' Liska corrected herself. The Poxpunk nearest to her looked up from where he was guiding the dead wyvern's head up the ramp to the trailer. He held a tattooed arm up in the air and the winching crew paused, leaving the wyvern's head dangling from the trailer edge. The Poxpunks standing on the baby wyvern stopped prodding it for a moment, leaving the poor thing whining and panting, it's football-sized eyes rolling in fear.

'Who the flum are you?' The Poxpunk with the raised arm turned to face them. He had crimson-dyed hair that trailed down his back in braids and was wearing a breastplate of hammered steel, flecked with rust and half-covered with fluorescent runes. His wyvern-skin trousers were spattered with neon paint and his armour-plated boots had spikes on the toecaps.

Even his face is tattooed, Liska realised. *He looks like he fell asleep and someone doodled all over him.*

'We are from Arborven,' shouted Liska, hoping that the Poxpunks knew of the tree-city. 'And we forbid you to slay that baby wyvern!'

'Wot, that puny runtling?' The Poxpunk pointed at the baby. It was trying to open its mouth to cry but they had now wrapped rope tightly around it, gagging the poor thing.

'Yes,' said Liska. 'We demand you let it go! By order of . . . um . . . by order of the treekeepers!'

'Oh, yeh?' The Poxpunk reached down to his belt and drew a wicked, curved knife with a serrated edge like shark's teeth. Two more jumped down from the truck, waving weapons of their own. Liska stared into their mean, tattooed faces and felt a flow of icy fear spread from her neck downwards. These savage hunters obviously had no idea who the treekeepers were, let alone any respect for them.

'Stay back!' A yell sounded from behind her. It was Lug, with a bristling Fishbone perched on his shoulders. He was holding his hands out in a spellcasting gesture, which also had no effect on the Poxpunks.

'Or what?' said the one with crimson braids. 'What are you bunch of snotty sniplings going to do to *us*?'

'This!' Lug crouched down to the ground, pressing his palms against it and muttering an incantation. When he stood again, both his hands were full of writhing earthworms. He hurled them at the Poxpunks with all his strength.

They pattered off their armour like wormy drizzle,

and then fell to the floor, weakly twitching. The Poxpunks laughed.

Something about those scrappy bullies laughing at her friend's brave stand made Liska's hackles rise. She swept her cloak around her and drew on its magic, folding herself like liquid into her griffyx shape. In a blink, she crouched before the Poxpunks, snarling, lashing her tail, wings spread wide in the fiercest pose she could muster.

The head Poxpunk stopped laughing and took a step backwards. 'It's . . . it's one of those shifters!'

His comrades stepped back as well, then began looking upwards, searching the skies for more shapewalkers. They must have clashed with guard patrols before. Liska noticed this and decided to use it.

'Yes, I am one of the defenders of Arborven! And there are many more of us on the way! We do not tolerate you hunting so close to our city! Leave the baby wyvern and begone!'

Still looking skywards, the Poxpunks edged back towards the smoking ship-wagon at the head of their trailer. 'Come on, you lot,' said the crimson-braided one. 'Let's take the big 'vern and scoot. Won't get more than a barrel of oil from the runtling anyway.'

To Liska's delight, the other Poxpunks jumped down from the baby wyvern's back and followed their boss into the wagon, glaring at Liska as they passed. She kept her snarl up, ready to nip any of them that got too close.

'You're welcome to it,' said the last Poxpunk as she passed. 'Thing's full of bloodbugs. More than half dead already, it is.'

'Keep moving,' Liska said, snapping her jaws. They watched as the Poxpunks climbed rope ladders and clambered through hatches, scrambling aboard their contraption. There was a hissing, creaking sound as more smoke billowed from its chimneys and then it rolled off across the Blasted Waste, towing the trailer behind it. The dead wyvern's head lolled off the end, bouncing against rocks as it went.

'Good riddance,' said Lug. He looked even paler than usual and was wobbling on his feet a bit.

'That was very brave, what you did,' said Liska, gently nuzzling his hand.

'Yes. Well.' Lug's voice was still shaking. 'Fishbone said he was going to catch a rat in the night and put it down the back of my robe if I didn't help. A fat, live one. With rabies.'

'That was before I knew your magic was just making tiny wrigglers,' said Fishbone. He had picked up one of the worms and was giving it an experimental lick. 'Your body-changing trick is good though. Kittimew is hearing stories about humies who can make themselves into monsters.'

Liska folded her wings and nodded at Fishbone. Then she turned to follow Elowen, who was already on her way over to the bound wyvern.

The baby creature gave a muffled, mewling howl and blinked at them all. Its long, spiny tail thumped at the ground. As Liska padded nearer, her foxy nose was filled with the smell of sulphur and reptile, brimstone and lizard sweat. And there was more: the sweet, rotten smell of sickness. The wyvern was indeed unwell.

'There's something wrong with it,' she said as they all gathered round.

'Yes, it's been tied up and jabbed with nasty spears,' said Elowen.

'No, some kind of disease.' Liska walked around the creature, still in her griffyx shape, sniffing it gently.

'Look,' said Lug, pointing at the wyvern's neck and chin. 'It's got lots of ... leeches ... I think.' Clustered around the base of its head, dug into the soft skin of its neck and behind its horns, were hundreds of fat grub-like things. They twitched and pulsed, their heads buried in the wyvern's flesh, sucking and feasting.

'Eww, maggots,' said Liska. The grubs smelt of pus and infection. She could see the skin around them was inflamed and sore.

'Can we pull them out?' Elowen asked. She prodded one and the wyvern gave a squeal.

'Not without hurting the poor thing even more,' said Lug.

'They look a bit like worms,' said Liska, an idea beginning to form. 'Do you think you could use your magic on them? Make them all drop off?'

Lug raised an eyebrow. 'I think they're the larvae of some kind of giant beetle,' he said.

'Isn't that wormy enough?' Liska butted him with her head. 'Come on. Your powers must be good for *something.*'

'Very well,' said Lug, clearly offended. 'I suppose I can try.'

Taking slow and very careful steps forward, Lug placed both of his hands on the wyvern's neck. He closed his eyes and began muttering under his breath.

Everyone else stared at the grubs, willing them to shrivel up and die.

At first nothing seemed to happen, but then one of the larvae gave a twitch. Another followed, and soon all of them were jiggling madly.

'... not quite worms ...' Lug muttered, '... but similar structure ... can feel them ... talk to them ... almost ...'

Beads of sweat broke out on his forehead as he focused harder. Finally, one of the grubs popped free from the wyvern's neck. It tumbled down, bumping over scales until it dropped on the ground and lay there, quite still. A thin trickle of blood ran from the wound it had left.

'That's it, Lug!' Elowen cheered and clapped her hands. 'You're doing it!'

Another grub fell away, then another. Soon they were all twitching free and falling, forming a snowdrift of dead larvae around the wyvern's head. More began to cascade out from between the baby's wings and the base of its tail.

'The dear thing was riddled with them,' said Elowen. 'It must have been so uncomfortable.'

When the last parasite had gone, the wyvern let out a

noise that might have been a sigh. A trickle of smoke rose up from its nostrils and its eyes half-closed with relief.

'If we untie it now, do you think it will eat us?' Lug asked. He took his hands off the creature's neck and began to edge away, just in case.

'I'm sure it won't,' said Elowen. 'But maybe you'd better stand clear, just in case.'

She rummaged in her pack and pulled out a clasp knife, which she unfolded. Being careful not to cut the wyvern, she began to saw through the ropes that bound it. One by one they dropped free until the wyvern was able to stand up, towering above Elowen. It spread its wings wider than the biggest oak tree, and gave its head and tail a good shake. Liska expected it to fly away, but instead it bent its neck down towards Elowen, its mouth beginning to open.

'Elowen, move!' she shouted, terrified the beast might snap her up.

'Big Mew's paws, I can't watch,' said Fishbone, hiding his face in his tail.

The wyvern's head was level with Elowen now, its jaws wide enough to eat her in one crunch. But to everyone's relief, it simply lowered its nose and rubbed it against Elowen's outstretched hand.

'It's alright,' she called over her shoulder. 'It's not going to eat us. I think it wants to say thank you.'

*

After all the excitement, they felt that they needed a rest. Making a quick camp, they shared some water and biscuits, while the wyvern coiled up beside them, licking its wounds. It seemed to know Lug had healed it and kept glancing over in his direction and huffing hazy clouds of grateful smoke.

Liska found herself wanting to curl up and sleep for a hundred years. She was too tired to even try changing back to her human form but, at the same time, she was aware of Thresher somewhere up in the mountains behind her, drawing closer every second.

'So,' she asked Elowen. 'What now? Is there a path we can follow north?'

Elowen looked around at the deserted, rocky wasteland, puzzled. 'Well,' she said. 'The last time I travelled this way there was a small trading town at the start of the northern road. It must have been around this spot, I'm sure of it.'

'No towns here,' said Fishbone, nibbling at a biscuit and wrinkling his nose. 'No roads, either. There was some ruins, back when I was being a young kitten. Just rocks now.'

He pointed with a clawed finger at a cluster of stones half covered by drifts of sandy earth and spidery gorse bushes. Liska had thought they were just more boulders but, looking closer, she could see they had regular edges, as if they had been carved and used as parts of buildings.

'Oh, great!' Lug waved his hands in the air. 'Our guide knows the way ... but only if we travel back in time five hundred years! How are we supposed to go anywhere now? There's no path! Just a wasteland filled with wyverns and those scary punk people!'

'I'm sure I can still find the way,' said Elowen, looking hurt. 'There must be traces of road. We can make our way if we're careful ...'

'No traces,' said Fishbone. 'Just dirt and sand. And poisonous snakes. Dune sharks, knife spiders, swoophawks ... Very dangerous out there.'

'And we can't "be careful",' Lug added. 'Thresher is after us! We shouldn't even be sitting here talking! Although if I take another step, my leg bones are going to crumble. My kneecaps are going to pop out. My toes are going to ...'

Liska had been half listening to the argument. She was looking at the baby wyvern with a thoughtful expression on her face.

'Do you think,' she said, 'that our new friend might be persuaded to carry us on its back?'

'Flying, do you mean?' asked Elowen.

'Oh, no.' Lug started waving his hands again. 'No way. I'm not going up in the sky. Not on that thing. You know I have vertigo!'

'Yes, flying,' said Liska. 'We could rig up a harness with this rope. You could sit on its back and I could fly ahead, leading it. Elowen could call out the route to me so I knew where to go. We could get to Nammu in no time.'

'That might be a problem,' said Elowen. 'From what I know of wyverns, they like hot, dry air. It might not be able to take us all the way to the north.'

'But it could carry us for a bit, surely? Imagine how much distance we could put between ourselves and Thresher. And you could all rest your feet at the same time.'

This last argument seemed to quieten even Lug. They immediately started tying knots in the discarded rope, trying to fashion a rough harness. Then they carried it over to the wyvern and stood there helplessly, wondering how on earth they were going to get it on the thing without being eaten or burned alive.

When Elowen held the rope up in front of it, a low growling noise came from its throat. Turning its massive head to Lug, it nuzzled him with its nose and blew steamy, brimstone breath all over him.

'I think it likes you, Lug.' Liska was finding it hard not to start laughing.

'Why don't you try putting the harness on it?' Elowen suggested.

'Oh, yes,' said Lug. 'So *I'm* the one that gets fried to a frazzle.'

Still, he took the harness and held it up and this time the wyvern didn't flinch. Wincing, Lug looped it over the creature's head, then stroked its nose as Elowen and Fishbone slid the collar down to the base of its neck and fastened the rope underneath its legs. When it looked as though they weren't going to be burned alive, they started loading their packs on its back.

'Do you really think this will work?' Lug asked as the wyvern nuzzled him some more.

'I think your new friend will do anything for you,' said Liska, sniggering. 'Perhaps you should give it a name?'

'Is it a boy or a girl do you think?'

'Judging by the way she's batting her eyelashes at you, she's definitely female.'

'We're ready to climb on,' Elowen called.

'Go ahead,' said Liska. 'Lug is keeping her occupied.'

'Big Mew's scratching post!' Fishbone leapt from the ground to the wyvern's knee, and then on to its back. 'No kittimew is ever riding on a sky lizard before!'

Elowen began to climb up as well, and the wyvern turned a curious head around to look. Luckily, with Lug still stroking her neck, she didn't seem to object.

'Your turn, Lug.'

Walking slowly to the wyvern's back, Lug reached up for Elowen's hand and began trying to scramble up the scaly stomach. To his surprise, the wyvern stretched her neck backwards, gently grasped his robes in her lips and lifted him up to sit with his friends.

'Well done, Gertrude!' shouted Liska.

'Her name is Myrtle,' said Lug, patting the wyvern's side. She blew out a trail of yellow smoke in appreciation.

'Here we go then,' said Liska. She began to

run across the sandy mud, heading away from the mountains. Her eagle wings beat hard, slapping the ground once, twice, and then she was airborne, climbing into the mist-free sky.

Looking behind her, she saw the freshly named Myrtle beginning to follow. The wyvern ran on her two hind legs – like an ungainly, sprinting duck – but then her powerful leathery wings began to beat, sending her upwards just as quickly as Liska had taken off. Soon they were circling together right at the edge of the mist-cloud that hid the Shield Mountains. Liska could see Elowen pointing the way from Myrtle's back, while Fishbone yowled with joy and Lug held on for dear life.

'Goodbye, home. Goodbye Mother, Father. Ylva.' Liska banked away from the sorcerous clouds that hid everything she had ever known, everything she loved, and headed off into the unknown, dangerous wasteland. She had a vision of her mother lying bandaged in an infirmary bed. Of her father and sister swooping down from the sky in their griffyx shapes, battling hordes of seepers. She wondered if she'd ever see them or Arborven again; whether the city would still be standing when they got back. Whether they would even return at all . . .

Fear mixed with nervous excitement at experiencing something so completely new coursed through her. It was almost too much for her, until she looked below and saw, on the mountain slopes, the tiny silhouette of a human figure flanked by a pack of hounds.

Thresher. Another few minutes and she would have been upon us.

Liska beat her wings harder, driving north as fast as the wind would take her.

9

'Welcome to Almberg, magical wonder of the
northern plains, with its glorious architecture
and tree of power. The pride of Skyra!'

Almberg Visitor's Guide

It was the longest distance Liska had ever flown.
Below her rolled endless miles of dry, deserted
wasteland. Nothing but rocks and sandy soil with the
odd patch of trees or scrubland. Crooked strips of stream
and river meandered here and there like lazy doodles on
a page. Once or twice, far below, they saw dust trails of
Poxpunk vehicles driving along hunting for prey. Apart
from that, the Blasted Waste seemed almost lifeless.

Except for wyverns of course.

Every now and then the sky was pierced by a roar. Myrtle usually replied and Liska spent a few terrified minutes looking around her, waiting for a titanic winged beast to swoop down and snatch her out of the air.

But, thank the Tree, they only saw one or two of the creatures and those were in the far distance. Just smudges amongst the clouds. Even so, they looked massive, gargantuan. Easily the size of the dead wyvern they had seen the Poxpunks carry away, perhaps even bigger.

They flew for hours and, other than a dull ache in her shoulders, Liska found that gliding was almost effortless. She just kept her wings spread and followed the breeze, gently rising and falling as the currents of air took her. Every now and then she circled around to see if Myrtle's passengers were coping. Lug and Fishbone were usually fast asleep, and Elowen was watching the ground far below, searching for a familiar landmark.

It was nearing dusk when she finally spotted one. Liska heard her anguished cry pierce the air behind her. She banked hard, swooping around to fly alongside Myrtle.

'What's the matter?' she shouted against the wind. 'What have you seen?'

'Almberg!' Elowen shouted back. 'It's gone!'

Wondering what her friend was talking about, Liska looked down at the ground below. Elowen was pointing to a sandy-coloured cluster of stone rectangles half buried by dirt and trees, scattered haphazardly at the edge of an ocean of forest.

'What is it?' Liska called. 'An old town?'

'It is ... it *was* ... a city,' Elowen replied. And then in a voice so quiet that only Liska's fox hearing could pick it out: 'It was my *home*.'

Sensing the place was important and realising that they wouldn't be able to fly on in the dark, Liska began a slow descent towards this Almberg. Behind her, Myrtle followed, letting out a trail of smoke as she dropped.

Within a few minutes they were gliding above the ruins. Liska spotted the shells of grand three-storey houses now reduced to one or two walls of ornately carved stone. Under centuries of dust, dirt and plant growth, she saw the outline of broad streets, circular structures that might have been theatres or stadiums and, roughly in the centre of it all, the lifeless trunk of a long-dead tree. One too big to have been anything other than a sacred tree just like the one at the heart of Arborven.

Liska landed on the plaza before it, kicking up a cloud of dust as she came down. Myrtle touched the ground a few seconds later, skidding to a halt in front of the tree itself. They all looked up at its bare, petrified branches as they stretched skywards. So similar in size to their own, but cold, dead and empty.

Liska shifted back to her human form, changing shape even as she walked over to where the others were beginning to dismount the wyvern. 'Is this Nammu? I thought we had much further to go!'

'No.' Elowen had hopped to the ground and was now staring up at the dead tree, with sad eyes, arms wrapped tightly around herself. 'This is Lysalm. Or *was*, I should say. Before it died.'

Liska spotted a gaping hole in the side of the trunk. She had a good idea what must have happened to it. 'They took its heart, didn't they?'

Elowen nodded. 'It used to be beautiful,' she said. 'Just like the Undrentree, except with golden bark and leaves the colour of sunrise and starlight. The whole city was perfect. Tall stone buildings. Statues, fountains, gardens. Such a wonderful place to live.'

'I thought you'd only ever lived in Arborven,' said Lug.

'No.' Elowen looked around her at the shattered houses and crumbled streets. 'I was born *here*.'

*

They made camp at the base of the tree, in between two roots that sheltered them like walls.

There was plenty of dead dry wood around, and even some pieces of what might have been furniture, now shattered and sanded smooth by centuries of wind-blown dust. They stacked it inside a circle of broken bricks and built up quite a blaze, then set about using their supplies to cook dinner. It mostly consisted of dried herbs that Elowen had brought but, after centuries of not having to eat anything, she'd forgotten what taste was, and they were all quite horrible. Liska was about to suggest she shapewalked and went hunting when Fishbone appeared out of the gathering darkness, carrying three dead furry things.

'Are they ... rats?' Lug asked, giving one a poke. 'I'm not eating rat. I don't care how hungry I am. I'm almost definitely allergic to them.'

'Fatter than rat,' said Fishbone, licking blood from his lips. 'Not as tasty.'

'I think they're groundhogs,' said Liska. 'They'll taste fine once they're roasted.'

Luckily her battle training had included some survival skills and she knew how to gut and skin small animals. Soon the unfortunate groundhogs were cooking over the campfire, giving off a delicious fatty smell that made everyone's stomachs grumble.

'Will there be enough to feed Myrtle?' Lug asked. The wyvern had curled up on the other side of the blaze, seeming to enjoy the heat.

'There's barely enough for us,' said Liska. 'I think Myrtle will have to go and hunt for herself. What do wyverns eat anyway?'

'Cattle. Deer. Things like that,' Elowen answered, but her eyes were fixed on the flames. All the excitement she usually bubbled with seemed to have drained out of her.

'Do you want to talk about it?' Liska shuffled closer to her, rested a hand on her shoulder. 'About what happened here when you were . . . younger. And alive.'

Elowen stared at the fire for a while longer, listening to it crackle, watching the fairy-like sparks and embers drift up amongst the bare branches of the Lysalm tree. The silence seemed to stretch off into the night, and then, as softly as the breeze blowing in from the desert, she began to speak.

'The people that lived here, they were very different from the mages of Arborven. The tree gave them magic and they used it to make treekeepers and shapewalkers, just like we do. But they didn't appreciate it the same way. They had no interest in living alongside Lysalm, in building their lives around it. The magic was a gift they felt they had a right to. They used it to make themselves more comfortable, to make everything easier. All these great stone buildings were made with it. They filled the city with lights, sounds, tastes and smells. It was a playground of wonderful experiences, all created by draining the tree's power. And the more they used it, the more they wanted. They became like spoiled children, thinking they were somehow entitled to live that way, just because they had the good luck to be born here.

'Anyway, as you know all too well, wherever there is a tree of light, there is also a dark sister. And that other tree will devote itself only to consuming and killing its opposite.

'Out past the forest there, a shadow tree grew. It became stronger and stronger, sending out its forces in waves. The Almberg shapewalkers fought them off bravely, but there are no Shield Mountains around this city. They couldn't hold them back for long.

'I remember there being attacks almost daily. Sometimes brief skirmishes on the edge of Almberg, sometimes battles in the streets. The treekeepers told the city elders to build defences, to come up with some plan to stop the invasion before it was too late. Before they had to use the heart of Lysalm to kill the shadow tree.

'But they didn't seem to care. They were quite happy for the heart of their tree to be cut out and used. They were sure that life would go on as before. They had even become so arrogant, they thought they didn't need the tree for magic. 'We'll find a way of getting it ourselves', they said. 'We're so clever and ingenious – how hard can it be?'

'So they took Lysalm's heart out and carried it to the shadow tree. Almost all of their shapewalkers died fighting through the seepers. Many of the treekeepers were also lost trying to get the heart close enough to do its work. In the end they succeeded, but at great cost. The shadow tree shrivelled up and vanished. And without its heart, Lysalm began to die too.'

'That must have been terrible,' said Lug. He gently

squeezed Elowen's shoulder. 'Did all this happen to the city when the tree died?'

Elowen shook her head. 'The city was still here when we fled. Treeless, magicless, but still here. Some of us were so disgusted with the way the elders had behaved. My parents had heard of another tree of light to the south – the Undrentree – and decided to live there. A group of us headed to the Shield Mountains to start afresh. In a way that would not repeat the mistakes of Almberg.'

'And that's why the whole of Arborven is built around the Undrentree like that,' Liska realised. 'It's the centre of everything. We all work to nurture and protect it.'

'Yes,' said Elowen. 'It was only a small thing when we got there. Just the size of a normal tree, really. And the kittimews kindly let us stay.' She paused to nod at Fishbone. 'We decided to use its magic to grow and care for more trees. In fact, our magic became that of the trees themselves.'

'And did you ever come back?' Liska remembered how shocked Elowen had been at the sight of Almberg in ruins. As if she'd been expecting the place to still be standing.

'Yes,' she said. 'Several times. Some members of my family remained here. And my parents' friends ... But each time we visited, the city was smaller. More and more of its citizens had drifted away. And those that remained had grown used to life without magic. They were coping, surviving ... The last time we came here was on our trip to Nammu. These buildings still stood then. There were roads and wagon trains heading north. Towns and villages along the way ...'

Elowen's voice cracked as she spoke. There were tears welling in her eyes. 'I'm so sorry. I led you here thinking the way would be easy. But everything I remembered has gone. We could be in great danger from all kinds of threats now. I misled you all ...'

Liska put an arm around her. 'Don't worry. We had to come anyway. And without you we would never have found the passage through the mountains.'

'Yes,' said Lug. 'I'm glad you're here with us.'

'She the only one clever enough to bring food,' added Fishbone. 'Even if it is tasting like dried mouse dung.'

'Forgive me,' said Elowen. 'Being here ... it reminds me of my old life. Back before the accident. When we were all just a normal family.'

'It must be hard,' said Liska. She had been trying not to think of her own family: the last glimpse of her mother as she was carried away on a stretcher. How they always seemed to quarrel. How, if they'd known they might never see each other again, they might have been kinder to each other instead. Being away from Arborven made it easier somehow. But the slightest sight or thought of something familiar would bring it all rushing back, just as it had for Elowen.

Sitting beside her, Liska could see Lug squirming, as if he was itching to ask something. 'I know it might be hard to talk about,' he began. 'And I really don't mean to be nosey ... but what was the accident? How *did* you go from being a normal family to ... you know ...'

'Dead?' Elowen finished his sentence and Liska glared at him, amazed that he could ask a question like *that* at this precise moment (even though she was curious herself). She thought Elowen might burst into tears or become cross, but instead she gave another sad sigh.

'Nothing went wrong,' she said. 'It was an energy spill. They happen every hundred years or so. Sometimes the magic builds up inside the tree and, instead of channelling it out to be used, there is a blast. Like a bolt of lightning from the sky. Usually it just shoots off into the air harmlessly. But on that day, for whatever reason, it arced down towards the ground. Into our house. We were just having an ordinary morning and then ... *zap!* The next thing I knew, we all woke up together in the family tomb underneath the temple.'

'Did it happen here as well, do you think?' Lug asked. 'Are there people in Almberg like ... like you?'

'I expect so,' said Elowen. 'I was really too young to remember. If there are, they are probably asleep. When you can't die, when you live forever ... the days just don't seem important any more. You start to sleep through a week or two, then a month, then more. Before you know it, a decade or a century has gone. Then you wake up and find out everything is still just the same as when you left. There doesn't seem to be any point in staying around to see it.'

It seemed so strange to Liska. Living forever was what most people wished for. She'd never considered what it would actually *feel* like. To know that there was no rush to do anything, see anything, because time was all you had.

'Is that why your family sleep all the time?' she asked.

Elowen nodded, throwing another stick on the fire. 'One or two of us used to be awake at the same time so we had some company at least. But they've started to sleep for longer and longer. I suppose, at some point, they just won't bother waking up at all. As if they were *really* dead.'

Liska, used to a fort filled with noise and bustle, found it hard to imagine. 'It must be very lonely for you.'

Elowen shrugged. 'I don't like to sleep as much as the others. I just snooze for the odd month here and there. Mother and I woke up a short while ago – that must be when Lug heard us talking – but she drifted off soon after. You get used to being alone after a decade or two . . .'

Liska looked around them, at the deep shadows in the shells of the buildings. There could be people here like Elowen, rising from centuries of slumber to peer out at these strangers suddenly appearing in their city. The thought made her shudder and shuffle closer to the fire.

*

Bright sunlight, shining through her eyelids.

Liska yawned and rolled over on her blanket, wincing at how much her back ached from sleeping on a stone-paved floor, and discovered the head of a half-eaten mouse had been left just inches from her face. Sightless eyes stared up at her and a tiny pink tongue poked out from a corner of its mouth.

'Yuck!' she shouted, jumping up. 'Who put that there?'

Fishbone was curled up next to her, watching her with a glinting, yellow eye. 'Me,' he said. 'Is a present. Or breakfast. Do humies eat mouse heads?'

'Not this one,' said Liska. 'Thank you, though. I guess.'

She stretched her arms and legs, feeling as though she had slept for hours and hours. Then she looked up at the sun and noticed it was nearly at its mid-day position. She *had* slept for hours! Why had nobody woken her?

She looked across the plaza, past the ashes of their campfire, and saw Elowen and Lug standing by Myrtle, stroking her nose as she made sad, mewing noises.

Still seething about the time they had wasted sleeping, Liska walked over.

'What's going on?' she said. 'Why did you let me sleep so late?'

'I'm sorry,' said Elowen. 'I spent the night wandering the ruins. I lost track of time.'

'Fishbone and I have only just woken up ourselves,' said Lug. 'We were so tired. If Myrtle hadn't started crying, we'd probably still be snoring now.'

'What's wrong with her?'

The wyvern was rubbing its nose up against Lug, whimpering softly.

'I think she's hungry,' said Lug. 'Poor little thing. I wish I could help but I have no idea what to feed her.'

'She should be able to hunt,' said Elowen. 'Baby wyverns hatch from their eggs and then fend for themselves.'

'Then why isn't she doing it?' Lug scratched her nose, looking worried.

'She doesn't want to leave *you*,' Liska said. 'But she knows she has to.'

Lug shot her a look, thinking that she was teasing him, but saw she was being serious.

'What makes you say that?'

Liska shrugged. She couldn't explain exactly. It was

how Myrtle was moving, the way she looked at Lug. It just seemed obvious.

'Liska is a shapewalker, remember,' said Elowen. 'She is more than part animal. She understands their body language and what goes through their heads.'

'Oh.' Lug looked even sadder. He wrapped his arms around Myrtle's neck. 'Then I suppose I have to make her leave. Although I wish she could stay forever. Do you think she'll be able to find us again?'

'Wyverns can't go north,' said Liska. 'It's too cold for them. I'm sorry, Lug, but you're going to have to say goodbye.'

Lug nodded, his eyes brimming with tears, and rested his forehead against Myrtle's nose. 'Farewell, girl,' he whispered. 'You're always welcome to come and see me in Arborven.'

That's not very likely, Liska thought, imagining how the mages would react to a growing wyvern landing in Undren Square. And that's if Myrtle managed to get through the choking mists that protected the city from her kind.

She kept her mouth closed, though, and watched as Myrtle turned away. The wyvern jogged across the plaza, beating itself aloft with strong sweeps of its wings. Soon she was circling above them. She gave a farewell puff of fire, and then headed south across the Blasted Waste.

Liska was about to turn back to their camp when she spotted a plume of dust on the horizon. It seemed to be heading in their direction.

'What's that?' she said, pointing. A sickly chill had begun to creep over her.

'Looks like one of those Poxpunk vehicles,' said Lug. 'I hope they haven't seen Myrtle.'

'I don't think they're after wyverns,' said Elowen. 'I think they're after us. It's coming straight here.'

'Don't be silly,' said Lug. 'It's miles away. It could turn at any moment.'

'Maybe.' Liska wasn't convinced. 'Even so, we need to break camp and get moving. Quickly.'

As they headed to pack up their blankets, Liska couldn't shake the feeling of ominous certainty that the Poxpunks *were* coming after them. And she thought she had a good idea who might be riding along with them.

*

Walking through the ruined city was slow and difficult. Many of the streets they started down turned out to be choked with rubble, forcing them to turn back on themselves.

More than once Liska suggested flying up to find a path, but Elowen insisted she knew the way. Every now and then she stopped to rest her hand against a wall, lost in sad memories. And all the while, Lug moaned about his blisters and aching feet. Didn't they realise they were being chased by a murderous hunter?

As they finally neared the northern edge of Almberg, they reached a point where the forest had begun to eat into the ruins, smothering everything in root and vine.

Unlike the neat, ordered and groomed trees of Arborven, this was wild growth. Mats of ivy and moss covered everything. Brambles knitted themselves across what used to be roads and alleyways. Anywhere there was a crack or a tiny scrap of earth, life had grown in it.

Trying to tear their way through was painfully slow, and eventually they reached a point where the undergrowth was just too thick.

'There *must* be a way in,' Liska said, wincing as she plucked a sharp thorn from the back of her hand. 'An animal path or an old road . . .'

Elowen was staring at a tumbled pile of stone, half

hidden under a thick layer of greenery. 'I think that used to be my school,' she said.

'I don't suppose your powers have come back yet?' Lug asked her. 'Maybe the memories have helped it along? If you know any arbomancy, you could move the plants out of our way.'

Elowen waved her china-white hands in the air but nothing happened. 'Sorry,' she said.

Lug leant close to Liska and muttered in her ear. 'Knowing our luck, she'll turn out to be a mossherder anyway.'

Liska rolled her eyes. 'Then I should definitely fly above now. See if I can spot a way through ...'

'No need,' said Fishbone. 'Save your magic. I is climbing up to see.'

Claws bared, he ran up the trunk of a nearby tree, then leapt from the branches on to the shell of a ruined building. Using the ivy for pawholds, he scrambled up to the top and peered out across the remains of the city.

'Path that way!' His voice echoed down to them and Liska could see him pointing off to the east.

'Look south!' Liska called. 'Is that Poxpunk craft still coming this way?'

Fishbone span around and peered out over the Waste. 'Sure is,' he shouted. 'Much closer now.'

Lug's face, rosy-cheeked after all their walking, instantly paled again. 'You don't think it's ...?'

Liska didn't answer. Instead, she began to clamber up the ivy-coated wall that Fishbone perched on. She could have just shifted and flown up, but Fishbone's idea about saving her magic was a good one. And besides, part of her wanted to show the cat-creature that he wasn't the only one who could climb.

Her feet dug out toeholds of missing bricks, her fingers clutched empty window frames and pieces of carved statue. Legs and faces, worn smooth by the centuries and with most of their bodies now missing, poked out of the ivy.

A few minutes later, she dragged her top half on to the small platform of brick where Fishbone was perched. He was licking his tail with his pink sandpaper tongue and giving her a look that said 'what took you so long?'

Liska ignored him, heaving her legs up after her and trying not to look as though she was panting for breath. Getting to her knees, she looked to the south, seeing the forest-coated ruins give way to the deserted stone jungle of empty Almberg. Beyond that was the dry, rocky Waste and there, streaming a plume of dust behind it, was a Poxpunk wagon ship.

Squinting, Liska could make out the sails and smoking chimneys of the vehicle as it chugged towards the ruins. Even as she watched, it ground to a halt, the dust cloud catching up with it and hiding it for a few seconds.

It had halted a hundred metres from the city, as if the drivers were scared to venture too close.

Perhaps they believe it's haunted, Liska thought. Then she remembered what Elowen had said about those like her, how they might be endlessly sleeping beneath those pillars of crumbled stone. *Perhaps it really is.*

As the cloud of sand cleared, Liska could make out tiny figures moving about on the craft's deck. A hatch opened in the side, dropping down to become a ramp. Liska held her breath, fearing what might emerge, and yet knowing at the same time just what she'd see.

And she was right. A tall, wiry figure stalking down the rampway, followed by a low, slinking, dog-shaped *thing.* Then another, and another and another.

Seven of them, Liska counted. *Seven seeper hounds for us to escape. Not to mention Thresher herself.*

'Well?' Lug's voice carried up to them from the mass of leaves and brambles below. Even from up here, you could hear the tremble in it. 'Is it her?'

'It's her,' Liska called back. Just saying it made her feel sick with worry. 'We'd better get moving.'

'But we flew for miles and miles!' Lug shouted. 'How can she have caught up with us?'

Liska could just about hear Elowen's reply to him. Calm and reasoned, as if she wasn't the least bit worried an evil killer was after them. 'If she stole a vehicle soon after we took off and drove all night she could have made up the distance. And we slept until noon, don't forget.'

'Worms take her!' Lug's curse echoed around the ruins.

Fishbone tutted, then silently moved to the edge of the platform, slipping over head first, flowing down the stonework like water. Liska moved to follow, allowing herself a last look over the ruins, at the cluster of figures heading their way.

How long before they caught up with them? How much time did they have?

She decided she didn't even want to think about those questions. There was only one thing they could do now and she hoped it would be enough.

They could run.

*

The path was nothing more than a muddy groove, worn bare by the paws of animals. Tall banks of thorny sloe and hawthorn trees pressed in on both sides, meeting overhead in a kind of low roof that would make everyone except Fishbone stoop or crouch to move along.

Liska sniffed. Her sensitive nose picked out a strong, musky odour. One she was familiar with from her scent lessons and survival training. One with a distinctly doggy hint to it. Fishbone recognised it instantly, too.

'Wolf! This path is being made by wolfses!'

'W-wolves? Wild ones?' Lug asked.

'Of course wild! Do you think they'd be like the dogses you humies keeps for pets? They is much bigger and bitier.' The kittimew hid behind Liska's legs, his claws digging into her leather armour.

'There were always packs of wolves in the forest, I remember,' Elowen said. 'And bears and wildcats. They never harmed anyone. Our shapewalkers used their skins for their beast forms.'

'No offence,' said Liska, 'but everything you "remember" so far has turned out to be wrong. The wolves might have been harmless then, but they could have turned into man-eating monsters by now.'

As if to answer her, a distant howl echoed through the forest. Fishbone dug his claws in harder and Lug began to tremble.

Liska knelt, peering down the tunnel into the deep woods beyond. Then she stood and looked back the way they had come, imagining Thresher and her hounds creeping closer with every second.

'Look,' she said. 'I don't see that we've got any choice. It's go ahead and risk the wolves, or stay here and face Thresher. I know which one I'd rather pick.'

'Thresher?' said Fishbone, hopefully.

'No.'

Wolves were living, breathing, natural creatures. If it came to it, she would rather they were the ones to tear her apart. With Fishbone still stuck to her leg, Liska ducked under the brambles and headed into the forest.

IO

'Better to be fried by a wyvern
than eaten by a wolvsie.'

Kittimew proverb

The path led down, down, through the last crumbling bricks of the city, winding between collapsed houses and the skeletons of staircases, their rickety steps leading up into the treetops.

After an age of cramped stalking, doubled over almost on to all fours, they emerged into the proper forest. Here, the trees were more established and there was space in between their trunks. It was still wild, though, with branches meshed so tightly overhead that only a few chinks of sunlight crept through.

The scent of wolf was everywhere and, now and then, a howl echoed through the trees. It sounded as if they were getting steadily closer.

At one point, Fishbone leapt up to Liska's shoulders and sat there, curled around her neck, claws pricking her shoulders. Every strand of fur on his body was puffed up and his yellow eyes blazed wide.

'Careful, cat,' she said. 'You're jabbing me with your needle claws. And you're blocking my hood. I won't be able to change shape if you don't move.'

'Kittimew. Not cat.' He spoke through gritted teeth and refused to budge an inch.

Lug and Elowen followed close behind, the ghost girl looking almost luminous in the gloomy, green light. Now she was out of the city, her melancholy seemed to have lifted. She peered into the shadows around her as if she could see treasure gleaming in the depths.

'Do you think the wolves are getting nearer?' she asked. 'I'd love to see one up close. They're such beautiful animals.'

'I'm sure you'll get a good look when there's one chewing your face off,' said Lug.

Liska picked up the pace, keeping an eye on the dark gaps between the trees. It wasn't long before she saw movement. And then twin, glowing pinpricks that gleamed back at her, leaving trails in the murk as they moved. Eyes. Wolf eyes.

'They're here,' she said in a low voice. Another howl sounded, this one close enough to make them all jump.

'Wh-what are they doing?' Lug had moved so close behind her, he was practically riding on her back as well.

'Circling us,' said Liska. 'Trying to see what kind of threat we are.'

'Are they g-going to attack?'

'Not here. Too many trees. They'll wait until we're more in the open.' Again, Liska couldn't say how she knew these things. It was part of the animal mind that they all shared. The dim memories of ancestors that had once run through the woods chasing down prey. Except in shapewalkers like Liska, those instincts were only half buried.

'Th-this is an open space,' Lug said, his voice squeaking. They had stumbled between two pine trees into a broad, church-like clearing. Branches met overhead like a vaulted ceiling, blocking out sun and sound. It was dark, ominous, empty.

But only for a moment.

From the edge of the treeline all around them, creatures stepped out of the shadows. Sleek grey wolves, big cats with dappled fur, hulking wild boars like barrels with legs. Hunkered down, ready to charge, they inched closer. *Pad, pad, pad.* They moved without taking their eyes off Liska for a second until, at some silent signal, they froze.

All except their leader. Striding through their ranks, towering over all of them, came a black bear, his thick coat rippling as he walked, long claws raking the forest floor. His eyes shone bright green, cutting through the murk like twin lanterns, and his mouth was full of gleaming teeth. Long as knives. Shining white like blades made of moonlight. He carried on moving, rearing up on his hind legs as he reached Liska, who tensed, ready for battle.

There is a small part of the brain that takes over when danger looms. It gives you two options: fight like hell or run for your life. Inside Fishbone's furry little head, that ancient underbrain took over, and it chose to fight.

Without warning, he launched from Liska's neck, hissing like a boiling kettle. A ball of electric fur and whizzing claws, he hit the bear's head and stuck there, yowling and scratching until the beast shook him off.

Fishbone thumped against the ground and bounced back up again, claws popped, teeth bared. The enormous bear stared back and the low rumble of a growl started in his chest. It sounded like a thunderstorm was gathering beneath his ribs.

Before he could lunge at Fishbone, Liska – her cloak now free – flipped her hood over and flowed into her griffyx shape. She dropped to all fours, facing the bear and was shocked to discover that he seemed *much* bigger than when she was standing. She spread her wings anyway and put on her best snarl, hoping that it might distract him at least. Behind her, she could hear Lug muttering prayers to his mummy and someone called Nematus.

The God Worm, she remembered. *We could really use that now.*

Her change had drawn the bear's attention. His gaze snapped from the hissing Fishbone to her and Liska noticed his eyes widen. The growl in his throat stopped immediately and he took a step backwards. Then he did something that made Liska yelp in surprise.

The bear opened his mouth in a yawn. A tremendous yawn that stretched his jaw wide open. Further and then further, until the fangs of his mouth dropped away. The skin of his face followed, peeling back from his head and shoulders, revealing a man hidden beneath. Tall, bare-chested with thick, corded muscle. He had skin the same colour as Liska's. The same tightly curled hair matted into locks, the same leaf-green eyes.

'A shapewalker,' Liska said under her breath. 'Just like me.'

Except the man's change wasn't like pouring your body from one form to another. It happened in jerks and jumps and seemed to be causing him pain. When it had finished, and his bear skin hung in a cloak from his shoulders, he almost fell to the ground, gasping with exertion.

Fighting for breath, he forced himself to stand upright and face Liska and her friends. He dipped his head at her in a polite bow, and then pointed deeper into the forest.

'I think you'd better come with me,' he said.

*

They walked in line, following the cloaked man and flanked on both sides by forest creatures. The animals, or shapewalkers in beast form, kept giving Liska curious glances. She stayed as a griffyx and matched their stares, taking the chance to snuffle at them when she could. Most of what she smelt was wolf or cat, but underneath were tones of human and also, very weak but definitely there, a hint of magic oil. Like that made from the Undrentree back home.

'Are these the shapewalkers of Almberg?' she whispered to Elowen as they marched onwards.

Elowen peered at the creatures, lifting a pale white hand to gently skim the fur of one that walked beside her. 'They must be their descendants. Amazing that they've survived in the forest for five hundred years! And still able to change their form.'

The cloaked leader shot them a look that told them to be quiet. Liska got the feeling they weren't quite prisoners, but not guests either. *There might be a way out of this,* she thought. *If we play it just right.*

They were led further into the forest, walking for what seemed like hours until they could hear noises through the trees. The laughter of children, crackle of fires, clanking of pots. Soon, they emerged into another clearing, this one filled with moss-covered huts. Liska could see they had been built with stone salvaged from the ruins of Almberg, but that had been a very long time ago, judging by the thick blankets of lichen that covered everything.

The village was bustling with shapewalkers, some in human form with cloaks of fur, some as beasts. They lounged in doorways and next to campfires, while children in clothing made from leather scraps ran in between the huts, clambering over animals that must be their mothers and fathers wearing their animal shapes.

The bear led them, still with their accompanying pack, to a long squat hut that stood in the centre. An old woman sat on a pile of furs at the entrance, white locks cascading over her shoulders and trailing across the floor. The skin hung from her bony arms in folds, but her green eyes were still sharp. They remained fixed on Liska as she approached.

'What is this you have found in our packlands, Beric? A winged fox? Like a beast from the old legends?'

'Deenai.' The shapewalker that led them bowed his head. 'We caught these strangers walking the path from the old city. They were on their own. No adults were with them. And ... there is something you should see.'

The old woman, Deenai, cocked her head as a curious wolf might. She made a motion with her hand, waiting to be shown. Liska had an idea just what the sight might be.

'If you wouldn't mind' – the shapewalker called Beric was speaking to her now – 'could you change for us? Back to your human shape?'

Liska nodded. It was a bit soon after her last transformation but not close enough to strain her too much. She closed her eyes, found the map of her birth form in her head – the exact pattern of cells and bones and organs she was most used to – and willed her body to twist itself into it.

The dizzy feeling as her muscles shifted, the stretching, pulling of her skin and hair and teeth. All was as familiar and easy to Liska as breathing. Within a few heartbeats, she was rising to her feet, reaching her freshly formed fingers up to push back her hood and shake out her locks over her shoulders.

From all around the camp she heard gasps and growls of surprise. When she opened her eyes, Liska saw everyone – beast and human – staring at her in awe. Even Deenai, the ancient chieftain of the pack, had her mouth hanging open in shock.

'But ... but how does she change so quickly? And without any pain?'

Liska frowned and shrugged her shoulders. What was the big deal?

'For us,' Beric explained, 'the change is very draining. It hurts badly. We can only shapewalk once every month, some less than that. Then we have to wait weeks before we can shift again.'

It was Liska's turn to widen her eyes. 'Where I come from, the shapewalkers can change easily. We only have to wait half an hour or so between shifts. And it definitely doesn't hurt us at all.'

'And your beast form,' Deenai pointed at Liska's cloak. 'Where does the skin of such a mystical animal come from?'

'They are handed down through our families,' Liska explained. 'They came from creatures that once lived in Arborven – our city. We have many other types amongst our people. Manticores, griffins, pantherines ...'

Deenai and Beric shared a look full of surprise, wonder and ... a glimmer of hope.

'Can you show us how to change like that?' Beric asked. 'How to flow between your shapes without pain?'

'I ... I don't know ...' Liska struggled to think

what to say. Shapewalking had always just been what she *did*. Like breathing or walking. She had no idea what made it happen, let alone how to teach it to someone else.

'Perhaps I could help explain.' Elowen, who had been watching the conversation in interested silence, stepped forward. Liska couldn't help noticing how different her friend looked compared to the tribe around her. How her bone-white porcelain skin stood out amongst all the fur and flesh. She looked like a walking, talking china doll. As if she had been carved from marble and then magicked into life.

The forest people must have thought the same. They tensed at the sight of her; Liska could sense their hackles rise. But Deenai nodded anyway, inviting her to speak.

'My name is Elowen,' she said. 'And I was once a citizen of Almberg. Back before the heart of Lysalm was taken. Before the city died.'

Growls and mutters came from the crowd around them, but Elowen ignored them and kept speaking.

'I know you think that sounds impossible. That I would have to be hundreds of years old for it to be true. Well, I am.'

'A deathless one,' Deenai muttered, making a gesture of protection with her hand.

'I can remember the days when the city was alive,' said Elowen. 'I can remember your people as its guardians. The shapewalkers of Almberg were fierce and proud warriors. They were able to change their forms as easily as Liska can. This was thanks to the tree that grew there. The oil made from its branches, filled with magic, was the thing that made the change possible. As babies, the shapewalkers were bathed in it. It soaked into their every pore. And the skins they wore – the very same ones that you wear now, handed down through your families – were drenched in oil too. Then magic spoke to magic. Fur spoke to flesh. Your people could flow between forms, their bodies remembering the shapes of both animal and human.

'But, since the city – and the tree – have died, the last shapewalkers moved into the forest. You must have lived here for centuries, forgetting much of your past. But some magic from Lysalm's oil is still in your blood, which is why you can change from animal to human. Except, over the years, it has faded and become weaker. The transformation has become more and more difficult, and that's why it causes you so much

230

pain. Without the oil it will never get any easier. Quite the opposite, in fact.'

'We will stop being able to change at all?' Beric asked, the blood draining from his face.

'Eventually, yes,' said Elowen.

There was more muttering from the gathered forest people. One or two of the younger children even burst into tears. Liska looked from face to tortured face, feeling a horror only another shapewalker could understand.

Being told you will have to stay with one form, she thought. *It would be like losing your sight or your hearing. Or never being able to walk again.*

As she watched the misery spread through the tribe, Liska felt a crushing wave of pity mixed with a twinge of guilt. If she hadn't come here, perhaps they would never have found out. Their changing might have slowly vanished, so slowly they might not even have realised it. If only there was some way she could help them. If only she could share her magic with them somehow . . .

And then it came to her. Perhaps there *was* a way she could share it . . .

'Listen,' she said. 'I've had an idea.'

*

231

She thought of Arborven, of her home, of the trees, the fortresses and the mountains surrounding it. And she thought of her family there, fighting for their lives even as she was standing in this distant forest, with these strange leftover people that were the past of Almberg and might be the future of her own kind.

What wouldn't the shapewalkers of the Undrentree give for more fighters to help them defend their own? And what wouldn't the forest people give to have their gift refreshed – to have a new tree to defend with their fangs and claws?

'Elowen,' she said. 'If these people were given fresh oil from another sacred tree ... would they be able to change shape like I can? Without any pain?'

Elowen paused for a moment, thinking. 'I don't see why not,' she said. 'The oil might be slightly different but it should have the same effect. The ability to shapewalk is in their blood, after all. And they have skins that are already bonded to them.'

'Then,' said Liska, 'Deenai: I offer you and your people the chance to join the shapewalkers of Arborven. If you travel to the south, across the Blasted Waste, you will come to a cluster of mountains, their tops hidden in thick mist. Inside is a living city, just like Almberg once was, with a light tree at its heart. If you will help our people defend themselves against the forces attacking them, they will give you oil that will return the powers of your ancestors to you.'

There was much chatter after Liska's speech, an excited bubble of voices getting louder and louder. Deenai frowned and nodded to herself through it all, before raising a hand for silence.

'This city,' she said. 'My folk are used to the forest and the wild. I do not think we would do well in a place of stone and brick like the ruins. It would go against our souls. Against our nature.'

Liska laughed at this, making the old chieftain frown even deeper. At least until she explained herself. 'No. No, it isn't a city of stone. It's made of trees! The mages live in houses amongst the oaks, beeches and elms. They care for them and build their homes amongst them. Just like this!' She raised her arms and gestured to the trunks all around them, surrounding the stone huts of the forest people.

Beric joined in with Liska's laughter, followed by the rest of the pack. Even Deenai was forced to smile.

'In that case,' she said, 'we would gladly help you. We will be guardians again, like the old stories of our ancestors. We thank you for this offer.'

'You're welcome,' said Liska, grinning. 'Just go to the feet of the mountains. One of my shapewalker kin is bound to see you and fly down. Tell them that Liska of the griffyxes sent you. And ... tell them that I am fine. Say that I am on my way to find Nammu's heart. They'll know what that means.'

Deenai's eyes widened in surprise again. 'The heart of the northern tree? I have heard of this legend. Why do you need it?'

The smile instantly vanished from Liska's face. 'Because my city is fighting against the shadow tree, Bitterblight. It is under attack even now. Finding the heart is the only thing we can think of to save it.'

On hearing this, Beric and the rest of the pack bowed their heads. Deenai reached out a gnarled hand and took Liska's in it, squeezing tightly. 'Brave child,' she said. 'We will do what we can to help you. And then we will go to fight for your city. It may be hundreds of moons since we battled the forces of our own shadow tree, but the stories have been passed down to us. We know of the danger and the fear.'

'We can take you through the forest,' said Beric. 'As far as the giant's territory at least.'

'Giant?' Lug spoke up. He had been trying to stand as still and unnoticeable as possible, casting the odd nervous glance at the fangs of the creatures all around him. 'Exactly what kind of giant are we talking about? Will it hurt us? Eat us? Pull our arms and legs off?'

'All of those, probably,' said Beric. 'It lives in the thickest part of the forest, between our territory and the open tundra, and it is very fierce. We often hear its screams and cries echoing through the trees.'

'It is an ancient thing,' said Deenai. 'Time and loneliness have hurt its soul, and it vents its anger on those that stray on to its patch. But it only roams the forest at night. If you wait here until morning and stick to the path Beric will show you, you should be fine.'

Liska's thoughts turned to Thresher and her skulking hounds, probably well inside the ruined city by now. Had they picked up their trail already? They hadn't even tried to hide their campfire or their tracks. They could be upon them at any moment.

'We really need to get moving as quickly as possible,' she said. 'Would we have time to cross the giant's part of the forest by nightfall?'

Deenai looked up at the speckled patches of sky visible through the trees. 'You have two hours or so,' she said. 'You might just make it. If you run.'

Liska grimaced. An impossible choice, but they would have to take a chance. After all they had been lucky so far, hadn't they?

'We'll go now, then,' she said. 'We don't have time to spend the night, but we thank you for your offer.'

'Oh, *please*,' begged Lug. 'We're safe here. Can't we stay a little while? Just for one decent sleep, and maybe a nice cooked breakfast in the morning?'

Deenai nodded, ignoring Lug's moaning. She motioned to Beric and he moved to the edge of the village, along with four fierce-looking pumas. 'Safe travels, Liska of the griffyxes,' she said. 'I look forward to meeting you again in a new forest. Maybe I will show you what a fine wolf I make.'

'I look forward to it,' said Liska. Then she grabbed Lug by the shoulders and pushed him in front of her, all the way out of the village and on to the giant's path.

*

They moved quickly, jogging between the trees, the pumas slinking beside them like a shoal of protective sharks. Fishbone had hitched a ride on Liska's back again. She could feel his paws trembling through the thick leather of her armour. Every time a puma swerved too close to them, he jumped out of his fur. *Poor thing*, she thought. To her, being around large, carnivorous animals was perfectly natural. And so was the fact that they were really people hidden inside the beastly forms like yolks in an egg.

Lug looked just as scared, but instead at the thought of being eaten by a giant. He was sticking close to Elowen, his fingers twitching, ready to call up his worm magic.

'Surely we *could* wait until morning?' she heard him whisper. 'It's so dark in these woods ... it's probably night already!'

Lug was right. It was gloomier than before and the shadows drew even closer as they went deeper. Up ahead, the trees turned to pines. Rows of straight, narrow trunks with branches meshed so tight that they seemed almost solid. A wall of needly darkness, wild and deadly. It sucked up the light like a sponge.

Beric stopped just in front of it, his wolves gathering around him.

'Oh, not in there,' whispered Lug. 'Please, not in there.'

'This is it,' said Beric. 'The end of our patch and the start of the giant's. The path is here: it's narrow but it runs straight through and out on to the tundra. You can probably make it in time if you're quick. Should you lose your way, just keep heading north.'

Lug backed away from the pine trees, shaking his head. 'North? How will we know which way that is? You can't see the sky, let alone the stars!'

'Look at the tree trunks,' said Beric. 'The moss grows on the northern side.'

'Thank you,' said Liska. 'You've been very helpful.'

'Anything for another shapewalker,' said Beric. He took her wrist in a warrior's clasp and shook it. Liska looked again at the bank of pines, and the narrow patch of bare earth that vanished in between them. She imagined them running through it, stumbling and tripping as Thresher and her hounds closed in.

Thresher.

'Beric,' she said. 'Before you go – there is something else you could do for us. Something that would really help.'

'Name it.'

'We're being chased. Hunted. By a woman with hounds ... creatures made from the shadow tree itself ...'

'Rot beasts? In our forest?' Beric curled his lip back in an animal snarl. One which was matched by the four pumas around him.

'Yes,' said Liska. 'She's been on our trail since we left Arborven. I don't suppose you could cover our tracks for us? Or maybe lay a trap or two?'

'We'll do better than that,' said Beric. 'We'll tear any creature of darkness we find to pieces. Our people still know the old stories. We remember what we were born for.'

'Thank you,' said Liska. For the first time since leaving the mountains she felt the weight of fear shift a fraction. 'Be careful, though.'

'And you, flying fox.'

With a final nod, Beric and his pumas turned back and disappeared into the forest, leaving Liska and the others poised on the edge of the giant's darkened world.

*

Run along the path.

They might as well have tried to run through treacle.

It must have been many years since any of the

forest people came this way. Meshed twigs and fallen branches blocked their progress every few steps. And it was so dark, nobody but Fishbone could see any further than a few metres ahead.

'I think I need night eyes,' said Liska. She pulled on her hood and fumbled her way into her griffyx form for the second time that day. It felt forced and clunky, her bones aching as they bent themselves into new shapes. When she stood on four paws, a wave of tiredness flooded over her. Just a taste of what it must be like every time Beric and his friends shifted.

At least she could see better now, although her delicate sense of smell was overpowered by the thick scent of pine sap that clogged the air.

'I can make out the path,' she said, looking at the others. Lug's pale face, poking out of his brown robes, seemed to hang in mid-air and Elowen glowed white like a candle.

'I can't see anything,' said Lug. 'I won't even be able to see the giant when it creeps up behind me and eats me alive.'

'Hold on to my tail,' said Fishbone. 'I will lead you. And then, maybe, you is stopping moaning all the time.'

'You'd moan too if you had any sense,' said Lug. He got down on his hands and knees and fumbled amongst the fallen pine needles, reaching for Fishbone's tail tip.

'It's *right* in front of you, for Tree's sake,' said Liska, growing impatient. 'We really need to get going. If Thresher somehow gets past the pumas, she'll easily catch us in here.'

As if in answer to her words, they heard a distant roar muffled by the pine branches. Another followed, and then the sounds of snapping and snarling.

'It sounds like our friends are as good as their word,' said Elowen. 'I do hope they won't get hurt.'

'*I* hope they turn Thresher into bear food,' said Lug. 'And then eat her. Is this your tail, cat? It feels more like rope.'

'Kittimew, not cat,' said Fishbone. 'And that is not me you is holding.'

Liska turned her night vision back to Lug in time to see him grasping a tripwire of twined ivy with his hand. It was tied to a wooden peg, pushed into the ground.

'Lug!' she yelled, leaping towards him. 'Don't pull that! It's a . . .'

There was a sudden *whooshing* sound and the forest

floor around them rose up, enfolding, enveloping them completely. Clouds of damp rotten pine needles poured over them, tumbling into their eyes, mouths and noses, and then they were swinging back and forth, squashed against each other too tightly to even move.

'. . . trap,' Liska finished. A net trap. It had scooped them up like a bunch of sticklebacks in a pond, and now they were dangling, stuck and helpless.

II

'He'll wear your fur, he'll eat your eyes,
He'll bake your bones inside his pies.'

Shapewalker tribe rhyme about the forest giant

Rotten pine needles, stinging her eyes, tickling her nose. They were even in her *ears*, for Tree's sake.

Liska sneezed and blinked. She tried to get a paw up to rub her face, but she was pinned between the net and someone's body. She smelt dust and age. A trace of mildew. *Elowen.*

Rope burned against the back of her wings as she swung from side to side. *Thank the roots I kept them*

243

folded. She could easily have broken one of the fragile bones when the trap sprung. And then she would be flightless for months while it healed.

'Is everyone alright?' Elowen asked. Her voice sounded muffled, as though something was squashed against her face.

'I is stuck!' Fishbone was wiggling in the net, hissing and scratching.

'We're *all* stuck!' Lug snapped.

'Quiet!' Liska tried to butt them all with her head. 'Do you hear that?'

There, further off amongst the piney darkness, came the sound of heavy footsteps. Footsteps coming steadily closer.

Lug began a low moaning sound that quickly built up into a full-fledged whine. 'It's the giant! We've been trapped by the giant!'

Thud. Thud. Thud.

The footsteps stopped outside the net. There was a jerk and then they were swung upwards.

Lug's screams blended with a terrified yowl from Fishbone. Liska turned her head, trying to get an eye to one of the holes in the netting. She had a brief glimpse of a craggy face: eyeballs as large as dinner plates and a crooked mouth wide enough to bite her in two. It seemed to be covered in green fur, stringy and wild . . . and then it was gone. The net sailed through the air and came to a bone-cracking halt, banging up against the giant's back. It was like slamming into a rock ledge on a bad landing.

'Owww! My leg! I think I broke my leg!'

'You is screaming in my ear!'

'Your stupid cat claws are digging into my neck!'

'Kittimew, not cat, you pasty worm fiddler!'

'QUIET!'

The last word was a thundering roar from the giant itself. Liska felt it buzz through her very bones and it was enough to silence Lug and Fishbone's arguing, at least for a moment.

With the four of them dangling over its shoulder, the creature began to stomp through the woods, the sound of crackling branches following as it passed. *Boom, boom, boom* went its feet as it marched and the darkness around them grew thicker and deeper with every step.

*

'This is all *your* fault,' Fishbone whispered at Lug, his voice hissing at the edges.

'How was I to know it wasn't your tail?' Lug whispered back. 'It was too dark to see anything. If we'd only waited for morning ...'

'I wonder what it intends to do with us?' said Elowen, sounding as though she was on some kind of fairground ride rather than in a giant's dinner satchel.

'Let's not hang around to find out,' said Liska. 'Can you reach into my pack? There's a pocketknife in there. We might be able to cut through the net.'

Elowen began to wriggle about, trying to dislodge Liska's pack from its place on her shoulder. But it soon became clear that she wasn't going to budge it. The net had her arms pinned to her sides, and both hers and Liska's packs were tangled in the mesh of ropy vines.

'That's it. It's over.' Lug began to sob. 'It's going to eat us all, I know it. Now my parents will never know what happened to me. I'll just be a heap of bones in this dark, creepy forest. And the rest of me will be in a pie. Or maybe some kind of soup.'

'I'm sure it won't eat us,' said Elowen. 'It might be just taking us out of its lands. Besides, there's a hint of the familiar about it, don't you think?'

Liska peered through the netting at the giant's back.

It was covered in green fur of all different lengths and textures. In fact, it didn't really look like hair at all . . . more like the moss that grew on the trees back home. Untamed, wild and straggly, but still moss.

She didn't have time for a closer look. The air around them suddenly became cooler, the faint traces of light blinked out like a snuffed candle. They had walked inside a room or cave of some sort. The giant's footsteps echoed as it trudged, and then it stopped.

'Here we are. The last few moments of our lives before we become casserole,' said Lug.

The net sack moved as the giant bent over. The sound of wood creaking filled their ears as it lifted up a door of some kind, and then they were tipped out, end over end, into a deep pit in the mulchy soil. A lid made of thick tree branches slammed down on top of them, shutting them in.

And then . . . silence.

*

'This is a larder, isn't it?' Lug's whisper came through the damp darkness. Liska was actually relieved that there was some noise – her heart had been beating so hard, she thought the others might be able to hear it and know how frightened she was.

'It might be,' she said. 'Can you have a look around outside? Try and find out where we are?'

'How can I do that?' Lug's whisper turned into a wail. 'There's a massive wooden door over our heads!'

'I meant with your worms, dunderhead,' Liska snapped. 'Using your "powers".'

'How can a handful of tiny worms help us now? We're doomed!'

Liska sighed. She climbed on to Lug's lap and poked his face with her wet, foxy nose. 'Stop that, now,' she said. 'This is one time your worms will be perfect. You can use them to listen in, can't you? Like you did when you spied on Elowen ...'

'Oh, right. Yes. Yes, I can do that.'

She could hear Lug muttering and sensed him moving his hands around in the dark. A few moments later, he whispered again.

'Well, there are lots of worms in the soil here. *Aporrectodea nocturna* and *Lumbricus terrestris* mostly. It's very moist and damp. Good conditions.'

'I don't care what types of worm there are, Lug!' Liska hissed. What tiny scraps of her patience that remained had now worn away. 'What's the giant doing?'

'Right. Yes. Giant. Well, I can't *see* it because worms have no eyes. But I can hear it out there. It's breathing. And muttering words I can't quite understand. Like its singing to itself. A lullaby maybe. Or a nursery rhyme.'

Liska remembered Deenai saying that the giant was deeply hurt. Not with broken limbs or battle scars, but wounds to its soul, to its core. Damage that years of loneliness had either caused or made worse. Which meant she had no idea what it might do next – what its plan was. Were they really in danger of being eaten? Or did it have some other, more grisly fate in store? Either way, they had to escape.

'If we make a hole, I can be wriggling out,' said Fishbone. 'Maybe I can get giant's attention – make it chase me so you humies can get away.'

'That's very brave,' Liska said. 'But I don't think it would help. We'd be running around in the dark forest alone. It could easily just catch us again.'

'Let's wait until morning,' said Elowen. 'Things always look better in the morning. And at the very least we'll have some light to see by. I want to get a close look at the giant if I can.'

'Why do you always want to look at things that are going to kill us?' Lug flapped his robes about, trying to get comfortable. 'And just how am I supposed to sleep in this place?'

'I'd have thought you'd be right at home,' said Liska. Although she wondered the same thing. It was damp and cramped, and the fear of what might happen to them bubbled at the edge of her mind, threatening to take over and make her start screaming for help.

Don't do that, she told herself. *There's nobody out there to hear you, anyway. And you might make the giant angry. Wait for a chance and then escape if you can.*

She secretly knew that if she could somehow get above the trees, she could fly out of the giant's reach. It would mean leaving the others behind, which would be cruel and awful. But she might be able to find the forest people again and persuade them to try a rescue. As horrible as the idea of leaving her friends behind was, it was the only thing she could come up with.

You'll think of something else, she told herself. *After all, you've got all night.*

Curling herself in her tail and wings, she tried to get comfortable and in spite of all the reasons not to, she somehow drifted off to sleep.

*

Liska woke with a jolt some unknown time later. Had there been a sound? A shout?

She could see a ghostly outline that was the pale face of Elowen, facing her on the other side of the pit. Her finger was raised to her lips. The yellow cat eyes of Fishbone blinked open beside her, seeming to float in the blackness.

'What is happening?' he whispered.

'Hush,' said Elowen. 'The giant is speaking. I think someone else is here.'

Liska froze, holding her breath, straining her ears. She could just about make out the sound of movement above their prison. Creaking and shuffling and ... an animal sniffing?

Then a deep, thundering voice boomed out, making her jump out of both her skins.

'I ASK AGAIN. WHO DARES COME INTO MY HOME UNINVITED?'

'Forgive me, great one. I am just a hunter tracking my prey. I follow the laws of the wild places. Once a hunt begins it must carry on to the end.'

The answering voice sounded strangled, raspy. As if the speaker had a hand clutched around their throat. *Or as if their throat was damaged somehow. Say, torn through by a wyvern claw, perhaps.*

Liska tried to stop her fox snout from snarling. She had a very good idea who the hunter was.

'THERE ARE NO LAWS HERE EXCEPT MINE,' said the giant. 'AND ALL THE PREY IN THESE WOODS BELONGS TO ME.'

'Of course. Of course. I would never hunt any creature that belonged to *you*. My quarry comes from lands far away. I have been tracking them for days.'

'NOTHING HAS PASSED THROUGH MY LANDS,' said the giant. 'TAKE YOUR HUNT ELSEWHERE.'

'Are you sure? I found their tracks next to a sprung net trap. And then yours led away. Heavier, as if you were carrying a load.'

The mud around them shook as something gigantic moved above. The giant was walking towards the speaker, his feet coming to rest very close to their pit.

'WHAT IS THAT YOU BRING WITH YOU? I CAN SENSE WRONGNESS ABOUT IT. A SMELL I REMEMBER FROM AGES PAST . . .'

'Oh, those are just my hounds,' said the hunter. 'An unusual breed. Nothing to concern yourself with.'

'SHOW ME ONE. NOW.'

Liska could hear the sounds of more footsteps and

muttered words from the hunter. It was definitely Thresher. She had somehow got past Beric and had followed them right up to the trap. And for some reason she didn't want the giant to see her evil slave creatures.

Whiskers tickled her cheek and she felt small paws on her neck. Turning, she found herself looking into Fishbone's gleaming, yellow eyes.

'Giant is distracted,' he whispered so quietly it was hardly a breath. 'We could try and escape now?'

Liska nodded. She reached up to touch the wooden hatch above. Stretching her hind legs, she pushed against it.

Solid. It wouldn't budge.

Perhaps if I changed to human form and got the others to help? There was a small chance they could lift it a bit. Maybe enough for Fishbone to escape.

Her thoughts were interrupted by a frantic tugging at one of her wings. She looked down to see the pale smudge of Lug's face. Even in the pitch darkness, she could tell his eyes were wide open in fright.

'Stop that,' she hissed. 'You'll pull my feathers out!'

He kept pulling.

'I felt something! Coming through the wall!'

'He's right,' said Elowen. 'There is. It's seeping through behind us!'

Everyone scuffled and shuffled over to Liska's side of the pit. She stopped trying to push the hatch open and sniffed at the muddy wall opposite. Immediately her nose was filled with the stink of oily rot, pungent and burning. There was only one thing in the world that smelt like that.

'It's a seeper!' She bared her teeth and growled. 'One of Thresher's hounds is trying to ooze its way in!'

It was too dark to see anything, but they could hear a soft sucking, squelching sound as the thing slowly bubbled through the soil towards them. Liska imagined its grey oily body forming into a tendril, then two, then three, as the thing nosed its way into their pit inch by inch.

'What can we do? What can we do?' Lug was starting to panic. Next to her, Liska could feel Fishbone's tail, puffed up as every hair stood on end. A low yowl had started to build up in the kittimew's throat.

'Get behind us,' Liska said to the others. 'We might be able to stop it.' A little cat and a fox against one of those creatures? They didn't stand a chance, but what choice did they have? 'Maybe you can call up that God Worm of yours. It could dig us a tunnel out of here.'

She said it as a half-joke but Lug started mumbling his incantations all the same.

'WHAT IS THIS? WHAT HAVE YOU BROUGHT INTO MY FOREST?'

Their panic was interrupted by the giant's voice. It sounded further away – outside the cave, maybe – but it was raised in anger. So loud it shook clumps of mud from the pit walls.

'They are harmless, I assure you! Don't hurt them! Please!' Thresher was shouting too. The louder her voice got, the more strangled it became. The giant must have seen the seepers and, from the sound of it, wasn't pleased.

'MONSTERS!' the giant raged. 'EVIL THINGS! THEY MUST BE DESTROYED!'

A *boom*, followed by a small earthquake. The walls around them shook, the hatch above creaked. Liska and the others clutched at each other in terror. From outside they heard a screaming, screeching howl. Someone was shrieking in pain, but it was a noise that no normal living creature could make.

'No!' Thresher yelled again. 'Stop!'

Another *boom*, followed by a second wail.

'The giant is killing the seepers!' Elowen shouted.

Liska had to admit that was how it sounded. Although she didn't want to get too excited just yet. They might be next on the giant's list.

'Curse you! Away, girls! Away!'

The squelching sound from the side of the pit grew louder, and then abruptly vanished. In its place was a gentle pattering of falling mud. Liska padded forward and sniffed – the oily rotten stink had gone.

'Thank the Tree, it's run away,' she said, letting all the breath she'd been holding out in one long sigh. 'I think we might be safe.'

'Safe? I haven't been safe since I left my nice marshy burrow,' said Lug before freezing in mid moan. The footsteps of the giant were stomping towards them again, and the wooden hatch of their prison began to lift. At the gap was a green-furred hand, gnarled fingers grasping, reaching to pull them out.

*

First Lug and Elowen were scooped, vanishing up out of the pit with Lug screaming as he went. Then the giant's other hand dipped in and Liska felt the long, bony fingers wrap around her and Fishbone.

She pushed against them but they were iron-hard. Jagged and knobbly with whorls and lumps, like the roots of a living, moving tree. The palms were covered with spongy layers of softness. It smelt of moss and lichen, of forest floors and tumbled, rotting trees.

There was a yowling in her ear from Fishbone as they were lifted up, up from the hole and into the cavern. Then the giant carried them across the floor and dumped them in a heap on the mulchy ground. As they tried to untangle themselves from the mess of robes, petticoats, tails and wings, the giant began scraping and scratching at the floor next to them. A moment later fire bloomed into life, chasing away the darkness and revealing their surroundings.

They were inside a wide ring of blackened rock that stretched upwards to a tattered roof made of rotten logs, roots and tangled pieces of vine. The space was very wide. Even with the light from the fire, it was hard to see the farthest edges.

Before them was an open crack that served as a doorway. Crooked and twisted, it looked like a knothole in a tree trunk and Liska could glimpse the dark forest outside.

A few metres away was the pit they had been trapped in, and beside them was a ring of stones that held the crackling fire. Standing over it, staring down at them, was the giant.

It was a hunched, lopsided thing, with crooked arms and legs. Shaggy streamers of green hung all over its face and back. They were clearly patches of overgrown lichen and tangled mats of vine and ivy. From beneath a heavy brow, two blank eyes glared. What could be seen of its face was gnarled and weathered, pocked with craters and cracks, speckled with moss, just like the ancient statues of Almberg.

'Pleasedon'teatuspleasedon'teatus ...' Lug was saying over and over as he clasped his hands together in prayer. The giant just stared, its long, rooty fingers twitching every now and then.

'This place,' Elowen said, looking around the cavern, 'it's the inside of a tree ...'

Checking the walls again, Liska could see she was right. They were etched from top to bottom with grain, just like wood. And the twists and bulges where they met the ground could be the start of roots. But for a tree to be this big ...

Elowen let out a gasp of shock. 'This must be the stump of the shadow tree! The one that Lysalm's heart was used to destroy!'

'YES.' The giant spoke but it seemed to be talking to itself rather than to its captives. 'SHADOW TREE. I ... I REMEMBER ...'

'And that means,' said Liska, realising why the giant seemed so familiar, 'that you must be a treekeeper! From Almberg before it was destroyed!'

'TREEKEEPER. YES. THAT'S WHAT I WAS.'

The giant's eyes seemed to spark at the name. Lines of runes could be seen now, glinting across its arms and body as they crackled with forgotten energy. It blinked and raised its hands to stare at them. Then it moved closer to the fire, peering down at Liska and the others.

'THERE WAS A CITY. AND A TREE OF GOLDEN BARK AND SUN-COLOURED LEAVES. THERE WERE OTHERS LIKE ME. AND ANIMALS WHO TALKED. MANY SMALL PEOPLE WHO MADE THINGS WITH MAGIC. I THOUGHT I HAD DREAMT IT, OVER AND OVER. WAS THIS ALL REAL?'

'Yes,' said Elowen. 'Yes, it was. I was there too when I was a young child. It was a beautiful place, full of light and happiness. And then the shadow tree tried to destroy it all. You treekeepers and the shapewalkers brought the heart of Lysalm here, and there was a mighty battle . . .'

The giant looked around the inside of the cavernous tree stump. It reached out a craggy hand to touch the soil.

'I REMEMBER WAKING UP HERE ALL ALONE. THERE WAS DEATH AND DESTRUCTION EVERYWHERE, BUT MY MIND WAS CLOUDY. THERE WAS NOTHING BUT CLOUDS FOR SUCH A LONG, LONG TIME. AND THEN I SAW THOSE CREATURES THE HUNTER HAD . . . THE THINGS THAT WERE MY ENEMY . . . AND THE MEMORIES STARTED TO RETURN . . .'

Lug leaned over to whisper in Liska's ear. 'Does this mean it's not going to eat us?'

She ignored him. There were things she needed to know. 'Can you remember how many seepers . . . creatures . . . the hunter had with her?'

The giant looked down at her, frowning for a moment at the sight of a talking, winged fox. 'YOU ARE A SHAPEWALKER. I CAN SENSE THE MAGIC FLOWING THROUGH YOU. BUT IT IS STRANGE SOMEHOW. DIFFERENT TO THAT I ONCE KNEW.'

'Yes,' said Liska. 'We come from another city like

Almberg. With a different tree. The hunter and her friends are trying to destroy it. Can you tell us how many creatures she had with her?'

'FIVE, I THINK,' said the giant. 'I KILLED TWO OF THEM. I CAN STILL SMELL THEIR POISON . . .'

'Five,' said Liska. 'That means Beric must have destroyed two as well. But she still has three left. And she knows we are here. She'll be on us as soon as we leave this place.'

'That's if we even *get* to leave,' Lug muttered. He was staring up at the giant in a mixture of fear and awe. It was colossal even compared to the treekeepers back in Arborven. In its prime, it must have been taller still, and brimming with power.

'WHY ARE YOU HERE, IN THIS DARK, DEAD PLACE?' the giant asked. 'WHY ARE YOU NOT WITH YOUR TREE?'

'Our tree is under attack,' Liska explained. She briefly told the giant about Bitterblight and their quest to find Nammu's heart. At the mention of what they were trying to do, great sorrow seemed to pass over the giant's face.

'I WISH WE HAD DONE THE SAME AS YOU,'

261

it said. 'BUT OUR MAGES WERE SO SURE OF THEMSELVES. THEY ORDERED US TO USE LYSALM'S HEART AND SWORE THAT THE CITY WOULD STILL STAND AFTER. WAS IT TRUE? DID MY HOME SURVIVE?'

'No.' Elowen's voice was quiet when she answered. 'Almberg is gone. I'm so sorry.'

The giant turned away and stared silently at the fire for a long time. Liska thought she could see glints in its eyes, as if tears were forming there. Could treekeepers cry? She'd never even thought about it.

'But there is good news,' she said, hoping to cheer it up. 'Some of the mages left and founded a new city to the south. It has a tree just like Lysalm. And it is full of life and magic, as Almberg must once have been.'

'THAT IS GOOD TO HEAR.'

The giant continued to stare at the fire, poking the embers with a long finger. Liska thought of the forest people and how her offer of a new home had given them a second chance. Might it work with the giant too?

'I'm sure, if you wanted, they would welcome you there. It's just a few days' journey away, across the Blasted Waste . . .'

'WELCOME ME? TO ANOTHER CITY?'

'Yes!' Elowen jumped up, clapping her hands together. 'That is a fantastic idea! You might even meet people you once knew in Almberg . . . my parents, some of the treekeepers there . . .'

'And they will need you more than ever now,' Liska added. 'To help fight against the shadow tree.'

'FIGHT.' The giant frowned, then rose up to its full height, stretching out arms that almost touched either side of the hollow stump. 'YES. I SHALL FIGHT. AND THIS TIME I WILL NOT FALL. BUT FIRST, I WILL HELP YOU ON YOUR QUEST.'

'Help? How?' Liska started to ask, but the giant was already moving, scooping them all up from the floor with both hands and striding out of the stump with them clutched against his chest.

'It's taking us out of the forest!' Elowen shouted, peering between the colossal fingers that cupped them. Liska looked too and saw the dense branches of pine trees whipping past as the giant strode northwards, cradling them like four tiny babies. Its steps ate up the path much faster than they could ever have run. Thresher would be hard pressed to keep up with them, not to mention being terrified of getting anywhere near the giant.

'We'll be out of the trees in no time,' Liska said. 'Then it's just across the tundra, and we'll be there!'

'Of course,' said Lug, 'there's still a *chance* it might eat us.' But even he was smiling for once.

12

'At the edge of the world, at the end
of all things, it is said there once
stood another tree of light.'

The Book of Undren

The giant took them all the way to the forest edge.
As it parted the dense branches of the last pine
tree, a vast open vista appeared before them, leaving
them blinking in the sudden glare of light.

The sun had just risen, shooting golden, gleaming
beams across from the horizon. It lit up a flat, endless
plain. A sea of grass dotted with clusters of heather and
lichen-speckled boulders. The air was sharp and cold.

A biting breeze sent ripples across the tundra, making the streaks of green, red and brown colour ripple like patches of water.

In the far distance, just a thin strip along the skyline, was a line of white ice.

The glacier, thought Liska. *The one that's about to swallow Nammu. If it hasn't already.*

That was their destination, their target. Having it in sight gave Liska a buzz of triumph. One that was quickly stifled when she worked out how far away it was.

'I WILL LEAVE YOU HERE,' said the giant, carefully setting them all down on the soft swaying grass. 'THIS COLD AIR HURTS MY BONES.'

Liska felt a stab of disappointment. She had hoped their new friend might carry them the rest of the way, striding over the plains ten times faster than they could manage on foot. But it *had* taken them through the forest – and also it hadn't eaten them for breakfast, which was one thing to be grateful for.

'Thank you,' she said. 'Don't forget – you must travel south to Arborven now. There will be a new home there for you.'

'HOME,' echoed the giant, a distant, dreaming

expression on its face. Then it looked down at them, raised a gnarled hand in farewell and disappeared back into the forest.

'Do you think it will head for the Undrentree?' Lug asked. 'Or will it just forget and end up sitting in that stump forever, stomping around the forest and scaring people?'

'I hope it does go north,' said Liska. 'I guess we'll find out. When we finally get back.'

They all spent a moment staring across the yawning plain, thinking about the distance they still had to travel.

'Yes,' said Fishbone quietly. 'If we is ever getting back at all.'

*

For the next five days they travelled ever northwards, growing colder and colder with each step. While they walked, Elowen practised gestures with her hands, as if she were summoning spells. Liska watched from the corner of her eye. Once or twice she saw a spark appear amongst the patterns Elowen drew with her fingers. But it always fizzled out after a few moments. Whatever powers the ghost girl had, they still hadn't returned to her.

They kept going through the sunsets into the nights, until it was too cold to move their aching feet. Then they lay under the wide-open sky, watching strange streams of coloured light flicker and dance above them.

Liska stayed as a griffyx because her fur coat and scales held in more warmth than human skin. She hunted groundhogs with Fishbone and they ate them, cooked over small fires made with dry grass and scraps of gorse, when they made camp. When they slept, Fishbone and Liska curled up next to Lug, trying to give him their warmth. He was wrapped in every spare blanket they had and still couldn't stop shivering. Elowen had torn up an old quilt and used her sewing kit to tack together some mittens for him. If it got much colder, Liska worried he might get frostbite, or worse. More than once she thought of telling him to turn back, but then he would walk right into the clutches of Thresher. Even though his lips were blue and frost clung to his hair, Lug kept stumbling on, too cold even to moan about how much he hated it.

Elowen didn't feel the temperature at all and her legs didn't seem to tire. In between practising magic, she chattered to them as they marched, trying to keep their spirits up, pointing out arctic foxes and ermines, bison, elk and wild horses.

Every now and then, Liska would take to the sky, flying above the tiny specks of her friends as the icy winds buffeted her, trying to gauge how far they had left to walk.

On the afternoon of the second day, she spotted a grey speck amongst the glacier ice. Halfway through the third it had grown to a splinter. There was definitely something big up ahead – surely it could only be Nammu?

The others were filled with excitement when she told them, and even found the energy to dance around in the grass and moss. Soon they could see it too, and the sight of it inching ever so slightly closer spurred them on.

But all their hope was shattered the day after when Liska saw four tiny figures emerge from the forest behind them. Smaller than grains of sand, she was still able to count them, and her eagle-keen eyesight could even pick out the way they moved. One stalking, striding, the other three surging and slinking. A hunter and three hounds.

It was a hard decision to stop that night, especially as Nammu was now so close. Near enough to see its trunk and branches. Near enough to hope that they could actually make it.

'W-will she c-come at us w-when we sleep?' Lug managed to stutter. He was sitting so close to their fire that Liska worried he might catch one of his many blankets alight.

'No,' she said. 'Not tonight. Even if they run without stopping, they're still four days behind.'

'And I shall be keeping watch,' said Elowen. 'I have had more than enough sleep for several lifetimes. Nobody will sneak up, I promise.'

'And I think we might reach the tree very soon,' said Liska, trying to sound as chirpy as possible. 'We could be camping there tomorrow night!'

But then we still have to face Thresher on the way back, she thought to herself. *Whatever happens, she is going to catch up to us. We could have the heart in our hands and still lose it unless we can find a way to dodge her.*

She threw a lump of dry gorse into the fire, sending up a column of swirling sparks. It just wasn't *fair*.

'Don't be afraid,' said Fishbone. 'There is only three hounds left. Liska and I can fight them off, no problems.'

Liska wasn't so sure. She gave Elowen a worried glance, but the dead girl was busy watching the spiralling embers as they blinked out in the cold air.

Why am I the only one who's worried? Am I turning into Lug? Liska nuzzled into her friend's blankets, curling up on his feet to keep his toes from freezing. The only course of action she could think of was for her to fly the heart home herself, up out of Thresher's reach. But that would mean leaving her friends to the mercy of the hunter and her seepers. There would be no chance of a rescue this time.

I won't do that, she told herself. *I would rather die first.*

A death which would mean the end of Arborven and all her family.

Sleep was a long time coming that night.

*

Liska woke to a potent musky stench that made her want to retch. The whole camp seemed to have been bathed in it.

'Eww!' she said. 'What's that smell?'

'I has marked our territory,' said Fishbone, wandering around from behind the campfire, buttoning up his trousers. 'You can thank me later.'

'That's ... that's disgusting.' Liska sneezed the scent out of her nostrils and stood up to look around. The first thing she checked were the figures closing in behind them. They were still specks, but they were definitely closer. Thresher was gaining on them. She must have marched on through the night, even though it was cold enough to freeze the blood in her veins. Her determination had to be admired, Liska supposed. Although it was a shame she and the hounds hadn't been turned into icicles.

Turning to the north, Liska judged the distance to Nammu. It looked as though they could make it by nightfall. If they got moving straight away.

'Come on,' she said. 'Let's make a start. We can eat breakfast on the way.'

Fishbone's stomach was already full of mouse but he had a pair of cooked groundhogs from the night before ready to share out. Elowen was up and ready to go, too. It was just Lug who was still huddled in his pile of blankets.

'Come on, Lug,' Liska said. 'One last push and then we'll be there.'

He didn't move.

Elowen went over to him and knelt down, peering

beneath the blankets. Her worried face made Liska rush over as well. Inside his snug cocoon, Lug's skin was pale blue, his lips and nose bruise-purple. He was struggling to open his eyes and his whole body was violently shivering. His mittens had been discarded and his cuddly worm toy was clutched in his arms.

'Oh, poor Lug!' Elowen pulled one of his hands out from the blankets. His fingers had also turned purple. 'What shall we do with him? His body is so cold!'

'Why did he take his mittens off?' Liska shouted. 'Of all the stupid things to do . . .'

'He must have been trying to cuddle Mister Wriggles,' said Elowen. She carefully prised the toy worm from his grip and eased the mittens back over his frozen hands.

'Rot take it!' Part of her felt like shaking Lug awake and yelling at him. But she was also angry at herself. He was her friend after all, and he wasn't made for adventuring outdoors. He wasn't made for anywhere except a marshy library, to be honest.

Liska racked her brains. If they built a huge fire that might warm him. But there was only dry grass and scraps of gorse to burn. By the time they'd made a fire hot enough they'd be sitting there like flightless chickens when Thresher and her hounds arrived.

'We need to get to Nammu,' she said. 'Maybe we can use some of its wood to build a bonfire. That would warm him up.'

'But how are we going to get him there?' Elowen asked. 'I can't carry him on my own.'

'I'll change,' said Liska. 'Between us we can manage him. And the walk might get his blood flowing again.'

Gritting her teeth, she shifted back from griffyx to human. When the arctic air hit her bare skin, it was like being slapped. Hard. So cold it hurt like a burn.

'Root and branch! No wonder he's frozen!' Liska wrapped her cloak around her, and then took Lug under one arm. With Elowen on his other side, they managed to get him upright and began the slow, stumbling walk towards the tree. Lug, half awake, muttered and moaned in between them, dragging his feet through the grass.

*

They made painfully slow progress, and for a long time the tree in the distance didn't seem to be getting any closer.

Patches of snow started appearing amongst the

gorse. Their feet stomped through them, breaking the icy crust on top and sinking through white crystals with the satisfying *scrrrunch* Liska used to love hearing when it snowed back home. Now it just meant that the temperature was dropping even further, filling her guts with fear for Lug.

To make it worse, Liska could feel the presence of Thresher behind her, burning into the back of her neck. She didn't dare look round, knowing it was useless. They couldn't walk any faster and their enemy was getting closer, closer all the time. Soon, she imagined, they would hear footsteps, the panting of the seeper hounds, the grinding of Thresher's teeth . . .

Liska risked a peek and saw they were still dots on the tundra. There was time to reach the tree and more. But then what? How would they get past them for the journey home?

Don't think about it yet, she told herself. *Don't think about how you'll have to fly away, leaving your friends, leaving Lug to freeze and the others to be torn apart by hounds. Just DON'T THINK.*

She concentrated on the tree. On the sound of snow beneath her feet, the icy wind chafing her bare face and neck. How she couldn't feel her nose or ears, and how Lug's dead weight was tearing the muscles in her shoulder. She kept her eyes focused on the grey shape of Nammu and just kept on taking step after step after step.

*

Dusk had begun to gather, the wispy clouds on the horizon darkening to violet, when Liska realised they were almost there. She had fallen into a kind of trance, hypnotised by her own footsteps and the strain of carrying Lug. Now they were within a kilometre of Nammu itself.

She stopped dead, staring at the thing she had travelled so far to find, drinking it in with her eyes.

It was smaller than the other trees she had seen, although still at least three times the size of the largest oak. Its bark was a deep stony grey, as if it had been carved out of rock rather than grown. Twisted, wind-tortured branches bent into strange contortions jutted out from it all over. Only a few of its leaves remained, dotted here and there on the odd twig. These were leathery brown and orange. The last leaves of an endless autumn stubbornly clinging on.

The ground around it was dusted with frost, icy crystals creeping over Nammu's trunk and branches.

And behind it was the cause. Crowding in, stretching off into the distance on either side, was a solid wall of blue-and-white ice.

The glacier.

A frozen tsunami, solid and unstoppable. It reminded Liska a bit of the granite walls of the Shield Mountains that surrounded her home. Except this towering mass was moving – too slow to see, too quiet to hear but moving all the same. Inching closer and closer to the sacred tree it would soon envelop and kill.

'But … why hasn't it swallowed the tree?' Liska stared closer.

The colossal block of ice seemed to have pushed forwards everywhere except around Nammu. The light tree was sitting in a scoop, as though the glacier was afraid to touch it.

'It doesn't matter,' said Elowen. 'As long as it's there. We aren't too late!'

'Yes!' Tears of joy froze at the corners of Liska's eyes as she cried them. 'And all we have to do now is cut out the heart—'

She stopped in mid sentence, a horrible thought creeping over her like ice from the glacier itself. *Cut out the heart*. But what with? All she had brought with her was a pocketknife. They should have had axes, saws, shovels . . .

She fell to her knees, Lug toppling down after her.

'What is wrong?' Fishbone had been staring at the tree too. He scampered back as soon as Liska knelt, his furry brow creased with worry.

'The heart . . .' she said. 'How are we going to get it out? We didn't bring tools, axes . . . How could I have forgotten that? How could I be so stupid?'

'Don't worry,' said Elowen, her voice as chirpy as ever. 'Let's just get to the tree. I'm sure a solution will present itself.'

'Or we could ask *her*,' said Fishbone.

For a horrid moment, Liska thought he meant Thresher, that the hunter might be standing right behind them ready to pounce.

But the little cat-person was pointing at the tree, at Nammu, to where a girl was standing, spear in hand. A girl with hair the colour of fire and eyes fixed right on them, poised in a warrior-stance, ready to defend her territory.

*

They started walking again, wary this time, staring at the fierce stranger waiting for them.

'Who is she?' Liska asked Elowen. 'What is she doing?'

'She must be one of the people that once lived in this place,' said Elowen.

'People lived *here*?' said Fishbone. 'Who would choose to be cold all the time when there's warm rocks to snooze on in the sunshine?'

'There were lots of people here once,' said Elowen. She pointed to the ground around them, where the earth was still scarred with squares and circles – the marks of tents and buildings that must once have stretched out from the tree in a small city. 'They wanted to be close to Nammu and its magic, just like the people of the other trees of light.'

'What happened to them?' Liska wondered. 'Why would they leave their tree? Especially when the shadow tree that might kill it was gone?'

'Some of them came to live in Almberg,' said Elowen. 'Others went to the east and west. They knew the end was coming. They just didn't know how long it would take.'

'Did they go to other trees of light? Are there more out there?' Liska looked eastwards but could see nothing except more tundra stretching off into infinity.

'Yes, I believe so,' said Elowen. 'I heard tales of a tree to the east whose people had found a way to destroy their shadow tree using magic. And of a place to the west where evil won, and the tree of light was devoured. Legends, probably, but there is often a grain of truth in them.'

Liska looked at the bumps and ditches on the ground, covered over now by grass and moss. She tried to imagine a sea of tents and log buildings here, the spaces in between filled with bustling people. Shapewalkers maybe, just like her. A whole city full of stories – of families, friends, enemies – that had sat here for many years, centuries even, and was now just ... *gone*.

She imagined how Nammu would see it, in the slow, creaking life of a sacred tree. The rise and fall of cities would probably just be a blink to Nammu. One day there was nothing, then a horde of swarming humans and then ...

... back to emptiness again – apart from a single girl with her spear.

Who was still watching them. Very closely.

Liska stared back as they stumbled nearer. She was young – perhaps close in age to Liska herself – but she was much stockier, with broad, muscled shoulders and thick arms and legs. She wore clothes of stitched leather, necklaces of bones and beads. Her eyes looked grey from this distance. They stared out from beneath a heavy jutting brow and either side of a wide flat nose. Her mouth was broad too and set in a stern line, jaw clenched. Traces of blue paint striped her cheeks, and her cloud of red tangled hair whipped back and forth in the wind, looking like a halo of fire raging around her shoulders.

They staggered the last few steps, in between the frosty roots of Nammu. Now the face of the glacier could be seen clearly, especially the part that surrounded the tree. The ice here was clear and fresh, marked all over with chips and slices.

Carved. Liska realised. *Someone has carved the glacier away from Nammu. They have stopped it from being frozen.*

She looked closer, spotting wooden scaffolding that ran up the glacier face. Stone tools – picks and axes – were resting up against it. Liska let out a whistle. How much effort must it take to cut away a glacier? How much sheer stubbornness to take on the most powerful force in nature? And to be done by just one girl?

Who was now looking down, probably just about to introduce them to the pointy end of her spear.

'Erm . . . hello?' Liska said.

The girl tilted her head to one side, sizing up the newcomers. She seemed particularly interested in Fishbone, who had made his eyes look as innocent and adorable as possible. He blinked them a few times for added cuteness.

'What do you want?' the girl said. Her voice was deep and gravelly, her accent thick, but they could understand her words.

'You speak our tongue?' Elowen asked.

The girl gave a nod and a grunt. 'Some of my people went to live in the stone city. They used to come back. Teach us things. Long before I was born. None of them comes here now.'

'The stone city is gone,' said Elowen. 'And the trees with it.'

The girl shrugged, as if this was no surprise.

'Are you the one who did this?' Liska asked. 'Did you cut the glacier back from the tree? All by yourself?'

The girl nodded. A brief, fierce dip of her head. 'My grandmother and I stayed behind to try and stop the walking ice. She died three winters ago. Now I fight it on my own.'

Fight is the right word. Liska still couldn't believe the effort, the determination it must take. But the girl was losing the battle. Ice had closed over all of the northern roots and was now reaching out to touch Nammu's trunk. An icy caress of death. One person on their own couldn't hope to hold it at bay for even a month longer.

An awkward silence began to stretch out, so Liska thought she should introduce herself. 'I am Liska, of Arborven,' she said. 'Another city far to the south. These are my friends Elowen and Fishbone, the kittimew. And this is Lug. He's very cold. We're worried about him.'

'He has the ice sickness,' said the girl. 'You need to build him a fire. Put him in a sweat lodge.' She pointed to a scraping in the earth next to one of the roots. It was stacked high with fallen branches. Then, as an afterthought, she added, 'My name is Embla. Last of the elk herders.'

'Embla, would you help us?' Liska asked. 'We don't know how to build a . . . sweat lodge.'

Embla grunted again, which could have meant

anything, but she moved to the log pile and started grabbing an armful of twigs.

Working quickly, they found a spot tucked in between two giant roots, sheltered from the wind on all sides.

Liska helped Embla drag branches, stacking them into a pyramid, while Fishbone piled handfuls of dry grass inside for kindling. They placed Lug as close as they could, and then set the blaze going. It went up in a tower of flame, blasting out a wall of heat that washed over them like a bath of summer sunlight. It was the warmest Liska had felt in days. Her bones began to thaw and she could see some colour slowly begin to bleed back into Lug's face, although his fingers stayed a worrying shade of purple. She hoped he wouldn't lose them. There were tales about shapewalker guard patrols getting lost in mountain snowstorms and having toes and fingers drop off from frostbite.

Poor Lug, she thought. *He really should have stayed back in Arborven. This whole quest has been so hard for him.* She gently folded his blankets around him, tucked his mittens on tight, brushed his tousled mousy hair away from his eyes.

'I'm sorry I made you come with us, Lug,' she

whispered to him. 'But I don't think I could have done it on my own. You're like a piece of home I brought with me. And we're here now. We did it! Please wake up so you can see . . .'

Liska had a sense of someone watching her and looked up to see Embla frowning down on them. The red-haired girl looked away and Liska blushed, worrying that she had shown too much of her vulnerable side. She was supposed to be a fierce warrior, after all.

Leaving Fishbone and Elowen to finish wrapping Lug up, she stood, wondering what she could say to this elk girl. How she could persuade her to give up the tree she had been fighting to save from freezing.

But Embla's attention was elsewhere. She was staring out at the tundra, where the figure of Thresher could be seen in the far distance. 'Who is that?' she said. 'Why do they chase you?'

'They are our enemies,' said Liska. 'They want to stop us.'

'Stop you doing what?'

Liska took a deep breath. She hadn't planned on bargaining with someone for Nammu's heart. She had no idea of what she would do if Embla refused to let them take it. Fight her? And then Thresher afterwards? She was too cold to even speak, let alone battle.

'We have a tree in our city. A tree like this one.' Liska pointed up to the branches above. 'But it is under attack from its opposite. The shadow tree we call Bitterblight . . .'

'You have come here for Nammu's heart,' said Embla. Her jaw was still set, her fist clenched around her spear. Liska sensed this wasn't the first time she had heard such a request.

'We thought there was nobody here.' Elowen finished covering Lug and came to join them. 'We thought it might even be a legend. But our city, our tree, is in danger. This was all we could think of to save it.'

'Where are your soldiers? Your army?' Embla said. 'When they came for Nammu's heart before, there were many fighters. The elk herders battled them and won. So the legend goes.'

'It's just us,' said Liska. 'Nobody would believe us. They thought Nammu was just a story.'

'And here it is only me,' said Embla. 'All the elk herders have died or moved away. The walking ice is eating Nammu. Already half her roots are dead. Soon the rest will be, too.'

'What will you do then?' Liska asked. She couldn't imagine how lonely it must be, living on these empty plains with only the wind and a dying tree for company.

Embla shrugged. 'Die too, I suppose.' She looked out at the tundra again, squinting at the oncoming hunter. 'What are those beasts that follow you?'

Liska shuddered at the thought of them, somehow feeling even colder. 'Seepers,' she said. 'Made by the shadow tree. Monsters like that are attacking my city even as we stand here.'

Embla's broad nose wrinkled in a snarl and her grey eyes flashed as fierce and fiery as her wild hair. She thumped the butt of her spear against the ground and spoke in her own tongue: a guttural mixture of grunts and clicking sounds.

She hates the seepers as much as us, Liska thought. *Even though all the shadow trees she could have known were dead generations before she was born.* It was an instinct. A loathing that ran through the very cells of those who lived near the sacred trees. And one that Liska might be able to use.

'Will you help us, Embla?' she said. 'Will you help us stop those creatures from killing our tree?'

'And us,' Fishbone added. 'They kill us quite a lot sooner.'

Embla's hand went to the layers of bone charms at her neck. Liska could see many were carved with pictures and symbols. Perhaps the very last artefacts of her tribe. 'Nammu is going to die soon,' she said. 'If I help you, Nammu dies now. Either way, she dies.'

'I'm afraid so,' Liska said.

Embla let out a sigh. A cloud of steam drifted from her mouth, up towards the branches above. 'But Nammu's death can help another tree if I give you the heart. And that is what Nammu would want. So take it.'

She bent to the ground and laid her spear at Liska's feet then stepped aside, head bowed. Liska thought she saw a tear or two fall from the elk girl's eyes.

'Before we do anything,' said Elowen, 'There might be a chance for Nammu to live on. And you too, Embla, of course. If you are willing to try. Although I cannot promise it will be a success.'

'What way?' Embla knuckled the tears from her cheeks and stared at the marble-white face of Elowen. Liska stared too, wondering what she was planning.

'I don't know if the elk herders knew the magic, but

in other cities there are special people who have joined with their trees. They become another kind of creature, part of both worlds. Treekeepers we call them.'

Embla nodded. 'There are stories of great elders who walked as wooden gods. Ours died when the walking ice first appeared. We did not know the ceremony to make more.'

Elowen gave a gentle smile. She moved to rest a hand on Embla's arm. 'Well, I know the ceremony. I can make you and Nammu join as one, if you wish it. Then you will both live on.'

'What?' Liska couldn't believe what she was hearing. 'How can you do that? Only an elder arbomancer has that power and there hasn't been one around for—.'

'Five hundred years?' Elowen smiled. 'Before our accident, my family were the elders. We knew all of the forms magic can take. We made the treekeepers soon after we arrived at the Undrentree.'

'You? Made the . . .? You know the . . .?' Liska gave up trying to speak and just stood with her mouth open. Of all the powers she expected Elowen to have, she had never imagined *that*.

'Yes, we made them from members of our family. Edda is actually my uncle.'

Liska tried to close her mouth but failed. All this time she had been walking around, talking to, sleeping beside ... Edda's *niece*?

'Now, my powers have been slow in returning since I last woke,' Elowen continued. 'But being this close to another sacred tree ... I can feel them waking, finally.'

To demonstrate, she closed her eyes and moved her hands through the air, tracing out an intricate pattern. As her fingers danced around each other, they left traces of blue light. A web of magical energy, hanging in space, quietly crackling. Liska smelt the familiar scent of potent magic tingling in her nostrils, sending sparks spiralling down her spine.

'Can you really do it?' Liska whispered to her. 'Are you sure you're strong enough to turn Embla into a treekeeper?'

'I think so.' Elowen was smiling at the thought but Liska wasn't quite as confident. She had seen how weak her friend's magic had been on the journey here. What if the process went wrong? What if something terrible happened to Embla? But then again ... if it *did* work ... they would have a treekeeper on their side. *That* would even up the odds against Thresher, for sure ...

Oblivious to their conversation, Embla had been

kneeling, pressing one of her hands to a root of Nammu. Now she stood again, a broad grin on her face.

'Nammu and I accept your offer with honour. We would like to join our souls together. And then we can face the walking ice and die as one.'

'Oh, you won't have to die,' said Elowen. 'You could come and live in Arborven, along with our treekeepers. You would be most welcome, wouldn't she, Liska?'

Liska was still having doubts about it, but she managed a nod. *If only Lug was able to hear this*, she thought. *Elowen – an elder arbomancer – he wouldn't believe it!*

'How long will this take?' she asked, trying to judge how far away Thresher was.

'Several hours, I should think,' said Elowen. 'Nammu has boosted my powers but they are still not at full strength. Besides that, I have to make a proper connection with the tree. Then we can sing together and knit Embla and Nammu as one. It is a slow process at the best of times. It can be done quickly but the danger of things going wrong is great if we rush.'

'I think we'll have enough time.' If Thresher ran all night, she would be upon them by the dawn at the earliest. Liska prayed that the hunter would be suffering from the cold just as they had. 'Come on,

Fishbone,' she said. 'We need to check on Lug. And then we have to prepare.'

'Prepare what?' Fishbone asked, eyes wide and hopeful. 'Supper?'

'For battle,' said Liska, feeling the fox within her begin to growl.

13

'And you shall become the Tree,
just as the Tree becomes you.'

The Rite of the Treekeeper

Liska sat by the fire listening to the snapping of the flames and holding on to one of Lug's mittened hands, gently rubbing his fingers. Her mind was playing through all the possible ways the coming battle might go. Unfortunately most of them ended with Thresher killing them all.

Unlike her, Fishbone had no worries. He was stretched out on his back basking in the heat. He opened one eye and looked at her hopefully. 'Belly rub?'

'You must be joking.'

Behind them they could hear Elowen crafting the magic that would bind Embla to her tree. Remake her in a new form: a thing of flesh and living wood combined. Just words at the moment, in a language that was dimly familiar to Liska. She had heard snatches of it used by stormsingers when they conjured the mountain mists back home.

The sound of it made her think of the Noon Fort. Of her family, her room, the view over Arborven. Was the battle still raging? Were her parents alive? And would they be worrying about her? She hadn't even left a note, she realised. Would they notice her things were missing and assume she had run off on her half-brained quest? Or did they think a seeper had snatched her on the night of the attack? Would they be mourning her right now? She wished there was some way to know. To have just a glimpse of them; to see that they were safe.

'I is going hunting,' Fishbone announced, breaking her dismal thoughts. 'Coming?'

Liska shook her head. As much as she would like the warmth of her griffyx fur, she wanted to watch over Lug. If he came round, he would need fresh water, maybe some bandages for his hands. Did frostbite make your fingers suddenly snap off, or did they shrivel up first? Either way, she thought someone should be here when he woke. She had many things to say to him and all of them began with 'sorry'.

She sat listening to the crackle of the fire and watching the stars appear as the sky darkened to black. At some point Fishbone returned with more groundhogs and a small pile of mice. They set about roasting them and melting snow in a pot for water to drink.

All the while, Elowen sang strange, arcane words, waving her hands over Embla as she stood up against Nammu's trunk. Sparks of blue-and-purple light hung in the air as she worked, but nothing else seemed to be happening.

Hurry up. It was too dark to see anything on the tundra now but Thresher was out there, edging ever closer.

As if summoned by her thoughts, Liska saw the gleam of a fire suddenly appear far out on the frozen plain. Her breath caught in her throat.

'A campfire,' said Fishbone, spotting it as well.

'She's stopped for the night?'

'Makes sense,' said Fishbone. 'She can't run on

forever. And she is a humie like you. She will freeze without heat.'

'And I suppose she doesn't have to rush any more. She knows we're at the tree. We'll have to go past her on the way back. She's got us cornered. She can just sit there in her camp and wait for us to come to her.'

'Or the f-fire's a t-trick and she's sneaking up to us right n-now.' Lug's weak, wavering voice came from inside his pile of blankets. Liska was so glad to hear it she didn't even mind that he was moaning again.

'Lug! You're awake!' She hurried over to him with a cup of snowmelt water and some roasted groundhog. Helping him to sit up, she put the cup to his cracked, frozen lips and then hugged him as gently as she could.

'I c-can't feel my h-hands,' he said.

Liska took a quick peek inside his mittens at his purple fingers and decided it was best to tell a white lie. 'They got very cold,' she said. 'Because you took your stupid gloves off. It might take some time for the feeling to come back.'

'I'm s-sorry,' Lug stammered. 'I j-just wanted to hold Mister Wriggles.'

'No, *I'm* sorry,' Liska interrupted him and then wrapped him up in another hug. 'I should never have made you come. But I don't think I'd have had the strength to leave if you weren't with me. So I'm glad I did, too.'

She felt Lug squeeze her back and then he spoke into the fur of her cloak. 'Did I m-miss anything?'

'Well,' Liska sat back and pointed to the giant tree and the cascade of magical blue light that was surrounding it. 'We're at Nammu! We actually did it! Oh, and Elowen is turning its guardian into a treekeeper with an ancient magical ritual.'

'What? H-how can she do that?'

'Turns out she's an elder arbomancer.' Liska grinned as Lug pulled the exact same face she had earlier. 'Her family created the treekeepers back home. Edda is actually her *uncle*.'

'An *elder*?' Lug blinked in disbelief. 'I thought she would t-turn out to be a sapsmith. Or maybe even a vermispex like me. But an *elder* . . .'

'I know.' Liska spread her hands and shrugged. 'And – even better – we'll have a giant tree person on our side when we have to fight Thresher. If Elowen finishes the spell in time.'

Looking up at Nammu, Liska could see that Embla had begun the process of changing. Her back, where it pressed against the tree, seemed fuzzy and blurred. As if she had started to merge with the bark. Her eyes were firmly closed, and Elowen was still making gestures and signing lost songs that sounded like lullabies.

'It's hard to believe treekeepers were once p-people,' Lug said. 'I used to think they just *were*. Like the m-mountains and the sky.'

'Maybe you should rest some more,' said Liska. 'It's going to take a long time and night has just started. I'll keep watch and feed the fire.'

Fishbone was already asleep, a deep purring noise coming from his throat. Lug snuggled back down in his blankets and was softly snoring in a few seconds.

Liska smiled over them both, then stoked the fire up and got ready for a long night of waiting.

*

At some point in the early hours, she dozed off, and was awoken with a jump by the snap of the fire.

Her hands went to her cloak hood, expecting to see Thresher leaping out at her, but there was only Fishbone, twitching as he dreamt of catching plump mice, curled next to the blanket mound that was Lug.

She turned around to see how Elowen and Embla were doing and was shocked at the change.

Blue light bathed the pair of them, and it was difficult to tell where Embla ended and the tree began. Strips of bark and tendrils of root were coming out of Nammu, wrapping and plaiting themselves into new arms and legs, swallowing up the human form of the elk herder and rebuilding it as something new.

As Liska watched, her left arm came free from the tree trunk with a slow, ripping sound. Embla gave out a low moan of pain and Elowen made a swirling gesture with her hands, building up the streaks of blue light that filled the air. More bark crawled over the fresh raw limb, coating it in new wooden skin.

It almost seemed wrong to be watching such a personal, private moment and yet Liska couldn't tear her eyes away. *This must be what happened to the treekeepers back home,* she thought. *All those hundreds of years ago. This was how they were born.*

She watched for a few minutes more, and then the fire began to collapse in on itself. Her duty wasn't over and if Elowen wasn't getting any sleep, then *she* shouldn't either. With a yawn she went over to the wood pile for some fresh logs.

*

Dawn was the next thing that woke her. She'd fallen asleep sitting up, doubled over so her head was almost in her lap.

She stretched and rubbed her eyes, squinting across the cloud of smoke from the dying fire to watch the first rays of the sun sparkle across the swathes of frost that covered the open plain before her . . .

And that was when she saw Thresher and her seeper hounds not twenty metres away, stalking towards them as if they were a herd of fat gazelles about to be slaughtered.

'Wake up!' she yelled at the top of her voice, stumbling to her feet. 'It's Thresher! She's here!'

Fishbone sprang up with a hiss and landed on all fours, his back arched. There was a mad tumble from the nest of blankets that held Lug, as he frantically tried to untangle himself.

Liska looked round to see – *please, Tree, let her be finished* – if Elowen was ready. Even knowing what Embla was being made into, the sight took her by surprise.

A towering treekeeper stood beside the trunk of Nammu. Three times taller than Embla had been, it was covered with fresh, gleaming silver bark. It had her same broad shoulders and thick, powerful limbs.

The face of living wood mirrored her strong brow and wide nose. There was even a cloud of red-leaved ivy curling wildly around her shoulders.

It took a moment for Liska to catch her breath, the change was so amazing. But Thresher was going to be amongst them at any moment. 'Are you done?' she called. 'Are you ready?'

Elowen was still standing by the tree, casting magic over Embla's right arm. She looked tired for once, the purple shadows around her eyes deeper, her shoulders slumped.

'Almost,' she called back. 'Her hand is still attached.'

Liska looked down to see Embla's fist was still joined to Nammu. Strands of wooden tissue were snaking themselves together, knitting palm and fingers. On the other side of the fire, Thresher was walking towards them, spear at the ready. Her three remaining hounds were hunkered down, slinking through the dry grass, their mouths hanging open. Liska could see fangs there, formed from grey sludge, which steamed in the chill dawn air. With every step they took, the moss shrivelled and died behind them.

'How long?' Liska shouted. If it was anything more than a few minutes, they weren't going to make it.

'Ten minutes!' Elowen shouted.

Curse it. Too long. Thresher was close enough now for Liska to see the smug smile on her face. She knew it too.

All Liska could do was flip her hood over and shift into her beast shape. Then with her fiercest snarl on her fox lips, she padded down to where Fishbone stood – his claws popped – ready to fight to the death alongside him.

*

'I finally caught you.' Thresher's voice, when it came, was husky and rasping. Liska could see the deep scars on her neck that caused it. *If only that wyvern had finished the job.*

'We're not caught yet,' she snarled. Two of the seepers had broken off, coming around from either side of the fire to flank them. She turned to face one, flaring her wings and snapping. She could hear Fishbone hissing at the other. Somewhere behind her there was a scrabbling and flapping as Lug clambered out of his blankets and started muttering prayers to his worm god.

'Shame,' Thresher continued taunting them. 'You got so close. The heart was here as well. All the time. Even Noxis thought it was probably just a story.'

The seeper closest to her took another step around the fire. It was only a pounce away now, waiting for orders. But if Liska could just keep its master talking for a few minutes more . . .

'Why are you doing this? You've betrayed your own kind for these . . . *things*.'

Thresher tried to laugh. It sounded like a crow being sick. 'You mages and half beasts have no idea of the *power*. Bitterblight has shown us what it can create. An empire that would put Arborven to shame. One that isn't ruled over by those walking wooden *monsters*.'

She pointed her spear at Embla, still joined to the tree, straining to pull her half-formed arm free.

'Instead you've chosen worse monsters,' Liska said. 'Evil, poisoned things. They stink of rot and death. Can't you smell it?'

'Oh, you get used to it after a while.' That tortured laugh again. 'I even quite like it. Better to be a lord among the diseased than a servant of the treekeepers. And now I'd best let my pets kill you before your tree girl can come to the rescue.'

She snapped her fingers and the seepers launched themselves.

Liska was ready. She saw one of the things leave the

ground and fly towards her, mouth wide open, seams of grey smoke trailing.

But she was already gone. With a beat of her powerful wings, she drove herself down, skimming along the ground underneath the seeper's feet, then digging her paws into the dirt to spin round, ready to attack.

The seeper landed, jaws closing on the flattened grass where Liska had just been. It tumbled over itself before jumping up, whirling round to face her . . .

. . . and met a cloud of sparks and embers that Liska had just scooped from the fire and thrown with her paw.

The red-hot charcoal dashed across the seeper's face, sinking into the gloopy liquid it was made of and *burning*. There was something in all that rot that liked fire. Liska could see flames start to form inside the creature's head. Sparks that landed in its mouth caught light as well and then it was rolling on the ground, beating its body against the earth, trying to put itself out.

Liska looked across to the second seeper and saw Fishbone on its back ripping out hunks of grey steaming goo with his claws and yowling fit to burst. The seeper danced around, trying to knock the kittimew free with its gummy oozing claws, but it was too slow. Fishbone danced up and down its back like a rodeo rider, scratching and tearing, clawing and gouging.

Lug was still praying, mittened hands raised to the sky, safe out of danger.

That just left—

Before she could turn to face the third seeper and Thresher herself, Liska was hit from behind. She was knocked to the ground, face in the cold moss, and a wave of rotten stink rushed over her.

Liska fought to get up but the thing was too heavy. A paw of rancid goo came down on one of her beautiful eagle wings, pinning it flat, crushing the delicate bone and tearing at the pin feathers.

'No!' she growled, seeing dripping jaws above, lowering towards her head. She looked across to watch Thresher leap the fire and swing her spear in a wide, flat arc that hit Fishbone across the back, knocking him off the seeper and sending him flying into one of Nammu's massive roots.

'By the sacred segments of Nematus, I smite you with the power of all wormkind!' Lug stood and threw a handful of stringy, pale things at the hunter – the best worms he could summon. They spattered over her shoulders then slithered off like slimy rain. She looked mildly surprised.

'Oh, not again!' Lug wailed.

Between them all, they had lasted two minutes, if that. Now Thresher just had to finish them off and her hounds could tear apart Embla before she was properly reborn.

Liska closed her eyes.

She could feel the seeper's jaw edging down, tickling the hackles at the back of her neck, ready for the final crunch that would crush her spine.

Closer . . .

Closer . . .

14

'Cats has nine lives. Kittimew has one.
But they gives it gladly for their friends.'

Kittimew proverb

Liska heard a sound. A ripping: a wet tearing,
splintering mixed with a scream of pure boiling
rage and agony.

She opened one eye a crack and saw Embla – or
rather the thing Embla had become – pulling at its
half-formed hand, wrenching it from the trunk of
Nammu.

Tendrils frayed and snapped; soft, white heartwood
splintered and flaked. Slowly, painfully, the fist came

free, breaking its last few connections with a chorus of pops.

And then Embla was charging towards them, her wooden face bent into a scream of fury, her new eyes glowing blue with pure magic.

She leapt from the top of the nearest root, three metres from the tundra floor, and landed with a *krump* that shook Liska's teeth.

The hand she had just torn loose was thick and clumpy, the bark already hardening around it. It looked more like a club than a fist, but that suited Embla just fine. She swung it high over her head and brought it down on to the seeper that Liska had burnt, crushing it into the soil, smashing a crater in the earth.

The seeper exploded, spewing globules of grey rot upwards in a cloud. They pattered across the roots of Nammu and Embla's fresh skin of hardened bark, hissing, shrivelling and falling away.

Liska saw the second seeper spring upwards, trying to strike Embla while her meaty fist was buried deep in the mud. But she had her other hand free. She swung it round and caught the creature by the neck, gripping it hard, as tentacles of grey sludge thrashed outwards from the thing's body.

The seeper pinning Liska made a wailing noise but didn't move from her back. She struggled against it but was held fast. It didn't look as though Embla would be quick enough to save her.

But there was still Elowen.

Liska saw a flash of white as her friend also dropped down from Nammu's root. Even though she must have been exhausted, her hands were moving in summoning patterns, making streaks and spirals of light in the air. She was using her arbomancer's powers to control Nammu itself, using the tree to fight against Thresher.

From the earth all around Liska, fresh roots burst, shooting straight upwards in an explosion of buds and vines.

They whipped downwards like striking snakes, wrapping themselves around the seeper that had her trapped. The thing was lifted clean off the ground, struggling and shrieking as the roots squeezed tighter and tighter.

Liska felt the weight on her back suddenly lift. She rolled out of the way just as Elowen's vines snapped shut, bursting the seeper into a cloud of rot.

Clots of the filthy stuff drizzled down to the ground

where Liska had just been lying, frazzling the grass there before shrivelling up and disappearing.

Liska flexed her wings, checking they weren't broken, then turned to see if she could help Embla.

There was no need. The giant treekeeper had freed her other hand and was holding the struggling seeper above her head. As Liska stared, she brought it down into the red-hot coals of last night's fire.

The creature instantly burst into flames, writhing about as its rotten body was eaten up in seconds.

That only left Thresher.

The hunter let out a strangled scream and threw her spear at Embla's chest with all her strength.

Liska winced, expecting the worst, but the spear tip simply bounced off Embla's silvery wooden hide. Then, copper-leaved hair swirling about her head, Embla took a giant step towards Thresher.

One trunk-like leg landed just in front of the hunter, and she brought her other foot swinging past it in an almighty kick. Thresher was caught in the chest and punted high into the air, sailing up almost as far as Nammu's topmost branches.

She flew up, over the lip of the oncoming glacier, and then began to tumble downwards. Liska closed her eyes, not wanting to see the landing, but she felt it through her paws. She flinched. There was no way a human body could have survived an impact like that. Even if it did, the ice would freeze it in minutes.

And just like that, Thresher and her hounds were gone.

*

Liska raced first to Fishbone, who still lay crumpled amongst the gorse after bouncing off one of Nammu's gargantuan roots. Luckily he was just bruised and winded, his side sore where Thresher's spear shaft had smacked him.

Next she saw to Elowen, who had stumbled to her knees by the fireside. She wasn't hurt, simply exhausted from channelling magic all night long.

'A short rest, I think, and then I shall be fine.' Her voice quiet as a sigh. Lug fetched his collection of blankets, Liska built the fire up again, and Elowen was soon fast asleep. Liska thought it was the first time she had seen her with her eyes closed. She looked more like a marble statue than ever.

Throughout all this, Embla stood silently by Nammu, one wooden hand resting on the great tree's trunk. Liska thought she ought to speak to her, given that she had saved all their lives. But what did you say to someone who had just become a magical being of immense power?

Although, Liska thought, *it's not that different from when a shapewalker changes. No matter what they look like, it's still the same person on the inside.*

She went to stand quietly beside her and cleared her throat.

'I ... um ... I just wanted to say thank you. For helping us.'

There was a creaking sound as Embla turned her head to look down at the small creature beside her. Her cascade of red leaf hair rustled as she moved.

'It is I who should be thanking you,' she said. Her voice was lower now, booming and thrumming with power, but Liska could still pick out a trace of Embla's human accent. 'You have made me a part of Nammu. Now she will never die. You have saved us both.'

Liska nodded, feeling the same awe and unease as when she met the treekeepers back in Arborven. But she was also filled with a burning curiosity. 'What's it like?' she asked. 'Being a treekeeper ... how does it *feel*?'

Embla's head, far, far above, tilted as she thought.

'It's strange,' she said. 'New. I have my old memories and feelings but also all of Nammu's. I can remember being a seed, growing in the soil right there. And I can remember my mother's mother, and all the mothers before that, going right back to the first elk herder who built her hut here. All the seasons, all the people. They are with me, woven into every grain.'

'That . . .' Liska fumbled for the right words. 'That sounds . . . nice.'

Embla smiled. A wide, wooden smile that lit up her face. 'It is nice, shapewalker. It is a history I . . . we . . . thought would be lost forever. And now it isn't.'

Liska nodded. The Undrentree must be the same, she realised. Not just a source of magic or a place to build houses around, but a living record of her people going back generations and generations. If it was lost, a whole chunk of the world would be gone with it.

If only they could get Nammu's heart back there in time to stop that from happening.

*

After just an hour of sleep, Elowen was up on her feet again. When Liska told her to rest some more, she shook her head.

'I've said before – I've slept enough for many

313

lifetimes. There are still tasks to do. Starting with us taking Nammu's heart.'

The death of a sacred tree. It was a sad, solemn moment, but also one filled with hope. Against all the odds, Liska's and Lug's gamble had paid off and they were finally here, claiming the thing that could save their home.

And yet there was Embla, the last trace of a whole civilisation, about to see her most precious thing in the world die.

They gathered by the trunk of Nammu, looking up at its timeless rugged branches, imagining them filled with leaves in warmer times when noise and life thronged the plains. Now there was just the biting wind whirling down from the glacier, the dusting of frost across the bark, and the last few brave leaves fluttering as if waving goodbye.

'Should . . . should we say something?' Liska asked as Elowen stepped forwards towards the trunk.

'Nothing needs to be said.' Embla nodded at Elowen to continue. 'Nammu knows what you ask of her. She has been waiting for her time to end for many years now. Everything is as it should be.'

'But dying is sad,' said Fishbone. 'We should at least do some yowling.'

'Please don't,' muttered Liska.

'All things die,' said Embla. 'But not many get the chance to help others live. It is an honour for Nammu to do this.'

Elowen, now calling on her magic as easily as breathing, stepped forward and laid her hands on the grey, frost-flecked bark of the tree. She began to sing in her arbomancer's language. The effect was instant. About halfway up the trunk a crack appeared. A split that yawned open, revealing the sap and wood beneath.

Layers and layers of tree flesh peeled backwards, like a flower unfurling. Deeper and deeper into the tree they saw, until a glowing seed about the size of a watermelon was revealed. Blue light poured out of it in rays, making them all squint. Liska's fur crackled with energy. It sizzled in her snout, it tickled her feathers. The power trapped in that small shell must be immense.

'Our thanks to you, Nammu,' Embla said, reaching in and taking the heart with her good hand. She carefully drew it out, cradling it to her chest. As soon as it had left the trunk, the last few leaves released their hold on the branches and fell to the ground like gently drifting snowflakes. The bark of Nammu seemed to lose its shine, becoming grey and lifeless. A stone tree in a frozen wilderness.

Silence enveloped them. Even the constant whistle of the north wind seemed to still. There was a sense that a momentous event had just happened. A change in the world that rippled through every atom.

'Well,' said Elowen when the stillness had gone on for a few minutes. 'Perhaps we should start walking home. We have quite a long journey ahead of us.'

'I can carry you all,' said Embla. 'If someone holds the heart.'

'Give it to Lug,' said Elowen. 'I think he needs it most.'

Liska looked hard at the worm caller and realised he had been very quiet since the battle. She noticed that his fingertips had turned dark. Perhaps the frostbite was setting in and causing him pain? She was about to ask when he began to sob. Big racking gasps that made his whole body shake as tears ran down his face.

'I don't deserve to hold it!' he cried. 'I don't deserve to even be here! I'm useless! A failure!'

'What are you talking about?' Liska put a paw on his knee but he shook it off.

'I can't do anything!' he wailed. 'Every time I've

tried to help, it just goes wrong. All I can do is throw worms at people. Worms! How is that meant to do anything?'

'Lug ... that's not true. You're just as important as any of us—'

'No, I'm not!' He began pointing at each of them in turn. '*You* can turn into a flying fox beast and fight and sniff things out. The cat has got claws and catches all our food. Embla is a giant treekeeper, for root's sake, and *Elowen* ... Well, it turns out she's one of the most powerful mages that has ever lived! How can I compete with all *that*?'

Liska was lost for words. It was kind of true, she supposed. Being able to talk to worms wasn't all that useful on an epic quest it turned out.

'You saved Myrtle from those parasites,' Elowen said, coming to the rescue.

'You spied on the giant,' said Fishbone. 'And is *kittimew*, by the way. Not cat.'

Liska nuzzled him with her nose. 'Do you know what?' she said. 'It doesn't matter if you haven't done anything amazing yet. We know you've been scared and uncomfortable and cold. But that doesn't stop you trying. Every time there's been danger, you've done your best with what powers you have. Just like when you stood up for me in the playground that day. You're as brave as any of us. Braver, even.'

'Yes,' said Fishbone. 'I is admiring the way you keep trying, even when you is always failing so badly.'

'But ... I can't just keep on throwing worms at people.' Lug sniffed and wiped his nose on his sleeve. 'It's pathetic.'

'I can show you how to channel magic properly, if that's what you're worried about,' said Elowen. 'I know lots of techniques the mages have long forgotten.'

Lug's eyes lit up. 'Will I be able to summon Nematus?'

'Well, let's not get ahead of ourselves,' she said. 'We'll see how things progress, shall we?'

Lug nodded and even gave Embla a graceful bow when she handed him the heart. He wrapped his injured hands around it and clutched it tight, the wispy hair on his head standing on end as the power coursed through him.

'Now,' said Embla. 'Let us leave this place.'

She reached down and lifted all three of them into her arms, holding them in a cage of wooden limbs, much like the giant had done.

As they arranged themselves comfortably in her grasp, she started to stride south, powering across the tundra as fast as the icy north wind. Liska poked her muzzle over the treekeeper's shoulder as they moved and watched the empty shell of Nammu growing smaller and smaller in the distance until it blended in with the white of the walking ice behind it.

*

They reached the forest edge by sunset and Embla showed no signs of tiring.

'I can travel through the trees by night,' she said. 'I can see their life glowing in the darkness. The whole place is alight with it.'

Liska looked and could see only thick dark branches. But she didn't want to argue. At the speed they were going they would be back in the Blasted Waste by morning.

Letting the rocking motion of Embla's footsteps soothe her, she curled herself up in between Elowen and Lug. She could feel the hum of energy from the heart, still tightly clenched in Lug's grip, and it gave her dreams of lost ages and secret veins of crackling power hidden beneath the ground.

At some point in the night she awoke and peered through Embla's wooden fingers to see she was passing through a clearing, dotted all around with lopsided huts of mossy stone.

'The shapewalkers' village,' she whispered.

'There is nobody here,' Embla replied as she strode through.

Liska sniffed the air and picked up traces of human and animal, the charred smell of spent fires and cooked food. But they were all cold scents, days old. The tribe must have taken her advice and headed for Arborven. Which meant her message might have been passed on to her family.

Liska snuggled back down, a warm tingle of excitement in her bones. *I'll see you all soon,* she thought, picturing her mother, father and sister in her mind. *Please be safe. Please be there to meet me. Please don't hate me for running off.*

*

Sunlight woke her next. She could feel warm rays, toasty on her fur. Hot – uncomfortable even. On instinct, she shifted back to her human shape, forgetting that there wasn't much space within the curled arms of Embla the treekeeper.

'Ow! Watch out!' Lug said, wriggling out of her way. 'You almost made me drop the heart!'

'Sorry,' said Liska, and then, 'good morning.' She

yawned and stretched, look around her as the dry, dusty wastes rolled by. Elowen had moved to sit up on Embla's shoulder and Fishbone was hidden in the mass of red ivy that was now her hair. Two slitted eyes peered out at Liska and gave her a wink.

'We're through the forest then,' she said, enjoying the feeling of warm air on her skin for a change. 'I was getting fed up of being so cold.'

'*You* were fed up of it,' said Lug. 'I nearly died.'

Liska looked at his hands and was amazed to see them pink and healthy. Not a trace of frostbite in sight. 'Your hands, Lug! They're better!'

'Yes,' he said, smiling and flexing his fingers. 'Thank the Tree.'

'I was hoping the heart might have a healing effect,' said Elowen from her perch. 'It worked even better than I expected.'

'It is so hot here!' Embla's booming voice made them all jump. 'Is it like this where you live? Because I think I might shrivel and die if it is.'

'No,' said Liska. 'It's much cooler in the mountains. Not as chilly as the tundra, but I think you will like it.'

'Have we got time for a magic lesson?' Lug asked Elowen. 'You said you would teach me.'

Elowen nodded and clambered down to talk to him. Liska took the chance to steal her perch. She let her cloak stream out behind her as she clung to Embla's shoulder, breathing in the scents of dry sand and baked rock. As she watched the wastes, keeping an eye out for wyverns or Poxpunks, she caught snatches of Elowen's advice.

'. . . and so the light trees draw up the energy we call magic from the core below. Then it leaks out, being stronger the closer you are to the tree. Which is why the most powerful mages are the ones that live next to it. But that's just laziness, really. The magic is there, deep beneath the ground, and anyone can draw on it if they can tune themselves properly.'

'So vermispexes don't *have* to be the weakest?'

'Not if they know how to feel the power below them.'

'But how can you do that? All I can sense in the ground is worms.'

'You already do it a bit just by using magic. And carrying the heart for so long should have made you a much better channel for energy. All you have to do is learn to sense it. Here, I can show you some exercises . . .'

They went on for what seemed like hours, talking

about spells and gestures, currents of power, shapes of force … Liska lost interest quite quickly. The only magic she needed was the cloak on her back and the fox shape hidden in her blood.

Instead, she watched the skies, blue and empty – until she saw a winged silhouette circling them high above.

'Uh-oh,' she said, pointing upwards. 'I think we've been spotted.'

Everyone looked skywards. 'Is it a wyvern?' Fishbone asked.

'I think so,' said Liska. 'It's dropping lower.'

As the dark shape came closer, they could see it was, indeed, a wyvern. Gliding on leathery wings, tail and hind legs stretched out behind it.

Nearer and nearer it came, closing on its prey, until they could see the shimmer of sunlight on its purple scales.

'I think …' Lug said, shading his eyes with his hand. 'It is! It's Myrtle!'

They all whooped and cheered as the wyvern flew so low it almost skimmed their heads. It banked, showing them a gleaming eye, and puffed out a small cloud of flame as a greeting.

'Myrtle! Hello girl!' Lug shouted, the happiest Liska had seen him since they left Arborven. 'Follow us to the mountains! I can't wait to show you to everyone!'

Liska thought that most of the mages would be less than pleased to see a fire-breathing wyvern up close, but she kept that to herself. She just hoped they would give Lug a chance to explain before they filled poor Myrtle with spears and arrows.

*

Even though Embla showed no sign of tiring, their trip across the Blasted Waste took longer than it had on Myrtle's back. They passed a cold night, tramping onwards, and it was halfway through the next day when the Shield Mountains finally came into view.

'That's it!' Liska yelled when she saw them. 'We're home! We're finally home!'

They all clambered up to Embla's broad shoulders to stare as the misty peaks grew closer and closer. Was their home still safe? Had the forces of Noxis and Bitterblight taken over? From this distance it was impossible to tell.

'Hey,' Liska said as she waited for the mountains to get near enough to see properly. 'I've just thought – how are we going to get Embla inside? She'll never fit into the secret passage we used.'

'There used to be a proper entrance,' said Elowen. 'At the north of the city. I believe they bricked it up a few centuries ago, but I'm sure we could persuade them to open it. The mages of Arborven need to know there is a world outside their mountains, after all.'

'At the north?' Liska said. 'By the Noon Fort?'

'Yes. The fortress was actually built as the gatehouse.'

Liska felt another buzz of excitement. That meant her family would be the first to see her arrive. On the shoulders of a treekeeper, of all things.

It seemed to take forever but finally they neared the long slope that led to the mountains. Liska stared up at the patch of mist that hid her home, searching for signs of burning or tumbled wreckage.

There were gouges in the earth all around, and patches of dry, seared gloop that must have come from the rot creatures. But no shapewalker bodies, thank the Tree, and no pieces of shattered brickwork.

'Do you think we won the battle?' Lug asked, mirroring her thoughts.

'I don't know,' she said, her voice wavering. 'If we

wait here, a patrol should spot us and investigate. Then we'll find out.'

Embla carried on striding, right up to the granite face of the mountain itself. It was raked with scratches, pummelled and chipped. The site of a fierce and recent struggle.

They stood there watching the swirling fog, expecting a manticore or griffyx to come swooping down. Waiting, waiting, waiting . . .

'Nobody's coming,' said Liska finally. Just admitting it made her feel physically sick. 'Something must have happened to them after all. We're too late.'

'Wait,' said Fishbone. He was sitting on Embla's head, ears twitching from side to side. 'Do you hear that?'

Liska strained her own ears, which weren't nearly as sharp as her fox ones. She thought she could pick out a dull sound, like a storm blowing through the forest. Or perhaps many voices roaring all at once.

'Is that . . .?'

'A crowd of humies,' said Fishbone. 'A big one. Off to the west.'

The west. Outside the mountains. *The Rotlands.*

'Embla!' Liska shouted. 'Follow that sound! Quickly! There's a battle going on – a battle for Arborven!'

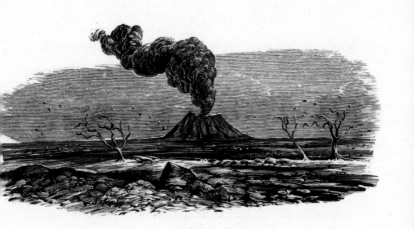

15

'Never have I seen such a sea of filth, death and corruption as the dreaded Rotlands.'

A Guide to Arborven by Obediah Dawnsoul

A sprinting treekeeper is an awesome sight to behold.

Embla leapt metres with each stride, heavy wooden feet crashing down on to the scree, smashing granite chips into sand.

Liska and the others clung on to her shoulders, their fingertips hooked around whorls of bark, hair streaming out behind them, wind whipping their faces.

They rounded the north-west mountains and turned

south, looking out over the stretch of waste known as the Rotlands. A place that had already been consumed by the shadow tree – a taste of what was in store if they should fail.

The red dirt and stone of the desert they had just crossed was covered in layers of grey and black slime. Like tides of dark vomit, it hung in strands and dribbles from every rock and stunted tree.

Half-formed clusters of diseased toadstools were clumped everywhere like blisters. Fat blowflies buzzed around, feasting on the gloop, bathing in the stink. It was a scene straight from Liska's worst nightmares, and it stretched all the way to the horizon, interrupted only by a single mound of earth. Some kind of stunted volcano with a crater at the top that wheezed out black smoke.

'The *smell*!' Liska clapped her hands over her nose. Fishbone's eyes were watering and even Embla had to stagger to a halt.

'What ... what is this place?' she asked, her wooden limbs beginning to tremble.

'This is the realm of Bitterblight,' said Elowen. 'This is how the shadow trees want to shape the world.'

'Big Mew's hairballs,' said Fishbone, coughing and

spluttering. 'It smells worse than a dead wolf's toilet parts!'

Liska didn't even hear him. Her attention was fixed on a crowd of figures gathered at the edge of the stinking rot. A massive crowd, thousands strong, facing out towards the sea of filth.

'Look,' she said. 'It's an army. *Our* army!'

Lug followed her gaze. 'Nematus below,' he said, his voice an awed whisper. 'There must be every mage in Arborven there.'

'But I fear it won't be enough,' said Elowen. 'See what faces them ...'

Liska tore her eyes away from her precious tree folk and looked across the plain. At first glance she had mistaken the heaving mass of grey ooze as part of the landscape. Now she could see it was moving, seething.

The entire plain, almost to the horizon, was choked with seepers of every size bleeding into one another: writhing, dripping, melting and re-forming. Amongst them were towering bulky slabs of fungus: hundreds of gorgaunts, each one even bigger than the creature they had seen in the Scrubbings that day. There were other things besides – monsters with three or more heads, tentacle limbs, spider's legs, barbs and spikes – all of them built out of chunks of mould and strands of putrid goo. And, watching over it all, like some kind of mad king, was a human figure held high on a throne of twisted black wood. Noxis himself.

'It *won't* be enough,' Liska repeated. 'There's so many of them!'

'I thinks I can help,' said Fishbone. He hopped off Embla's head and began scampering down her body, round and round in spirals like a squirrel.

'Where are you going?' Liska called after him as he reached the ground and began to run on all fours back towards the mountains.

'Reinforcements!' he yelled back, before disappearing amongst the boulders. Liska felt strangely abandoned. Fishbone had been there through so much, she was used to having him at her side.

'That's the last we'll see of *him*,' said Lug. 'Can't say I blame him though.' He went to staring at the army of Bitterblight, the heart of Nammu beginning to shake in his trembling hands.

Liska looked towards them as well. A sickening thought had just occurred to her, one which began to swell and bloom into full panic. 'They're all here,' she said. 'Everyone. Which means this is a last stand. You don't think—'

'That they've already taken the heart from the Undrentree?' Elowen finished.

'We're too late!' Lug wailed. 'After all that, we didn't get here in time!'

'Maybe,' said Liska. 'Maybe not. We'd better deliver Nammu's heart and see.'

Embla nodded and began marching towards the gathered armies.

*

As they got closer, Liska could make out ranks of coloured robes amongst the Arborven forces.

The mages stood in lines – arbomancers, stormsingers, barkmages – all the way back to the lowly mossherders. In front of them, towering above, were the treekeepers. Edda was there right in the centre. And, to her delight, a new addition: the hunched mossy back of the giant could be seen standing amongst its brothers and sisters.

Ranged in front of the mages were the shapewalkers, the front line of defence. There were hundreds of them – every warrior from each of the four towers.

They stood in human form, cloaks at the ready.

Manticores, cockatrices, pantherines ... and the griffyxes. Liska strained her eyes for a glimpse of her parents, but the first familiar faces she spotted were wearing wolf and bear skins. It was Beric and Deenai, along with all their tribe. They turned as Embla's heavy footsteps approached and greeted them with a cheer.

'Look!' Deenai shouted. 'It is Liska of the griffyxes! And she has a treekeeper of her own!'

Suddenly all eyes were staring in their direction. Gasps and whoops could be heard, followed by a scream of joy.

'Liska! Liska, is that you?'

A trio of people were running at them from among the ranks of the shapewalkers, fox-fur cloaks flapping behind them.

'Mother! Father! Ylva!' Liska shouted back, scrambling over Embla's shoulder and tumbling head over feet to land in her family's arms. She felt herself being squeezed, kissed and slapped on the back, all at the same time.

'Oh, Liska! Liska!' her mother was saying. 'Where did you go? What happened to you? I thought you were dead until the forest people arrived!'

'Hello, Mother.' Liska grinned up at her, pointing to Lug and his precious burden. 'I brought you the heart.'

*

Even though they faced an unstoppable army, there was pause for some rejoicing. Lug's parents were fetched and there was much crying, hugging and scolding.

Liska learnt that the attack on the Noon Fort had been beaten back around dawn on the day they left. Since then, there had been several more battles. Many people had been wounded or lost, or had simply vanished in the chaos. That was what everyone had assumed had happened to Lug and Liska, right up until Deenai's people and the giant arrived.

Liska's mother had a bandaged arm and leg and half-healed wounds on one side of her face. But she had dragged herself out of the hospital to fight again. Her father and sister were scraped and battered but otherwise uninjured. They listened to a brief version of Liska's adventures with a mixture of amazement and pride on their faces.

At some point Edda the treekeeper came over. When he saw Embla and the heart, he bowed low before speaking to her in a language of creaks and rustles that only the pair of them seemed to understand.

'You're welcome,' Embla replied. Liska realised Edda must have been thanking her for Nammu's heart. The greatest gift one treekeeper could give to another.

Then Edda spotted Elowen and rested a twiggy hand on her shoulder.

'Lady Dawnsoul. Niece,' he said, in his creaking voice.

'*Lady*?' Lug gawped. 'You never said you were a lady!'

Elowen just gave a knowing smile.

'I know,' said Lug. 'It's because I never asked.'

Finally Edda turned to Liska. 'I owe you an apology, young shapewalker. I believed – we all believed – that the story was just a myth. I should have had more faith. And now, thanks to your bravery, we might have a chance.'

'Are we still in time, then?' Liska asked. 'You haven't sacrificed the Undrentree, have you?'

'Not yet,' said Edda. He pointed a gnarled finger at a group of manticore shapewalkers who were standing apart from the rest of the forces. 'We had a team ready to do just that should the battle fail. But now we won't need to.'

'And how will you get to Bitterblight?' Lug asked. 'There's seven million seepers in the way!'

334

'We will distract them if we can,' said Edda. 'And try to clear a path. The shadow tree is growing inside the crater of that volcano. A squad of brave warriors will be needed to take Nammu's heart there.'

'If you please, Uncle,' said Elowen, tapping her fingertips together as she did when excited. 'I think that Liska should be the one to do it. This was all her idea after all.'

Liska's mouth hung open, as did her mother's. 'Me?' she finally managed to say. 'Kill Bitterblight? But ...' She was about to say, 'I'm only a child', then remembered that it was the exact saying of her mother's that used to infuriate her so. Instead, she bit her lip.

'I can carry her,' said Embla. 'At least until she is safe to fly.'

'And I will go too,' said Elowen. 'My magic has fully returned now. I can feel it.'

'If it's all the same,' said Lug, 'I think I'll stay here with my family. I might try and use my worm powers. I have a good feeling about it this time.'

'We'll need the special one, Lug,' said Liska, taking the heart from him. 'We'll need the god worm.'

'I'll do my best.' Lug gave her a lopsided smile and then surprised her by throwing his arms around her in a tight hug. She squeezed him back. After everything they had been through together, everything they had seen ... it felt wrong to be leaving him behind.

'To your positions then,' said Edda, interrupting the moment. 'And good luck, everyone.'

Liska was just being lifted back up to Embla's shoulder by one of her massive hands when a hideous cacophony of screeching and yowling ripped through the air. Everyone looked back towards the mountains where the sound was coming from, and saw a bounding flock of at least five hundred kittimews flowing down from the slopes towards them.

Many mages stepped into a combat stance ready to defend themselves, but Edda himself bellowed at them to hold.

'Stay your spellcraft! These are kittimews! Our first and oldest friends!'

The group tumbled and scampered over to them, clustering around Embla and Liska. Looking down, she could see fur of every colour and pattern, clothes made of knitted and patched odds and ends and armour cobbled together from pieces of junk and unwanted kitchenware.

'I is back!' one of the kittimews shouted, standing

on the shoulders of the others. He wore a helmet fashioned out of an old teapot, topped off with a crown of broken glass and wire. Peering closer, Liska could see it was Fishbone himself.

'Thank the Tree!' she called down to him. 'I thought you'd run away for good!'

'Run away?' The furry little cat man looked offended. 'We is here to fight for Arborven like all the humies!'

'How did you get so many ca— I mean kittimews, to come with you?' Lug asked, staring at the spears and spiky clubs they carried with some unease.

'Because I is their king, of course!' Fishbone puffed out his chest and his people all yowled at the top of their voices. It was a sound that could curdle wyvern milk. Liska shook her head. She had been travelling for days with both Arborven and kittimew royalty without even realising it.

'We're going to take the heart to Bitterblight,' she said. 'Stay here and look after Lug.'

Fishbone rolled his eyes. 'My army can do that. *I* is coming with you!'

Before Liska could stop him, he skittered up Embla's back and took his usual place on top of her head, poking out from the nest of scarlet ivy. He raised both of his paws, claws out, and shouted, 'Charge!'

As if at his signal, the treekeepers began to stride towards the enemy, making the ground shudder with their mighty footsteps.

The shapewalkers began to fold themselves in their cloaks, twisting their bodies into fighting shapes. They *whooshed* up from the ground with sweeps of their wings, filling the sky with creatures from ages past. Pantherines, cockatrices ... Liska even saw some lamassu, the winged lions with human faces from the southern guard tower.

'Be careful, Liska!' her mother shouted up to her before shifting herself.

'We will watch out for you from above,' her sister added.

Liska waved back as Embla started her own march, waved also to Lug who was already beginning to start his summoning surrounded by a horde of fierce scruffy cat warriors. An honour guard of tails and whiskers.

All the other mages had begun their magic too. The battlefield lit up with streaks and flashes of coloured light. Strange, arcane symbols floated in the air. A mystical fireworks display.

The ground rippled as roots and vines pushed up from below, lashing their way towards the enemy. Clouds of mist, crackling with trapped lightning, started to form in the sky. The stunted, poisoned trees of the Rotlands were once again filled with life. They sprouted arms and legs, their bark hardened into spikes and blades, turning into walking wooden war golems. They snapped themselves off from their roots and joined in the march.

The air was thick with magic, the smell of it almost overpowering the putrid rot.

For a moment at least.

And then the army of Bitterblight attacked.

*

Seeing the energy of Arborven, feeling the static tingle of power in the air, Liska had thought – just for a moment – that they might simply tear through the seepers and win.

But that, she realised, had been stupid.

As powerful as her people were, their numbers were nothing compared to the sheer mass of the enemy.

The shadow tree's forces waited until the treekeepers were well out on to the plain of rot, until their feet splashed through thick puddles of poisonous goo, and then they surged forwards.

Shrieking and howling, they rose up behind a waft of stink, boiling forwards like an exploding drain. Seepers piled on top of one another in waves, in crests, and crashed down on the treekeepers, swallowing them completely.

For a second Edda and the others were gone from sight, and then they burst free, lashing about themselves with their trunk-sized limbs.

The liquid bodies of seepers flew through the air all around, but there were always hundreds more to replace them.

Then gorgaunts stomped forwards, picking up handfuls of their smaller comrades and hurling them at the mages like deadly snowballs.

They crashed into the ranks, breaking spells, lashing out with their rubbery tentacles, causing massive damage everywhere.

The mages struck back with bolts of lightning from the gathered storm clouds. Their wooden golems fought tirelessly, hacking at the gooey creatures that swarmed all over them.

And from the sky, the shapewalkers swooped, biting and clawing, snatching and gouging. They flew around the gorgaunts in fierce swarms, aiming for their eyes, tearing at their legs and shoulders. More than one of the giants toppled over, crushing hundreds of seepers into liquid beneath them.

But none of it was enough.

For every enemy that was defeated, three more took its place. Nightmarish things tottered towards the treekeepers on spider legs, poisonous barbs and stingers flashing. Four-armed beasts with serpent bodies reared up, snatching shapewalkers from the sky as they flew past. Dragon-shaped masses of living fungus spat missiles upwards – great clods of grey jelly that burned flesh and melted armour.

'There's too many!' Embla shouted. She had been swinging with her club fist as they marched, sweeping enemies out of their path. They were behind the main force of treekeepers, out of the thick of battle, but were still getting swarmed.

'I'll try to make a gap!' Elowen called. She was moving her arms in patterns, casting hexes that hung in the air, glowing. Roots whipped all around them as they walked, tearing through seepers. Still some got through.

'Take that!' Fishbone yelled, slashing at a creature that had managed to clamber up Embla's back. The thing dodged around the treekeeper's neck, coming close to Liska, who held the heart up as a shield. Beams of light shot out from it, searing the seeper into dust.

'Don't let them see we have the heart!' Elowen warned. 'We have to slip through without them noticing!'

Liska nodded, tucking her precious cargo underneath her cloak. 'Can anyone see Noxis? Is he fighting too?'

She scanned the hordes in front of them, looking for that evil throne. Noxis knew they had gone to fetch the heart and he knew what they looked like. If he spotted them, they were done for.

'Wyvern!'

A cry went up from a soaring squad of pantherines just above them. Liska saw them bank left and wheel away, coming back in a defensive pattern designed to fight the flying lizards.

'Wait!' she shouted up to them. 'It's on our side!'

They hovered, staring down at her in surprise as she pointed to the purple-scaled wyvern that was swooping down towards them, shrieking in fury.

'It's Myrtle! Attack, girl! Attack!'

Myrtle zoomed over Embla's head, wind rushing behind her, and flew low over the ranks of the seepers.

She opened her mouth wide and let out a cone of blasting fire. It cut through the beasts, setting them ablaze. Then they scattered, screaming and writhing, spreading the fire amongst their own ranks.

'Hooray, Myrtle!' Liska whooped and cheered as the wyvern passed low again and again, burning great holes in the enemy forces each time.

Then, after her fifth attack, she ran out of flame. She circled for a moment or two, gave an apologetic wave of her tail, and left.

'If only we had an army of Myrtles,' Fishbone said, tail drooping. She had done impressive damage to Bitterblight's forces, but not enough to turn the tide of battle.

'They've regrouped already,' Liska said. The wall of grey troops ahead of them had flowed back together as if Myrtle's attack had never happened. If anything, there were *more* of them than before.

'Your treekeepers cannot break through,' Embla said. She had stopped marching, watching the brave force of Arborven giants battling against the seepers. The giant they had met in Almberg forest fought hardest of all, his powerful, mossy fists smashing enemies all around him. But there were just too many of the foe. As they stared, one of the treekeepers fell backwards, toppled by the weight of evil creatures swarming all over it. And it didn't get back up.

'We need a miracle,' Liska whispered, looking back to where the mages wove their spells, where Lug's personal guard of kittimews dashed about like furry whirlwinds, shredding with their claws. Amongst it all she could just about see her friend crouching with both hands pressed to the ground, his eyes closed in concentration.

His lips were moving as he repeated his familiar prayers to the worms. But this time something different happened. An orange glow began to flow from his palms, down into the soil. A deep rumbling could be heard, as if the very bones of the earth were grinding and shaking.

'Well, *that's* new,' said Liska. Could Elowen's magic lessons have actually worked? Or maybe holding Nammu's heart for so long had changed Lug somehow?

'Elowen.' She tugged at her friend's tattered white dress. 'I think Lug's magic is finally working!'

Elowen paused in her own spellcasting and the two of them watched Lug as the aura of orange light spread outwards from him, growing more and more intense.

The ground under the battlefield was starting to buck and roll now. Cracks appeared, tearing the layers of goo apart like soggy sponge. Sparks of energy began to crackle, streaming out of Lug and zipping off towards the hordes of seepers. Something *huge* was coming.

KRA-KA-KOOM!

A thunderclap tore the air, orange lightning arcing down from the sky, striking the very centre of Bitterblight's forces.

Precisely where it hit, the ground rose up into a hummock, a hill, a mountain ... and then it broke open to reveal a worm. The biggest creature the planet had ever seen. An earthworm the size of a city, each segment taller than a treekeeper. It loomed over the battlefield like a colossal tower, head waving this way and that. At the tip of its nose was a star-shaped mouth, gaping wide and lined deep into its throat with teeth like razor-sharp tombstones. A roar blasted out from the thing's maw, one that shook the earth and pounded the air.

Every single being stopped their fighting to gape.

'*Nematus,*' Liska whispered in awe. 'The god worm.'

She looked back at Lug, standing now, his arms moving, controlling the epic beast.

'Do it, Lug,' she mouthed. 'Crush them.'

He brought his hands sweeping downwards and as he did so, Nematus followed. It toppled over, hitting the ground with a thud that knocked everyone off their feet, sending a cloud of pummelled seeper particles into the air.

And then it began to writhe and roll, smashing and smearing, crushing and rending – mashing all the rot beasts into paste.

The mages cheered, the shapewalkers roared. They redoubled their attacks, beating down their enemies even as they tried to flee the worm.

'This is it!' Liska shouted. 'This is our chance! We have to get to Bitterblight now!'

'Charge!' Fishbone shouted again and Embla began to run at full speed into the thick of the fleeing seepers, heading straight for the volcano.

16

'Black are the roots of the Shadow Tree.
Whoever they touch will never get free.'

Arborven children's rhyme

Dodging lunging rot beasts, smashing seepers away with her fist, Embla loped up the steep edge of the volcano. Most of the enemy creatures were at the bottom of the slope, slamming into each other as they tried to avoid the thrashing, crushing body of Nematus. The topmost section of cracked and blasted rock was clear. Liska held her breath as Embla scrambled up it, wondering what her first glimpse of the dreaded Bitterblight would be like.

It was every bit as horrible as she feared.

They cleared the crest of the volcano and paused on the rim, looking down. Below them was a steep slope of blackened stone. A deep bowl shape and, at the bottom, filling the crater completely, a twisted thing from her worst nightmares.

The shadow tree was a writhing, jittering mess formed of patches of the deepest night. Like someone had scratched and scribbled at the surface of reality itself, tearing through to the dark emptiness beyond.

Whereas the Undrentree and Nammu had poured out magical energy, this *thing* sucked it all in. It drained everything around it – Liska could feel its hunger pulling at the marrow of her bones.

Could it even be called a tree? It had branches of a sort – jagged, bent things like shards of broken glass – and some kind of trunk, but the wood moved over itself, slithering like the scales of a coiling snake. Liska thought she saw glimpses of faces there. Things with wide-open mouths lined with shark's teeth. Hints of spider eyes, glassy and empty of all feeling. Clawed hands pressing against the bark from within, trying to escape.

Above it hung a cloud of greasy smoke, pulsing in

gusts and eddies, rising up from the volcano's mouth and coughing outwards.

Spores, Liska realised. The thing was constantly spewing out millions of rotten particles that would land and spread poison. And it would never stop, she knew, until the whole world was covered in death.

Everyone was frozen in place, staring in dumb horror, fighting against the waves of sickness and revulsion that flowed over them.

The tree seemed to stare back, willing them to come closer, hungry to corrupt them, to kill them and then suck all the goodness out of their bones as they lay amongst its roots.

And then there was movement: a figure cloaked in a torn black robe, stumbling out from behind Bitterblight and looking up at them with eyes that bubbled with madness.

'Noxis,' Liska managed to say. She clutched Nammu's heart tightly to her chest, feeling its flow of magic ease the nausea a touch.

'Is that it?' Noxis was shouting up at them, his voice teetering on the edge of hysterical laughter. 'Is that all Arborven has to attack me with? One lonely treekeeper and some children?'

'M-monster,' Embla stammered. She took a step down into the crater, battling against the waves of evil power that pulsed out at them.

Elowen was struggling too, her hands shaking as she tried to form a spell. Her jaw clenched with effort, her eyes flashed blue ... but nothing happened. 'There's nothing here,' she said. 'No roots or seeds to control. Arbomancy is useless.'

'Your tree magic won't work here.' Noxis could see what she was trying to do and found it hilarious. 'There is only the power of Bitterblight!'

He cast a spell of his own, bursting the rocks in front of them with a serrated tendril of dark energy. It rose up, just as Nematus had done, waving in the air, ready to strike them.

'Not trees, perhaps,' Elowen muttered, 'but storms might.'

She raised her hands to the sky, drawing down a vortex of clouds. Electricity sparked and crackled within before shooting down in a bolt that struck the tendril, bursting it into fragments.

'You can call storms?' Liska said, staring at her friend in awe.

'I can use all kinds of magic,' said Elowen. 'That

was the way with all mages when we first came here.'

Bitterblight was not as impressed, though. It sent out a shockwave of pure hatred that was enough to knock Embla off her feet. She fell to the ground and began to tumble and slide down the steep slope of the crater, her passengers bouncing free and falling along with her.

Liska felt herself roll over and over, pointed shards of rock scratching and jabbing her as she tumbled. She kept tight hold of the heart all the way, even though it meant taking blows to her head.

When she finally stopped, she struggled to her feet, finding herself just metres away from the shadow tree, blood streaking her face from several small cuts. Elowen and Fishbone were close by and Embla almost on top of Noxis himself, but the mage's eyes were fixed on Liska alone. Her cloak had fallen back, revealing Nammu's heart. A single gleaming point of light in that dark smoky pit.

'*You*,' Noxis said. 'You're the ones my son warned me about. You're the ones that I sent Thresher to catch.'

'Thresher is gone,' said Liska, that final image of her sailing through the air fresh in her mind. 'And everything else will be too if you carry on. Your own son will be killed! Doesn't that bother you?'

A flicker in Noxis's eyes. Perhaps the last shreds of his humanity fighting back, but then it was sucked under. Eaten. The veins on his neck and bald head pulsed a sickly grey, and his eyes blazed with pure madness.

'I don't care! I have no son!' he screamed. 'And it doesn't matter that you have that tree's heart! It won't be enough to save you!'

Liska couldn't believe he had turned against his own kind, his own blood, so completely. 'Why?' she shouted. 'Why are you doing this?'

Noxis pressed a palm to the trunk of Bitterblight and grinned. 'Can't you feel it? The power? It dwarfs the magic from the Undrentree. If we give ourselves over to it, we can crush the Poxpunks and the wyverns. We can make the whole world bow down to us. Why live in pathetic tree houses when we can have towers crackling with dark energy? Why settle for a tiny, hidden city when we can have an empire that rules all?'

'But at what cost?' Liska pointed to the blackened, scarred rocks around her. 'What good is all that power if everything gets destroyed to earn it?'

'You wouldn't understand.' He sneered down at her like she was some kind of insect. 'You're just a child.'

Just a child. Those words again. As if she was too small, too weak to matter. As if adults like Noxis had the right to throw away her whole life without even consulting her. As if her opinion was worthless.

Well, it was her world too. And she wasn't about to give it up without a fight. 'We'll show you what children can do,' she said, nodding to her friends. 'Do it *now,* Elowen.'

Elowen nodded, throwing out her hands in a gesture that brought down a bolt of lightning right on Noxis's head. At the same time Liska flipped her hood over, shifting forms even as she leapt into the air. Her body folded into its griffyx shape, her paws clutching the heart of Nammu tightly as she beat her wings, soaring up and around Bitterblight in a tight arc.

From above, she saw Noxis juddering as the lightning ripped through him. She saw smoke stream from his robes and the shadow tree behind him flicker as if in pain.

As it flinched, Embla regained her strength and began to charge forwards. It looked as though she might reach Noxis in time to crush him completely, but Bitterblight wasn't beaten so easily.

Shoots burst from one of its roots, zipping towards Elowen as she channelled the lightning. Fishbone leapt to stop them, slashing with his claws, but he wasn't fast enough to block them all. One or two wrapped around the ghost girl, dragging her to the ground.

In the same instant, the trunk of the tree seemed to open, wrapping itself around Noxis, coating him in strands of toxic wood.

It was like watching the ceremony that turned Embla into a treekeeper, only much, much faster. The evil mage screamed in agony as he was transformed against his will. Liska remembered what Elowen had told her about the dangers of rushing the bonding magic. Bitterblight clearly didn't care about that. It spat layers of bark over Noxis, winding them around him like a hungry spider binding a juicy fly. He span in its grip, bones cracking, limbs swelling, becoming half-man, half-darkness. A ruined mirror image of Embla, who was standing before him staring on in horror.

Knowing the magic could finish at any moment, Liska swooped in, trying to get Nammu's heart close enough to kill the shadow tree.

She dodged the clouds of spores, not wanting them to touch her fur let alone get inside her lungs, and wove amongst the shard-like branches. They moved from one place to another without warning, making her swerve hard left, right, then right again.

They were as sharp as the broken glass they resembled. One of them caught her hind leg, snagging it and slicing through the scales into her skin. Liska yelped, almost dropping the heart from her paws. She veered out, away from the tree, looking for a better gap, a way in. But with the branches shifting and blocking her, it was impossible.

Glancing down, she saw Elowen still trapped by the crushing tendrils, grimacing as she tried to summon more lightning. Fishbone was on her shoulders, trying to free her with his claws.

Meanwhile, Bitterblight had finished building its vile treekeeper. The new Noxis stumbled away from the trunk – a misshapen thing of charred wood and thorns, with limbs of odd sizes and a face frozen in a scream.

Despite everything looking wrong, he still brimmed with power and burning rage. With a terrifying roar, he launched himself at Embla and the two began to battle.

Liska flew around them, coming in for another run at Bitterblight. She watched as they pummelled each other with blows strong enough to smash boulders into dust.

Embla swung with her club fist again and again, cracking the poorly formed skin of Noxis and breaking off jagged chunks of living wooden flesh.

But the evil mage was doing damage of his own. The jagged thorns that lined his arms tore at Embla's bark. His fingers were also barbed like claws and he raked at her face, tore out clumps of her ivy hair.

They both roared and howled with pain and fury, making the whole crater shake. And mixed in with it all were the screams of Elowen, wailing as Bitterblight squeezed her tighter and tighter.

There wasn't time to wait for Embla to win. Liska *had* to get to the tree.

She flew low, beating her wings for speed, aiming at the legs of the battling treekeepers. Just as she was near enough to touch them with her whiskers, Embla struck Noxis with a mighty blow that cracked one of his wooden arms in two.

He bellowed in pain and Bitterblight juddered along with him. For a split second, its branches blinked out of existence.

Now's my chance! Liska aimed herself like an arrow,

tucking her wings in and using her speed to shoot straight between the legs of both Embla and Noxis, right up to the trunk of Bitterblight itself.

She hit the wooden surface with her shoulder, jarring her whole body, bouncing off again to tumble down between the roots. She curled her wings about her, keeping the heart tucked safely inside, but no sooner had she landed, she saw grasping tentacles begin to form on the surface of Bitterblight's bark, reaching out for her, slashing at the air with their razor-blade thorns.

Desperate, Liska tried to spot a crack or knothole she could push Nammu's heart into. A way to get it inside Bitterblight so it could do its work. All she could see was solid wood, pulsing and twitching like black jelly.

'Where do I put the heart?' she shouted across at Elowen, who had been lifted up in mid-air by the roots that were crushing her.

Her friend couldn't find air to speak. But even as a tendril wrapped itself around her neck and began to squeeze, she lifted up her hand and pointed. With her last scrap of strength, she summoned a bolt of electricity that crackled out from her finger, hitting

Bitterblight a metre up from where Liska crouched. The bark puckered and split, peeling back a fraction to show the withered flesh within. A small hole, but maybe just enough to get the heart started . . .

It was too high up for Liska's griffyx form to reach. She would have to shift back and hope she had enough strength left to perform her task.

Gritting her teeth, she shrugged off her enchanted skin, jolting her body into the change. She felt her bones scream out in shock, her muscles pull and tear as they suddenly began to warp. Her heart pounded, her blood rushed. Sparks flashed in front of her eyes and her vision swam, but she could see clearly enough to notice that Bitterblight's tentacles were on her. She could feel them wrapping around her leg even as it twisted from paw to foot.

Halfway between fox and girl, she heaved herself upright. She clutched the heart in fingers that were still tipped with claws, still shedding their coating of fur.

The tentacles cut into her calves, her thighs, burning the skin. Her whole body shook with the effort of changing itself so rapidly, but she fought to stay awake.

Just a bit further . . . Somehow she found a last scrap of strength, enough to shove Nammu's heart up against the bark of Bitterblight, to nudge it into the hole that Elowen had started.

As she did, she saw the blue light begin to melt away the darkness. It crackled and hissed like burning hair and the air was filled with a chemical stench. The wood around the heart began to fold in on itself, collapsing in chunks that rapidly became bigger and bigger. A chain reaction that grew faster than Liska's eyes could follow.

In an instant the heart of Nammu had been swallowed, tumbling into the very core of Bitterblight and pulling every atom of the horrid thing in after it. Screaming filled the air, and Liska couldn't tell if it came from Noxis or the tree itself. She had a sense of things whipping past her faster than the wind, as the roots, branches, tendrils, spores ... everything that had filled the bottom of the crater ... was sucked away into a tiny point in space.

Her last sight, before her legs turned to jelly and she fell, was of Nammu's heart hanging in the air as the branches and roots around it snapped and broke, tumbling into the blue light and vanishing. And then the heart itself blinked out. Gone.

Liska hit the ground with the smile still spreading on her face.

17

'I have seen shapewalkers fly into the very
jaws of death just to win themselves a stripe.'

A Guide to Arborven by Obediah Dawnsoul

Liska only had a dim memory of what happened
after the battle. She was sick with dizziness and
every part of her ached from forcing herself to shapewalk
before she was ready. There were bumps, gashes and
scratches all over her face and arms, and her legs burnt
where Bitterblight had wrapped her in its shoots.

Patches of things came back to her after. Glimpses
she saw and heard as someone – Embla? – carried her
out of the volcano crater and back to her home.

Noxis, or the thing he had become, had been shattered by the battle and the death of Bitterblight. A limbless chunk of living wood remained, with his screaming face trapped in the middle, wailing and gibbering. It would, perhaps, have been better for him if he'd died.

Elowen and Fishbone had been with her as they walked down on to the battlefield. She remembered the kittimew's sandpaper tongue cleaning a cut on her forehead, and how cold Elowen's hand had been as she held it.

She had a half picture of the Rotlands as they staggered across it. It was empty now. The giant worm had left, leaving a crater almost as wide as Bitterblight's volcano. All the seepers and gorgaunts were gone too. Smashed to pulp by Nematus, or blown into mist when the shadow tree died – there was nothing but a crust of grey slime to show they had ever been there.

She remembered the cheering as they reached their friends. Lots of blurry faces that swam into view above her. Kisses from her parents, Lug laughing and whooping ... the celebration as they all marched into Arborven together.

After that, she had fallen into a long, deep sleep.

*

It was several days later when Liska awoke and found herself in an unfamiliar bed. She was in a room built from wooden planks and beams. Light poured in from a tall window filled with panes of coloured glass. It painted patches of colour all over her white sheets.

She sat up, wincing as every muscle in her body blared with pain at the same time. She felt like one enormous living bruise.

Looking around, she noticed an entire wall of her room was covered in bark decorated with patterns of coloured moss. She was in the tree! In the infirmary of the mages no less. Her arms were bandaged where the blade branches of Bitterblight had sliced them, and she was wearing a simple green nightshirt.

My cloak! She panicked, looking around for her second skin and quickly spotting it draped over a chair by the window. She was just about to totter out of bed and put it on when the room door opened and three familiar faces walked in.

'Lug! Elowen! Fishbone!' She croaked their names as they ran to her and the four of them bundled each other into a tight hug.

'Stop! You're hurting me!' Liska had to cry out

when the squeezing got too much. Then they perched on the end of her bed, broad smiles all round.

'You're finally awake!' Lug said. 'It's been days! Did you see me summon Nematus?'

'I certainly did,' said Liska. She noticed how Lug's chin was held a little higher, his shoulders more square. He finally had a bit of confidence in himself.

'He is not stopping yowling on about it ever since,' said Fishbone, rolling his yellow eyes.

'Well, it was very impressive,' said Elowen. She wore a new dress. Cleaner, but just as lacy and frilly as her old one. 'Almost as impressive as Liska destroying Bitterblight.'

'Yes, well . . .' Liska blushed. *So it really happened then,* she thought. *It wasn't just a dream.*

'You're the hero of Arborven,' said Lug. 'Well, we all are, kind of. But you most of all.'

'Have I really been asleep for days?' Liska asked. 'Have I missed anything?'

'Lots!' Lug waved his arms in the air, robe sleeves flapping. 'My family have been invited to move out of the Scrubbings! We're being given a mage house in the first circle. The *first circle!* We're as important as the arbomancers now!'

'That's amazing,' said Liska, chuckling.

'Not a big deal,' said Fishbone, wrinkling his nose. 'Us kittimews is being invited as well. But we has the decency to refuse. We is much happier in the caves. There is not as many juicy rats where you humies live.'

'Does that mean I won't see you again?' Liska asked.

'Of course not!' Fishbone reached up and took one of the rings from his ear. It was a silver hoop with a bright blue bead of lapis on it. He handed it to Liska with a bow. 'This is token that marks you as honoured guest of kittimew. When you visit our patches, some mew will spot you and bring you to my palace. And you must promise to visit lots.'

Liska laughed. 'I promise,' she said. 'And you are welcome at the Noon Fort any time as well.'

Fishbone bowed again. 'I will come. As long as there is rat for dinner.'

'And what about you, Elowen?' Liska asked. 'Or should I call you Lady Dawnsoul?'

Elowen gave one of her smiles. 'Just Elowen, if you please,' she said. 'My news is that my entire family have awoken! The death of Bitterblight disturbed their slumber. Now they are all going to attend the ceremony together!'

'Ceremony?' Liska wondered what she was talking about.

'A ceremony for *you*!' Lug shouted. 'And guess what you're going to get?'

Liska stared, speechless. She hardly dared think it. *A stripe?* It seemed like a lifetime ago when that had been her dream. Half the reason she wanted to go on a crazy mission to find Nammu's heart in the first place.

'It's in two days,' said Elowen, patting her arm. 'We'd better let you rest. The best mages in the city are caring for you and they won't be pleased if we get you too excited.'

But there wasn't much chance of resting once word got out that she was awake. Her mother and father were by her side soon after, bringing her a set of new leather armour. They spent a long time telling her how proud they were of her and how brave she had been. Liska soaked it in, knowing that it would be a long time before she was called a child again. Even Ylva treated her with new respect, offering to take her cloak and have it spruced, groomed and freshened with a dose of tree oil so that it sparkled with magic. They were going to be at the ceremony too. Along with *all* the other shapewalkers.

'I can't wait to see the look on the manticores' faces,' said her mother as she left. Liska thought she'd never seen her so happy.

Deenai and Beric came to see her also, full of news about their journey south and their new home amongst the trees. The northern gateway had been opened and the forest shapewalkers had been given the task of patrolling the foothills outside the city. The magic of the Undrentree had refreshed their powers and they could shift form just as easily as Liska, a trick that they took great delight in showing her. Deenai's form was a sleek white-furred she-wolf with deep green eyes. She nuzzled Liska's hand before trotting off back to the cool shadows between the trees.

Once or twice, as the healers came to check on her, Liska caught sight of a treekeeper outside her room, bending down to look in. Embla had been there, with her clubbed fist and cloud of red-ivy hair, as had Edda. Liska was sure he had winked at her with one of his glowing eyes.

Apparently Lug had even suggested that Myrtle came to visit, but the infirmary mages managed to persuade him otherwise. The young wyvern hadn't actually been allowed into the city yet, but they had made a landing pad for her just outside the new gate. Lug met her there every day to groom her and keep her free of parasites. He usually had an audience of terrified onlookers. It was going to take a little while before the tree-dwelling mages learnt to accept a wyvern as an ally.

And then the day of the ceremony came around.

She stood in the hall just as before, only now it was packed with shapewalkers as well as mages. All the treekeepers were there too, including Embla and the giant who was now affectionately known as Mossy. They waved as she looked at them, and Liska grinned back.

Her family and friends were in the front row, looking proud enough to burst. She even caught sight of Odis amongst the black-robed arbomancers. She half expected him to cast a spell at her, but instead he nodded before looking away. A respectful truce then. Probably the best she could hope for.

Edda himself was going to be performing the stripe giving, which was apparently a great honour. The hall fell silent as he entered, taking his place at the front where Liska was kneeling, ready for the ritual. He said some words in his rumbling voice but Liska didn't really hear them. She was too busy wondering which leg the stripe should be on, what colour it might be. Her thoughts were interrupted by her mother's frantic whispering behind her.

'Liska! Change your shape!'

She realised, with a cringe, that the entire hall was staring at her in silent expectation. 'Oh,' she stammered. 'Yes. Sorry.'

She drew her cloak about her and shifted until she stood on all fours before Edda, her tail twitching nervously back and forth, her eyes scrunched shut. Was it going to hurt? Burn? Tickle?

None of those it turned out. The ancient treekeeper crouched down, dwarfing her completely, letting sacred tree oil fall from a flask. She felt it land on the top of her right leg and sizzle there. A pins-and-needle tingle that slowly faded before happening again a little further down.

When she lowered her head to look, there was not one, but *two* stripes of the brightest leaf green wrapped around her foreleg.

'*Two* ...' she breathed.

'One for bringing us Nammu's heart and one for using it to destroy Bitterblight,' Edda said, and laughed.

'You are now the youngest shapewalker ever to have two stripes.'

A cheer went up then, one which shook the roots of the Undrentree itself.

Liska blinked back hot, happy tears. *Two stripes*. It had happened. The thing she had lain awake nights, plotting and praying for. Double that in fact.

The funny thing was, now it finally had, it didn't seem that important. And why had it been so vital in the first place? Just so she could show everyone how brave she was, she supposed. That she was someone to be admired.

'Now all Arborven will see how courageous you have been,' Edda was saying as if reading her mind.

Her eyes went to the cheering crowd, fixing on the three figures who were standing at the front, whooping louder than anyone, not caring who noticed or stared.

And what others might see as just a worm caller, a ghost girl and a talking cat, were so much more precious than stripes, fame or glory.

'You don't need to count someone's stripes to see what kind of person they are,' she said to Edda, looking up into those immense, powerful eyes.

'Oh, really?' He smiled back down at her. 'What should you count then?'

She smiled back at him. The answer was simple.

'Their truest friends.'

Read on for an extract from *The Legend of Podkin One-Ear*. A bard is about to tell the story of a young rabbit who must face the most horrifying enemy rabbitkind has ever known . . .

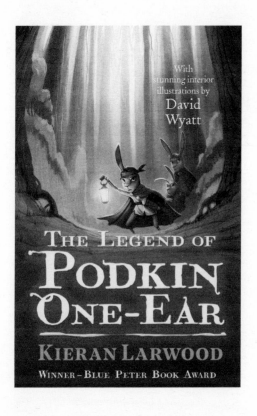

CHAPTER ONE

A Bard for Bramblemas

Crunch, crunch. Crunch, crunch. The sound of heavy footsteps, trudging through knee-deep snow, echoes through the night's silence.

A thick white blanket covers the wide slopes of the band of hills known as the Razorback downs. Moonlight dances over it, glinting here and there in drifts of sparkles, as if someone has sprinkled the whole scene with diamond dust.

It is perfect – untouched except for one spidery line of tracks leading down from the hills towards the frosted woodland beneath.

Crunch, crunch. Crunch, crunch go the footsteps of the track-maker. He is hunched and weary, using a tall staff to help him through the snow. He might have been an old man, if it hadn't been many hundreds of moons since men trod these lands. Move closer and instead you will see he is a rabbit, walking upright in the way men once did, his ears hidden beneath the hood of a heavy leather cloak, fierce eyes peering out at the wintry midnight world.

The thick fur on his face and arms is dyed with blue swirls and patterns, which marks him out as a bard. A travelling, storytelling rabbit. A wanderer with nothing on his back but a set of travel-worn clothes and a head stuffed full of tales and yarns: old, new, broken and mended. Just about every story you ever heard, and many more yet to be told.

Don't worry about him being out in the cold on such a wintry night. His trade will see him welcomed in any warren. That is the tradition and the law throughout all of the Five Realms of Lanica, and woe betide anyone who doesn't keep it.

Crunch, crunch. Crunch, crunch. His breath steams out behind him as he forces his way through the snow. Listen closer and you can hear him mumbling curses with each hard-fought step. Closer still and you can hear the strings of wooden beads around his neck clicking and clacking. The bone trinkets and pouches around his belt knocking and niggling.

He marches with a purpose, as if he has someplace to be and he is already late. But where is there for him to go? There is nothing but snow and trees from here all the way to the horizon. Until, of course, you remember that he's a rabbit. Rabbits live underground, in warrens and burrows: warm and safe, out of the winter ice and frost.

And that is indeed where he is heading. Into the woods and through the trees until he stops before a pair of huge entrance doors, set into the side of a little hill. Behind them is Thornwood Warren, and there had better be a warm welcome for him, or there will be serious trouble.

Boom, boom, boom! He smacks the end of his staff against the oak and waits for an answer.

Back when rabbits were small, twitchy, terrified things, warrens were little more than a collection of holes and tunnels in the ground. Now, in this new age, they are something different altogether: there are entire villages and cities built under the earth, completely out of sight.

The bard knew that behind those wooden doors would be nest-burrows and market-burrows, workshops, temples, libraries, larders, pantries and a dozen kitchens to feed them all. There would be soldiers and healers, servants, cooks, smiths, weavers, tailors, potters and painters. Old rabbits, young rabbits, poor rabbits and noble rabbits. All walks of life hidden away in cosy, torch-lit, underground houses; all arranged around every warren's hub: the longburrow, a great feasting hall with a huge fireplace, rows of tables and nearly always music. Music, noise and merriness – that is what rabbits love. Especially tonight, for this was Bramblemas Eve: the night on which the winter solstice was celebrated with a special feast, and the promise of presents in the morning, left behind by the mysterious Midwinter Rabbit.

And stories of course. Special stories, told by a visiting bard – that is, if he ever got inside the place.